ETERNAL LIGHT

THE LIGHT ONE SAGA

ETERNAL LIGHT

The Light One Saga

KASSONDRA SHOBERT

atmosphere press

Prologue

I'm over 300 years old, but I do not physically age with time. After I reached the age of twenty-eight, roughly 274 years ago, my natural appearance never changed again. It's as though my body remains in perfect preservation. *Divine immortality is only a fraction of what you're granted when you become the Light One, amongst many other rewarding factors*—or so I'd been told.

Most of us expect an endless life to be phenomenal; to live eternally and reside in a world of serenity with no possibility of an end. Others, however, surmise it as no more than a torturous curse; permanent solitary confinement as you watch those around you die ceaselessly. I, too, believe just that, and this is why I endure no desire to be the everlasting Light One. Nevertheless, what I've been doomed with is far worse. The consequences of my decisions during my eternal life are the *real* curse.

My name is Evelyn Walsh. I'm not human, and I possess the power to demolish every bone in your body with the electricity that I can easily produce with just the slightest touch of my fingertips. I'm a monstrosity. I've been like this for a very long time now, and I should be feared.

Every two years I am forced to leave this life, shunned to a desolate and hollow dreamscape where I lay lifeless and watch as another two years pass before I can return. So I live, and I die, incessantly. It's tormenting, the fact that I'll never find true peace. I'll never perish for good. I'll never escape from forever.

Are you curious why this happens? As of the year 1892, during my immortal life, I'd grown vindictive while searching for a way to make a final exit and relinquish what I suspected then was a burden. I just wanted to die indefinitely, especially after losing someone close to me to a morally corrupt government system.

"*Your duty is to protect elementals,*" the Elemental Elders had informed me. "*You are prohibited from harming humans unless they have harmed an elemental. When doing so, you must go about it judiciously. If you do seek out justice against our command, there will be consequences.*"

This human—Mayor Clarence Howard—had it coming to him. Though there had been rules, I broke all of them. I was deemed a mishap. I'd reached my fate per the Elders' judgment—an infinite existence of interminable suffering, reminding me I couldn't elude who I was or what I'd done.

For years I pursued retaliation as a relentless monster while in search of the Dharo Dagger, the one weapon that could ultimately end my existence. That is until one day in the 1900s, I abolished my heinous sacrilege. Now with every life I leave, I also return with overwhelming remorse for the ones I've hurt. This shatters me to the core. *How's this any way to go on,* you wonder? It's dreadful and harrowing, yes, but I don't have a choice. Nothing hurt worse than the last time I left.

I remember that very night of my previous death; it was in the year 2022. The storm was powerful that night, as always, but the potency of guilt and shame I felt was beyond the physical pain I feel when I'm cast away. It all happened so fast, too fast. I wasn't ready to leave—not because of the deep affliction of misery that occurs every time it happens, but because I did the one thing I shouldn't do while I'm alive: fall in love.

Yes—I was loved back by the most exquisite, beautiful, and kind person I've ever known, just to be taken away by my curse once again, and I never got to say goodbye. My disappearance broke her heart. She didn't know who or what I was; I somehow managed to conceal it from her for two years, as I've hidden it from almost everyone for countless decades now.

Today, in the year 2024, I have awoken. I'm alive again. The upsurge of blood flows vehemently through my veins as my old soul prevails and my heart that was once indifferent beats ardently. I feel the air pervade my lungs as they desperately expand with every viable breath that I inhale.

She needs to know who I really am. I know it'd be for the better if I refrain from returning to her, but she's the only reason I want to live on. I'm alone right now, and it's all I can do not to just whisper her name...

"I'll see you again soon, Carson."

Chapter 1

Carson Miles sauntered inside her apartment after a busy and mentally exhausting day. Carson worked as a charity manager and had begun numerous local charities in Tree Heights as well as some surrounding towns. Carson loved her profession and the obligations that accompanied it. That didn't mean there weren't days that drained all of her energy. Although many days were pleasant and equanimous, every so often she did encounter tough situations.

Some days would reopen the wound of her freshly mended broken heart, and today had surely been one that twisted the knife. Earlier in the day she had addressed an altercation with an intoxicated, homeless individual who initiated verbal aggression with the crew. He screamed and cussed in their faces as he took swigs from a glass bottle in a brown, crinkled-up paper bag. Donnie, a retired combat veteran, husband, and father of two, suffered from severe PTSD, depression, and alcoholism.

Of course, none other than Carson herself spoke empathetically to this man, as she always did with everybody. Donnie broke down in tears, revealing to Carson he desperately missed his kids and wife and just wanted to get back onto his feet. He only needed a boost in the right direction. She thought back on the conversation.

Carson chose a spot across from Donnie in the middle of the floor while everyone gazed upon the situation.

"My wife, Stacey, tried to help me. She called doctors and specialists, but nobody could take away the images in my head. The medications wouldn't even work. It feels like I'm trapped in a prison and I can't get out of my own thoughts. What I've experienced overseas is haunting me. The more I would think about it, the more I would drink because it would numb me. I was constantly drinking, and that's why Stacey kicked me out," Donnie cried, his tears splashing onto the linoleum floor. "She said I couldn't put her and the boys through this anymore. That was three months ago. It's been downhill ever since. I have no money. I can't get a job, and I have nowhere to go but the streets. I don't want to live like this anymore. I want my life back. The one with my twin boys and my wife."

Carson gently placed her hand in Donnie's. "I know you feel like you've failed, Donnie, but that isn't the case. The system has failed *you*. This is what we—" Carson gestured to her and the other surrounding bodies, "—are here for. To help you get your life back on track."

"Thank you." Donnie offered a nod as he sobbed. "Can I ask you something?"

"Anything you want, sir," Carson answered.

"Do you ever feel like we are the players of one giant board game?"

Carson tilted her head in an attempt to comprehend his theory.

"I feel as though I just keep losing, so I have to keep starting over, and I get farther and farther away from the 'Finish.' I'm so tired of playing."

"I can see that," Carson concurred. "But Donnie, I'm pretty sure you've just won the game today."

Donnie looked up into Carson's eyes as if realizing the same.

Carson continued, "Donnie, we are going to make this transition as easy as we can for you, but we are going to need you to try your best too. That means we need to try to stop drinking."

"I'll do anything. Whatever it takes."

"When you feel that urge coming on, I want you to think

of your family. Every time you say no to a drink is a step closer to them," Carson stressed.

"I can do this. The last thing I want them to think is I abandoned them; just up and left."

That last comment, however, triggered Carson in a way in which she could feel herself starting to tremble. She stood up and motioned to her team to begin working on things for Donnie.

"Donnie, they're going to begin the process. I will talk to you again in a little while."

He nodded. "Thank you, Miss Carson."

Carson quickly made her way to the back of the building and slipped outside. Donnie's words echoed in her mind.

"The last thing I want them to think is I abandoned them; just up and left."

Tears swelled behind her eyes. She jammed them shut and forced herself to breathe, attempting to push her own feelings of personal abandonment away. Images of Evelyn, the only woman she'd ever loved and the one person who claimed she'd never hurt Carson, flooded her mind.

Carson shook her head. She wasn't going to let her humiliating past ruin her day, not when she worked so hard to get where she was now. She took one more large breath in and, upon exhaling, she opened the door and headed back inside.

Fortunately, the plan for Donnie's current situation moved along progressively well. Carson was able to give him a hot meal, a shower, and a place to rest until the proper transportation was arranged for a rehab facility, which Donnie further agreed to. There was something about the way Carson could speak to others in distress that eased their minds, which was probably why she did so well running a charity. But even as a child, she was always interested in charity work and constantly volunteered at animal shelters, food banks, and soup kitchens.

Carson was originally born in Oakland, California, and lived there until her early teen years. Her family had been debating the possibility of moving somewhere safer because the crime rate was skyrocketing just before her twelfth birthday. After a nearby school shooting, her parents decided that was it for the "Golden State." They packed up their two kids, cats, and dogs and headed east. Her parents chose Pennsylvania—a small town named Tree Heights, specifically, in the northeast. It developed its name from the fact that it possessed the loftiest trees in the state. Although it had significantly sizable trees, that didn't quite make up for the sparse population of people. It took some getting used to, but Carson seemed to fit right into the small, friendly town. It didn't take long for her to notice that the seasons were magnificent. It was nothing like California, but the picturesque falls, glistening winters, rainy springs, and evergreen summers grew on her.

Shortly after she turned eighteen and became a woman, she turned heads in ways that could break necks. At five-foot-six, she blossomed with long, chestnut-colored hair that she often styled in loose, pristine curls. Her dark hair brought out her chocolate-brown eyes, with flecks of gold speckled throughout the irises that emerged in the light. Her skin was naturally tan, probably from growing up in California, so it welcomed the sun. But it wasn't just Carson's beauty that captured the attention of others; it was her benevolence that made her so unique. In a world where everyone else put themselves first, Carson always strived to invest her time in aiding the creation of others' happiness.

During high school, Carson had come to the realization that she was attracted to those of the same gender. Fortunately, she had a family that supported her, no matter what sexual orientation she chose, not that she really believed it was a choice to begin with. Carson knew she'd been born that way, and she revealed it to her family when she entered the tenth grade. Of course, most of them already knew, including her mother.

"The gender of the person you love does not make a difference to your father and me," her mother had reassured her. *"The only relevance is if you find happiness with that person, regardless of how they appear on the outside. If you can give your heart to someone, my dear, you'll discover there's nothing else in this world that's more important than that."*

After that day, Carson found security in her own skin because she knew she was blessed with a supportive, loving family.

Later that afternoon, while Carson was cleaning up for the day, she got a text message from her brother, Graham:

Hey Car, I'm at the charity firehall, a few blocks down from you. Can you come help me with something after you're done at work?

Carson sighed. All she wanted at the moment was to go home and fall asleep, turn off her mind for a few hours. But being the dependable big sister she was, she quickly texted him back that she would.

Several minutes later, she arrived at the firehall. Oddly enough, it appeared to be closed. It was pitch-black inside. She pulled out her phone and texted her brother:

Where are you? This place looks closed.

As Carson waited outside for his text back, she crossed her arms in an attempt to get more comfortable and decided to look around. Traffic was steady, with cars zooming by on the streets. People passed her on the sidewalk, laughing, chatting, and enjoying themselves. Typical Friday afternoon behavior.

She then cast her gaze across the street, spotting a young

woman sitting on some apartment steps carefully watching her, or so it seemed. Carson couldn't make out who it was. The woman was wearing sunglasses, concealing her identity. It didn't help that she was thirty or forty feet away. Carson did, however, recognize a few minor details about this person. She studied her from across the street, noting the ocean-blue denim jacket she wore, which complimented her tanned skin. Her mocha hair was pulled up in a messy bun. All ordinary things, except for one: the wide, cordial smile plastered on the woman's face as her eyes lingered on Carson. It was almost as if she was excited to see her. Was this normal?

Carson watched as the woman offered her a friendly wave. Puzzled, Carson looked behind her, wondering if maybe she was waving to someone else. Once she realized there was no one else around, she turned in the direction of the woman and yelled across the street, "Um, hello. Do I know you?"

Just before the woman had a chance to reply, the firehall doors banged open, startling Carson.

Graham poked his head outside. "Hey, Car! Did you not get my text? I told you to come in. It's open."

"Um, no, I—uh," Carson stuttered as she gazed back in the direction of the woman, but found no one there. The woman was gone and there was nobody sitting on the steps. "Did you see that woman sitting over there earlier?"

Graham glanced in the direction she was pointing. "No, Car. Matter of fact, that old apartment building has been deserted for a long time. Something about severe water damage."

Carson was stumped. "Huh. That's weird. I just saw someone sitting there and she waved at me."

"That's cool and all, Carson, but come on. I need your help." Graham gestured for her to follow him.

Carson peeked one more time across the street, studying the large, unsightly structure. How hadn't she noticed the grossly neglected building behind the woman on the stairs? The woman obviously didn't live there, and by the excitement on her face, it was almost as if she had specifically chosen that spot just to watch Carson.

She shrugged her shoulders, deciding to let it go, and followed Graham inside the firehall.

Once inside and just past the doors, she hesitated, standing in complete darkness. "Graham, where are you going? I can't see a thing. What's wrong with the lights?"

Graham didn't reply, but she could hear his footsteps as he easily strode through the darkness. Carson was almost sure he had somehow developed night vision as he ever so effortlessly walked on.

Carson faltered before finally deciding to take a step forward. She carefully reached out in front of her as if protecting herself from running into an imaginary wall. "Graham?"

In an instant, the lights flicked on, momentarily blinding her. "SURPRISE!"

Carson opened her eyes to find her family and friends surrounding her, including Graham and her best friend Rikki. Her smile widened. "Aw, you got me!"

Graham giggled as he, Rikki, and Carson's parents hurried over to greet Carson. "Happy birthday, Car!" he blurted.

"Merry Christmas!" Rikki exclaimed, which made Carson laugh even harder.

Carson pulled them all in for one big hug. "You guys are the absolute best!"

"Just wait until later, when the stripper pops out of your birthday cake—"

Carson's mother, Jan Miles, shot a look at Rikki that cut short her very comical remark.

"Just a joke, Jan," Rikki giggled, her amber eyes dancing.

That's what Carson loved about Rikki. She never held back.

"Carson, everybody would like to say hello. Come, come," Jan insisted as she gently guided her away to welcome the guests who had come to celebrate her special day.

After about three drawn-out hours, Carson finally finished

acknowledging, thanking, and expressing her sincere gratitude to multiple groups of people for coming to her party. She, by no means, felt ungrateful for the time her family spent planning this party, but she was exhausted. It wasn't their fault; Carson's mind would not stop racing.

Although she had pep-talked herself into having a pleasant day, and pushed Evelyn as far out of her thoughts as she could, it took much out of her to try so hard. What was so different about today that she couldn't focus on much without letting Evelyn cross her mind?

"No girlfriend, I take it?" an overbearing male voice asked, pulling Carson from her thoughts and back to the moment at hand. "And I don't see a ring on your finger."

Carson turned to find her brother's old high school football friend, Todd Jenkins, standing there.

Carson cringed internally. Over the past few years, Graham and Todd had drifted apart. It was most likely because Graham had grown up fast, and Todd still wanted to party every weekend as if he was living in a frat house. Todd was arrogant and obnoxious, while Graham was mature and respectful. This day was not letting up.

"Hello, Todd. Nope. Still single since the last time you asked me."

Todd grinned confidently, which just about caused Carson to shudder in disgust. "Then I suppose you wouldn't mind going out with me?"

"I'm sorry, Todd. I don't think so," Carson politely declined.

"Why not?" Todd's expression became cold. "Oh, don't tell me you're still hung up over that bitch that left you?" he snapped.

At this point, everyone quieted, probably to eavesdrop on the embarrassing situation.

Carson felt a brick in the pit of her stomach as she struggled to hold her composure.

Within a matter of seconds, Graham stood in front of

Carson. He glared at his old friend. "Todd, you need to leave. You are not welcome back here, and if you ever talk to my sister like that again, you will be sorry."

Todd shook his head as if he was appalled. "Wow. You have to be kidding me. What a waste." He poked his head around to look at Carson, blatantly ignoring Graham. "Call me when you wise up. Women are supposed to be with men." Todd spun around to leave, but halted abruptly to avoid running into Rikki, who was standing inches away from his face.

"It's Tiny Todd, right? You know what they say—guys that have a big, bad attitude like yours are usually compensating for something much smaller," Rikki spat out.

"Excuse me?" Todd squealed as his eyes scanned the room full of staring people.

"Oh, you know what? Now I'm sure that was your name." Rikki shook her head in disbelief. "The things the girls used to say in the locker room." She pinched her pointer finger and thumb so close together, they barely touched. "Tiny Todd."

Cackles and laughter echoed throughout the room as Todd rushed out the doors in humiliation.

"And that's the show, folks," Rikki blurted. She bowed sarcastically.

Everybody laughed louder and harder.

"Thanks, I'm here all night." Rikki hurried over to Carson, intertwining her arm with hers. She shook her head once more and sighed. "Men."

Hours later, Carson slumped down onto her kitchen chair. Today, she turned twenty-seven. She genuinely appreciated the birthday party, but she didn't like to celebrate the truth; she was getting older. In her mind, birthdays were just a discreet way of sugarcoating the fact that everyone was dying slowly. Time flies by; it escapes from your grasp no matter how hard you try to hold on, and you can never get it back. What's the point of celebrating anyways when you aren't celebrating with the one you wish was still around? It certainly wasn't the most optimistic way of portraying reality, but it was how she perceived it, especially after the last few heart-rending years.

Carson had mastered quite the successful exterior facade lately. With time came experience; experience in pretending someone didn't just suddenly whip the rug out from underneath you. Her resilient, career-thriving, and compassionate charisma masked the vulnerable, discomfited, and isolated person she also was. But that person—the latter—exposed themself more recently as she thought about the past.

Carson flicked her eyes over to a book resting on her kitchen table. She snatched it and opened it slowly. To most it was just an ordinary cookbook—only Carson knew what was hidden inside. Sitting in the very back of the book was a withered, folded-up note. Carson studied the outside of the thin paper, acknowledging the transparency. She could see the smudge of ink that had soaked through from the inside. She jammed her eyes closed, unable to bring herself to open it. She eventually slammed the book shut, trapping the note inside, got up, and tossed it inside a drawer. Two years had drifted by, yet she still had the same reaction when it came to Evelyn Walsh.

Carson thought back on the day before their second anniversary. Evelyn had disappeared, leaving just a small handwritten note behind with a few mindless words inside it, requesting forgiveness for her sudden departure.

After that day, Carson entombed and buried her broken heart so deep and distant from another human being that she felt like she'd never unveil it ever again. And even after all the anguish from rejection and tears throughout multitudinous sleepless nights, that woman was still all she thought about to this very day.

Chapter 2

~ Evelyn, 2020

"Ugh," Carson grumbled as she trudged out of Tree Height's Business Hall. "I don't know if I can go another minute in there listening to them argue with each other."

She had agreed to meet with some out-of-state charity runners about possibly cohosting a universal charity, but the evening wasn't going as planned. All they'd been doing the last few hours was fighting back and forth about funds. Why was money such a priority to some people? She had been taught to make do with what you have; the smallest amount of money could go the longest of ways, especially if you put your heart into it. All Carson ever really desired was to help the community. In a room full of avaricious, money-hungry people, her philanthropic nature and moral integrity outweighed all their bad qualities combined.

Carson marched over to a bench just a few feet from where she'd been standing. Luckily for her, the meeting was almost over, but she desperately needed a few minutes of fresh air at least to clear her mind from all the heated controversy. Not only was the seat very welcoming, but the view of the horizon ahead was breathtaking. Pinks and oranges radiated prevalently with full, white clouds strewn throughout the sky. It was a picture-perfect view and reminded her of the skies she had relished as a child in California.

Carson gazed at the lovely scene. The sun was about to go down, so she savored the sight, not taking immediate notice of the stranger who joined her at the other end of the bench.

When she snuck a glimpse of him, she assumed he was perhaps in his late thirties, maybe early forties. The man stared straight ahead with his eyes fixed, unfazed, on the skyline. There was something about him that made Carson feel uncomfortable, but what troubled her the most was the pronounced scowl on his face.

"So you're the Marked One." The man's voice was low and raspy, the way one would sound after screaming for hours. It was harshly uninviting to her ears.

When he finally turned to face her, she took note of a few prominent features beyond his sinister expression. His whiskey-colored eyes were bloodshot, as if highly irritated. Her first guess was intoxication. She noticed his dark orange irises seemed to glow, wavering with an unusual hue of red at times. Her mind was playing tricks on her, she was sure, but his eyes were nevertheless astonishing. He smelled of something sweet; she couldn't put her finger on it, but his demeanor was hard and cold.

"I've been waiting for the chance to meet you."

Inwardly, she cringed, but she refused to let him know he made her feel uneasy, so she spoke reticently. "Do I know you?"

"You will," he hissed, disgruntled. His obvious impatience didn't leave him any time to hesitate between breaths. "Expect to know all of us very soon."

Carson, frightened now, responded, "What are you talking about? All of who?" She felt her heart pounding in her chest, and her breathing quickened. She'd failed at her attempt for a guarded exterior, and she was now sure that he'd picked up on her feelings of trepidation.

The man eerily moved closer to her with every word he spoke. She became dizzy and lightheaded. She couldn't tell if her sudden disorientation was caused by her present angst or the overbearing aroma she was inhaling. Either way, her head was spinning.

She made an effort to slide down the bench farther from

him, but his malicious tone drew her in, and she froze instead.

"It's all coming to an end. *We* will take over. When that day comes, the 'Light One' won't be able to stop what—"

A loud, sonic boom of thunder cut the man off mid-sentence. Carson watched as a large white lightning bolt flashed across the sky. More roars of thunder followed. She peeked over at the strange man, witnessing a conspicuous shocked expression on his face.

The tone in his voice changed drastically—a mix between a perplexed and outraged inflection—and he shrieked, "What? No! It can't be! It is not yet time!"

Carson quickly glanced at what he was referring to. It was gloomy, as if a storm was rolling in. *This doesn't make any sense,* she thought. The sky had just been a beautiful palette of colors minutes ago. When she turned to face the creepy man again, she discovered she was now alone.

Did he flee in fear? Endless questions bombarded her. *Did the lightning scare him? What was he talking about? Who's the Light One? What does that even mean?* She thought about calling the police. Frantic, Carson got up before he decided to reappear.

"Excuse me, are you okay?" asked a warm, pleasant voice behind her.

She turned around to look at the person to whom the mystery voice belonged. A woman—probably in her twenties—stood near the bench with a concerned expression on her face. Attractive was an understatement. She was dressed in a pair of fitted, dark blue jeans that plunged into black combat boots with buckles on the lateral sides. Her tight, black shirt fit elegantly over her shapely upper body. She wore a black leather jacket consisting of numerous buckles, snaps, and zippers.

"Yes, I'm fine, thank you. It was just some crazy man. He must've been drunk or something. He said some really bizarre things. I mean, if not drunk, then drugs for sure," Carson informed her.

The lovely stranger stepped forward, closing some space

between Carson and herself, but Carson didn't mind. "Are you sure? Did he scare you? I was standing right over there—" she motioned to a tree near the Business Hall, "and you looked, um, afraid."

"He did a little, but I think the lightning frightened him off. Can you believe there are grown men out there who are actually still afraid of thunderstorms?" Carson giggled light-heartedly, but still felt a little uneasy over what the strange man had said to her. "Um, but he said something about taking over. It wasn't the normal, everyday conversation you have with a stranger, you know?"

"Must've been the drugs." The woman smiled engagingly, easing Carson's tension. Her voice was charming, and those full lips of hers were clearly inviting Carson's eyes to stare.

Stop being a creep, Carson scolded herself. It wasn't helping that the woman smelled wonderful; a subtle scent of some sort of blended musk and eucalyptus, if Carson had to guess. Of course, she didn't mind breathing it all in. Everything about this woman evoked her full attention.

Attempting to distract herself, Carson turned her gaze away from the beautiful stranger and back to the sky. Much to her surprise, the sky was clear, and there was no sign of rain or lightning, let alone any storm.

"Um, that's strange. It looked like a storm was coming," Carson commented, supremely bewildered. "Did you see the sky a few minutes ago?"

The woman glanced briefly in the same direction. "No, actually, I didn't. I suppose I was distracted." She winked at Carson.

Carson's heart walloped, and she felt the warmth in her cheeks from blushing.

"I'm Evelyn, by the way," the woman continued. "I'm new to the area."

"Uh—" Carson stumbled over her words. "I'm—uh, Carson. Welcome. I've lived here several years. Kind of small, but everybody is friendly and hospitable." She paused and corrected herself, "Um, everyone with the exception of *that* guy."

They both laughed, and Carson noted the substantial, comfortable feeling of security that this young, beautiful stranger provided.

"Good to know since I'm just settling in right now. I decided to go for a walk and seemed to stumble right into your problem." Evelyn chuckled again, her eyes dancing unreservedly as she spoke.

Carson studied her eyes. Piercing blue irises stared profoundly back into hers; an unusual, rare shade that was almost...indescribable. If she had to think of a word, though, what could she really say? Beautiful? *No, not good enough.* Captivating? *Yes, absolutely captivating.* But words didn't even do them justice. What was it with the eyes of everyone she encountered today?

After gazing admirably at Evelyn's eyes, Carson explored the rest of her, beginning with her other facial features. Evelyn possessed full, luscious lips, the kind you craved kissing, and the kind that Carson herself witnessed forming a very alluring smile. Evelyn was blessed with a full head of luxuriant blonde hair with highlighted strands scattered throughout. Loose curls fell down her back and the sides of her lovely face. She had vibrant, healthy skin. Her beauty was radiant in all aspects.

After staring, beguiled, Carson finally snapped out of the trance at the sound of Evelyn's voice.

"Do you think you'll be okay tonight? I mean, after that little scare?"

Carson blinked a few times. She'd forgotten all about that man. This new stranger—Evelyn—consumed all of her attention now. She liked it. "Oh, yes. Thank you. There are a ton of weirdos out there." She flashed another friendly smirk. "Just add it to the list."

"Okay." Evelyn bit her lip as she glanced downward and to

the left. "Um, so maybe I'll see you around?"

Carson decided to go out on a leap of faith. "Well, if you're interested, I'm just about to leave my meeting. Want to grab something to eat? I know all the good restaurants in this town."

Evelyn was clearly pleased with Carson's offer, and she grinned with utter satisfaction. "That would be great, honestly. I'm not really familiar with the area. Maybe you could show me around?"

Carson's smile widened. "Yes, of course. I mean, I'd love to." By this time, she didn't even try to hide the excitement in her voice. "Let me just go grab my things, and I'll be right back."

Evelyn nodded and sat down on the bench, waiting patiently. "I'll be right here."

Carson swiveled around and headed back toward the building she'd exited ten minutes earlier. She could feel Evelyn's eyes on her, watching her as she walked, but she enjoyed it. She wanted more.

Carson sank down into her comfortable living room couch, accompanied by a hot cup of tea. Her body was spent, so she was hoping her mind would allow sleep. Lately, Carson had been having odd dreams, and they'd even startle her out of a sound sleep. She didn't remember much except for the overwhelming sounds, for the most part. Sometimes a crackling noise blared as if she were near a campfire. Every now and then it was almost as if she felt the warmth on her skin. Other times she heard the pleasant, sonorous sound of water splashing and waves crashing, just like she experienced during childhood trips to the ocean. She recalled the soothing, gentle breeze of wind that whistled and roared around her. There was also this vivid buzzing sound, similar to static.

Thankfully, those dreams weren't the ones waking Carson. As a matter of fact, they calmed her, until the other one would commence—the one in particular that would frighten her. An awful, tumultuous scream would usually wake her, leaving her to catch up with her heartbeat. Unfortunately, after Carson would wake, she never remembered anything but darkness. She didn't understand why she had these dreams.

She took a big, satisfying sip of her chamomile-and-honey tea. Everything felt content except for one thing—one thought she couldn't shake off. She knew how much better it could have been if the one person who lived in the back of her mind was still in her life. *Why did she leave?* This question remained indefinitely. Carson never understood what caused her to go. Evelyn had loved her. Carson knew she did.

Carson and Evelyn's relationship had been perfect during their time together—pluperfect, in fact. Their love was significant, and Carson cherished it in its entirety, but great love stories always seemed to expire with some bitter ending—which was true in Carson's case, and it played on repeat every time she closed her eyes.

Fortunately, the last six months had been getting a lot easier for her. She could finally get out of bed without the fear of collapsing. She fought hard to push her thoughts and feelings aside with time when it came to Evelyn, but today was somehow different. Evelyn was the only thing on her mind, as though she could feel her standing right there.

CHAPTER 3

"Hey, Carson, can you unlock the door? You do this to me every time I come over." Graham pounded on her door so loudly that the next-door neighbors would have had the right to complain.

It was 2 a.m., but that was becoming the norm for Caron's younger brother. He'd usually stay at Carson's if he was out late rather than wake up their parents when he was in town.

Graham was twenty-four, five-foot-eight, and very handsome. It was safe to say that the Miles blessed their children with good genes. Graham's eyes sparkled in the light like two bright brown marbles. His midnight hair was chopped short but still long enough for him to pull off the "effortless bedhead" style. He possessed dark facial hair that was trimmed neatly, refusing to let it get too long. He cared a lot about his physical appearance because he grew up as an overweight child, and it made him insecure. He went to the gym almost six days a week. Being fit was a priority to him, even though his family had always made it apparent they loved him no matter what size he was.

Carson slithered off the couch and staggered over to the door, attempting to unlock it despite still being half asleep. Eventually, she managed to get it open. "Sorry, Graham," she apologized, wiping her eyes. "It's just a habit."

He barged in and threw his backpack on the couch. "Well, what if someone was chasing me? I'd be dead by the time you got to the door," he quipped, sarcasm evident in his deep voice. His attempt at a sobering expression, though, made it all the more amusing, and he knew that. He marched over to the fridge, opened the door, and rummaged around. He finally decided on a gallon of milk, unscrewed the lid, and drank from the jug itself.

"What if there was already someone inside my apartment waiting for your macho ass because I decided not to lock it?" Carson asked him gravely, but broke into laughter as soon as she saw the look of defeat that cast itself over his face. "What're you doing out so late anyway? And geez, use a glass." She rolled her eyes.

Graham wiped his mouth with the back of his hand like a little kid. "Oh, I went out with Amy. She and I decided to go for a late walk." He took another gulp from the jug, ignoring her demand.

"Is everything all right?" she asked, concern evident on her face.

He trudged over and sat an arm's length away from her on the couch. "Sometimes she's a bit hard to get ahold of. I just try to convince myself that she's busy with work."

"Graham, don't be the guy who's just 'good enough' for the time being. I don't want to see this girl hurt you. I know how it is," she told him, sincerity in her tone.

Graham couldn't keep the irritation out of his voice as he lashed out almost immediately. "Carson, Amy is *not* like Evelyn. She's not just gonna disappear into thin air," he snapped, and watched as Carson's expression changed from concern to affront in a matter of seconds. He instantly felt guilty.

Before Carson had the chance to reply, Graham spoke again. This time, however, his tone softened. "Um, I'm sorry, Car. I didn't mean it like that. I just meant Amy may not turn out to be like, uh...Ev. I'm sorry. I didn't mean to bring up a touchy subject. I know Todd probably did enough of that earlier tonight."

She smiled at him and nodded in warm rapport. "I know, Graham. That's okay. And to be honest, I'm the one who's sorry. I shouldn't have brought her up. I haven't in months.

It's just that I've been thinking about it a lot today. I don't know why. Do you think something could have happened to her?"

Graham didn't want to make Carson feel worse, but he knew she needed to hear what he was thinking—well, *some* of what he was thinking. He'd watched his big sister go through so much pain in the last couple of years that it hurt him even thinking about that troublesome time. Just within the last several months, she'd shown so much progress in getting over the breakup. He didn't want her backtracking.

"Listen, Car, I love you. You're my big sister, and I'll do anything I can to make you feel better. But you know Ev's not coming back." His jaw tightened as he spoke. "And if she did happen to go through anything, well, it's called regret. I hope she feels regret and shame every day for leaving the way she did." He shook his head in disapproval. "It's been two years, Car. I know you loved her, but you need to let this go. You deserve better. You know you do."

When he thought about Evelyn, all he could muster up were spiteful feelings of despise and fury for the way she'd left things with his sister. Evelyn had stuck around for two years, made Carson fall in love with her—tricked the whole family into completely adoring her, for that matter—and then just up and left them all as if the previous two years had meant nothing. If it weren't for Carson's parents, Graham, and her best friend Rikki picking her heart up off the floor for months, Carson still wouldn't be the same person.

Graham and Rikki had been the ones who took time off work to stay with Carson after her breakup. They took shifts and even became close friends during that time. They'd literally drag Carson out of her bed, order her to get dressed, and then show her that the outside world still goes on after a heartbreak.

In Graham's mind, Evelyn was damned if she ever thought she could come sneaking back into Carson's life as long as he was around—and as long as he was alive, he was going to be around *permanently.*

"You're right, Graham. I don't know what it is. I'm just a little sensitive today." Carson shook her head slowly, disappointed in herself. "But thanks for having this talk with me. I know you care about me. I love ya too, bud. Now go to sleep. You know where the extra blankets are." She pointed to the closet in the hall, then stood up, stretched, and moseyed off in the direction of her bedroom.

Graham caught her attention again. "Hey, Car?"

She turned around to face him, all ears.

"I want you to know I'm here. I know I act intolerant when it comes to her, but you can talk to me, even if it's about her. About anything for that matter," he emphasized. The guilt really kicked in when Graham thought about all the times Carson took care of him through their childhood, and the least he could do was listen to her when she spoke on her birthday, whether it was about Evelyn or not. "But when I said you deserve better, I meant it. You do."

Carson smiled faintly. "Thanks, Graham, but you really are right. I need to let this go." She turned around and scampered off to bed.

Graham stole a few blankets and an extra pillow from Carson's hallway closet. He began to make his bed on the couch. He lay down, struggling to collect positive thoughts. He didn't mean to hurt his sister's feelings. It's just that he didn't even like hearing Evelyn's name.

Carson had been through enough. Graham wanted what was best for her, and that was to get Evelyn off of her mind, ultimately forever.

Chapter 4

Evelyn pulled Carson back in for another kiss as if she was afraid she wouldn't see her for days.

Carson giggled, "Babe, I'm just running to the bathroom." But then she threw herself back into Evelyn's arms and placed her lips onto Evelyn's compellingly. She lingered before finally forcing herself away and smiling warmly. "Be right back."

Evelyn watched Carson in adoration as she walked through the crowd of people, who were jostling into one another. She'd never fallen for another person like this before. They'd been inseparable for months, and she relished every moment she spent with her.

Carson wanted to spontaneously get out of town for the weekend and take a break from life's duties, so they had driven a few hours to the club they were currently at, the first place that caught Carson's eye. A few drinks accompanied by dancing would even loosen Evelyn up, Carson had reassured her. Little did Carson know that alcohol didn't affect Evelyn in the least.

The women's restroom was on the other side of the club, but not too far. It was dark inside the club, with only the bright strobe lights that emitted red, blue, green, and purple beams, which flashed intermittently over the large swarm. The music blared, so it was almost impossible to have a conversation with someone, but that didn't make a difference when it came to Evelyn's senses. She could hear, see, and even feel things ordinary people were incapable of sensing. There wasn't a whole lot of distance between herself and the restroom doors, so she knew for sure that Carson was safe inside. She stared down at the table, waiting patiently for her girlfriend's return. She began to feel the ambiance of the atmosphere; she could sense the club's mood. There were many cheerful attitudes, and some drunk and emotional ones as well. It appeared like the usual, ordinary bar scene for the most part. That was until she heard a voice, a man speaking to someone on his cell phone.

"Jimmy, it's Arthur. Yeah, yeah. I got it. Yeah, Jimmy, there are two. Give me about an hour, and I'll bring them back. I have the drinks just about ready."

Evelyn's head remained in the same position, but her eyes shot over to another table in the corner. She watched as a heavyset man—possibly in his fifties—dropped something into a few glasses in front of him after he hung up his phone. He wore a gray suit with a red tie that hung loosely and neglectfully around his neck. Whatever he released in the glasses fizzed momentarily. It was too dark for anyone to notice; anyone except for Evelyn. The thing about her eyesight was that she could see effortlessly in the dark. At times like these, night vision had its advantages.

She observed discreetly as the man hooked his stubby fingers around the glasses and glanced out at the crowd of people. He locked his eyes decisively on some young girls dancing and goofing off carelessly. They were obviously intoxicated and not paying a bit of attention to anyone else, and he was indeed on his way to further complicate their night.

"Great," Evelyn sighed and rolled her eyes. This man, Arthur, reminded her of somebody she hadn't thought about in a very long time—Mayor Clarence Howard. Arthur was bringing back sensitive memories, and Evelyn wasn't about to relive the past, because it didn't turn out so well for Evelyn, and, well, it turned out much worse for Mayor Howard. She glanced over at the bathroom door again. Carson was still inside, so she had some time. She took a deep breath, attempting to pacify her sudden anger.

Arthur deviously began to move in the direction of the two girls, but halted when he heard Evelyn speak.

"I probably wouldn't do that if I were you," she warned. She offered a cunning smile and leaned her elbows on the table beside him, surveying his every move.

"Excuse me?" he asked, scrutinizing her with his beady eyes.

"We both know that wasn't an antacid you dropped in those drinks." She shot her gaze down at the glasses he was holding, as if to reveal something he didn't already know, and then back up at him.

He looked around to ensure no one else was listening, then took a hulky step inward, close enough for her to feel his breath on her face. "Unless you want trouble tonight, I suggest you mind your own damn business," he hissed, glowering down at her.

She sighed. "You know, I was. I *really* was. But your little cat-and-mouse game here partook in quite the interruption of my evening." She glared back at the lewd man, and when she did, he saw real, tangible sparks in her eyes. "So, unless *you* want trouble tonight, I suggest you call Jimmy back and tell him you aren't going to make your double date."

The man stiffened. His mouth dropped open, and he gasped. "What the... Wh-who are you?"

She gestured to the door that displayed "EXIT" in large, brightly lit red letters directly above it. A few policemen stood on each side of the doorway, conversing. "I'm just that irrational story you'll attempt to explain to those cops over there if you don't leave right now." Her eyes flashed with sparks once again.

Frightened, the man's gaze jittered back and forth from the cops to her. "Uh—okay. Y-you got it." He snatched the glasses and hurried off, but before he got very far, he heard her voice again. Every coarse hair on the back of his scraggly neck stood rigid as he sank in perturbation.

"Oh, and Arthur?"

His eyes widened with shock as he looked up to find her standing right in front of him, just inches away. He turned around frantically to look at the table they were standing at moments ago and then back at her. "Wha—how did you do that? How do you know my name?"

"Just a good guess," she teased, then pointed to the glasses in his hands. "The glasses. Dump them."

He nodded tensely, fear evident on his face. He quickly dumped both drinks in a large garbage can beside him and even let go of the glasses themselves. They broke once they hit the bottom of the large bin.

Evelyn grinned shrewdly at him. "Good boy," she bantered. "Now run along. And Arty, you behave tonight. You don't want me paying you a home visit. Your wife wouldn't appreciate that." She winked at him, and he shuddered. He couldn't get out of there fast enough, rudely bumping into people as he desperately rushed to the exit.

Carson sat at their table with her phone. She wasn't sure where Evelyn had gone because she'd just come from the restroom, and she was sure Evelyn wasn't in there. *Maybe she's getting us drinks?* She glanced in the direction of the bar and didn't see her there, either.

She pulled Evelyn's contact up on her phone, ready to call her, but paused once she felt two arms wrap around her body from behind. She heard a familiar voice.

"Hey, you."

Carson turned around to find Evelyn there, smiling affectionately at her. Evelyn lowered herself to Carson's level, kissing her lightly.

"There you are," Carson said, relieved. "I got worried. Where did you go?"

"Oh, I'm sorry, Car. Some guy needed help leaving. He realized he'd had too much to drink, so I called him a cab. I'm sure he'll undoubtedly feel rough tomorrow, though," she muttered earnestly.

Carson stood up and turned to face Evelyn, tangling her arms around her waist. "Aww, baby. That was very kind of you."

29

CHAPTER 5

The next morning, sunlight streaked through Carson's bedroom blinds as she opened her eyes. Although she was still dead tired from the busy day before, she couldn't force herself to fall back asleep; thoughts about last night's dream flooded any chance. Like the others, this one provided no real meaning. Only this time she specifically recalled feeling as though she couldn't breathe, like her lungs were being polluted and she was suffocating. *Strange.* She decided to push it to the back of her mind for now because she had another busy day planned ahead of her.

It was Saturday, which meant Carson had the town picnic to attend. She was volunteering with Rikki and meeting Graham's girlfriend, Amy, for the first time. She casually rolled out of bed and set off for the kitchen, craving her first cup of coffee to start the day. She glanced in the living room on the way to the kitchen. The couch was empty, despite the few slovenly folded blankets and pillows sitting on top. Graham had already left. She wasn't the least bit surprised though, because he was an early riser. He always hit the gym in the mornings. But he did the honor of making sure the coffee was on and ready for Carson when she woke up, and for that, she was grateful.

Carson staggered over to the kitchen window after she poured herself a steaming cup. She took a peek outside. The spring-like sweater weather would soon transform into shirtless-with-shades days. Not too humid, not too cold; just right. It reminded her of the weekend club getaway she spent with Evelyn. She tried to close out those thoughts, but she couldn't forget her if she tried.

It was nearing ten o'clock, and Carson needed to be at the town park by noon; she was assisting her best friend at a vending booth all day. She jumped in the shower after she picked out her outfit: a pair of distressed blue-jean shorts with a maroon T-shirt displaying "*Tree Heights Picnics since 1963*" on the front.

After a quick attempt at looking somewhat presentable for the day, Carson grabbed a bottle of water and her keys and rushed out the door. Once she started her car, her heart jumped at the realization of what was on the radio. It was a particular song that Evelyn had said—just a few nights before she left—reminded her of Carson.

The music echoed throughout her car, tugging at the strings of her freshly mended heart. She hadn't heard that song in months. After Evelyn disappeared from her life, she avoided anything with sentimental value altogether, especially songs that brought back memories like this one. It was now just a useless reminder of someone who had let her down disgracefully.

Carson shook her head in disgust as she quickly turned the station. She buckled up and headed off to the town park to meet her family and friends. She didn't have time to reminisce on disconsolate events from the past, either.

As Carson pulled into Tree Heights Diamond Park, she caught a glimpse of Graham with his new girlfriend, Amy, their arms locked as they walked over to greet Carson. Amy possessed jet-black hair that fell straight down her back, and she was lean with a sharp, feminine curve to her body. Her well-exposed toned legs demonstrated visibly contracted calf muscles as she strutted along, plunging down into black wedge heels that she glided in with ease. Her perfectly polished, florid toenails exposed themselves at the toe-cap. She wore a provocative black dress that was thin and ever so revealing. Her manicured nails were black at the bases and gradually faded into bloodred at the tips. A pair of large, black, thick-framed sun-glasses sat on the bridge of her nose, hiding her eyes from view. Carson noticed Amy had pointy facial features, despite the portion of her face that the glasses masked. Although Carson couldn't see her eyes, she assumed Amy possessed a self-loving, pretentious expression underneath. Carson didn't want to draw a critically unjustified conclusion, but Amy appeared as high-maintenance as they came, smirking those salient red lips egotistically.

"Finally decide to get here?" Graham joked and shoved Carson as she got out of her car.

Carson shot him a teasing I'll-knock-you-out-bro look. "I woke up late. Someone decided to knock on my door in the middle of the night." Her eyes darted over to Amy. "You must be Amy. It's nice to finally meet you. I've heard a lot about you. Glad you could make it today."

Amy took a few steps toward Carson, but she didn't bother to remove her sunglasses. She did, however, offer her a formal smile. "Hello, Carson. Pleasure's all mine." She closed some distance between them by taking another step forward. Carson still couldn't see her face clearly, but she did notice the movement of her eyes that traced her up and down as if examining her.

Carson shifted uncomfortably, but then Amy held out her hand with courtesy, so at least she presented *some* manners. Carson gripped her hand lightly and shook it without a word while watching Amy beam with satisfaction. Carson figured Graham too would notice her odd behavior, but when she glanced over at him, his expression seemed content as ever.

Amy finally broke the silence. "Oh, that's right. Happy belated birthday. Sorry I missed it. Had to work late."

"That's okay. It's understandable. It's nice of you to take the time to volunteer with Graham at the picnic today."

"I'm happy to oblige. Wherever Graham goes, I go. That reminds me...we should spend some time together, just us girls. Graham always mentions how important you are to him, which means you are important to me too." She smiled a little too widely, her straight white teeth exposed.

Carson offered a closed smile and nodded. "Right. Um, yeah. Sure. We should do that."

Amy had the strangest way of exchanging small talk, but Carson didn't want to make her uncertainty obvious to Graham, so she politely changed the subject. "So where are you from, Amy?"

"All over. I like to travel often. Never really found any reason to settle in one place, until I met Graham." She looked back at Graham, who was smiling at her with admiration. "I moved here a few months ago. It's not exactly my thing, you know, a small town. But Graham *is* my thing. So I decided to stay."

Carson forced a smile this time. "Well, anyone who makes my brother happy is worth having around." She decided it was time for her to head over to the vendors to join her best friend. "Again, it was great meeting you. Maybe I'll run into you guys later?"

"Same to you. Oh, and Graham told me you've had a rough couple of years. So, if you need someone to talk to I can—"

"Excuse me?" Carson's voice converted from mild friendliness to vast defense in a matter of seconds. Her questioning gaze shifted from Amy to Graham. It was clear Graham had confided in Amy a little too much already; she didn't only hear about the family's holiday traditions and their favorite childhood memories this early in their relationship, but all about the failures of Carson's personal business as well.

By the sudden fearing yet guilty expression on Graham's face, Carson could tell he wanted to stop Amy from saying another word. *Too late.*

"Your ex. It sounds like she really messed things up. You know, disappearing and all the way she did. She sounds like a coward." Amy actually sneered, as if she had something against

Evelyn. She didn't even know Carson, let alone Evelyn. What gave her the right to make any assumption at all? Carson was beginning to not feel so bad about her earlier prejudgment on this girl.

"Uh, thanks for the concern, but that's actually something personal Graham probably shouldn't be letting the entire world know." Carson glared at Graham pointedly. "Graham, come find me later. Rik and I are grilling today."

He nodded in guilt-ridden agreement.

Humiliated, Carson finally excused herself, but before she turned around to leave, she noted the sly grin on Amy's face. Was all of this really normal behavior for somebody who was practically a stranger? Was Carson just overanalyzing this girl because she was protective of Graham? She decided to give her the benefit of the doubt. "Again, it was great meeting you."

"Same. I'm certain I'll see you in the near future, Carson."

After that, Carson walked immediately over to where the booths were, where she watched as her best friend set up.

"Car! Over here! Can't you see me? I'm right here!" Rikki theatrically waved her arm as Carson walked in her direction. She didn't stop until Carson was just a few feet from her side. She slapped her hand onto her chest in overdramatized relief. "Oh good, I thought you were gonna walk right past me. So what's up, lesbo?" she uttered, exhibiting a comical grin. Her sarcasm and humor always made Carson laugh and thus put her in a better mood.

Rikki, who was around the same age as Carson, had ginger hair that she'd frequently leave down in naturally wild curls with the attempt of taming them with some mousse and hairspray. She was also about the same height as Carson, give or take an inch. Rikki's curvaceous body fit snugly into some black spandex tights and a loose, green T-shirt with "*Tree Heights Picnics since 1963*" also displayed on the front. She had rusty-brown eyes and freckles sprinkled upon her face, which were made particularly prominent by the sunshine.

Rikki had been raised under the impression that over-dressing is always better than underdressing, so she usually went above and beyond to look flawless. However, she dressed a little more casually for the occasion today. Her shimmery green eyeshadow and black mascara praised the glint of her eyes. The blush she wore complimented the contour of her delicate cheekbones, and her lip gloss made her plump pink lips shine beautifully on that Saturday afternoon.

Carson and Rikki met a couple years after Carson moved to Tree Heights, so they had been friends since their teenage years. Rikki was no less than that obnoxious, charismatic, and eventful guest you wouldn't regret bringing to your favorite resident at the nursing home's ninetieth birthday party, or so Carson found out when Rikki persuaded most of the elderly crowd to dance with her. Carson had laughed so hard tears streamed down her face during this entertaining moment, although she was secretly afraid of someone breaking a hip. Fortunately, though, everyone returned to their rooms with all brittle bones intact.

Aside from her charming and amusing personality, Rikki had a slight attitude problem—that was only beginning to worsen—to say the least. She never had any trouble asserting her duty as an honorable friend when it came to Carson, and this even included lashing out on some poor, harmless gentle-men who would ask Carson out innocently. Most of the time, these guys were unaware of Carson's sexual orientation, and it was usually a common misunderstanding. As for the pushy, arrogant ones who still felt entitled and were bound and determined for an explanation—such as Todd—Rikki would fly off the handle. During times like these, Carson would pac-ify the situation and, once Rikki cooled down, they'd both laugh hysterically as the guys would helplessly scamper off with everything but their pride and dignity.

Although the outbursts on strangers were likely avoidable, Carson knew it was Rikki's solidified way of expressing her loyalty. She believed everyone needed a person in their life who'd demand justice when it was deserved as well as someone who could rein the other back in when they'd jumped a little too far in the deep end of confrontation. Despite being somewhat polar opposites, they knew each other well, and their relationship thrived naturally.

Rikki, who had stood by Carson's side after Evelyn left, never once acted like Carson's restless nights full of tears during their adult sleepovers or her sluggish moods on shopping trips were ever nettlesome. She never revealed a sense of impatience or irritation when Carson called her in the middle of work just to vent or cry about her recent breakup. Rikki provided what knowledgeable advice she could, though she herself didn't "do" relationships. What Rikki did superlatively, though, was listen, and that's what Carson needed. She remained a reliable friend and for that Carson couldn't thank her enough.

"So what are we in for today?" Carson asked her.

"Well, basically we're just in charge of the grill. Hamburgers, hot dogs, chicken. All the good stuff." Rikki led the way over to the grill. "So what's up with the new chick Graham's dating?" she asked Carson curiously.

"I have no idea. She's odd, Rik. And you know me, I don't judge. But I just don't feel right about her," Carson explained. She crossed her arms. "Oh, and it doesn't help that she knows all about my business with the breakup. Graham filled her in entirely. I've yet to speak with him about that." She shook her head.

Rikki eyed her inquisitively. "Maybe he's just concerned about the way you've been lately. I think he needed someone else to talk to," Rikki explained.

Carson turned to face her. "What do you mean 'the way I've been'? Is this something the both of you have been discussing?" she interrogated her.

"Car, I want what's best for you just as much as Graham

does. He texted me late last night. He just wanted to make sure you were okay, like that there wasn't anything you weren't telling him."

"What does he think? Just because I've brought her up a few times lately doesn't mean—"

"Hey, girls!" Rikki's mother rushed over to greet them.

Rikki rolled her eyes almost instantaneously. Rikki's mother, Sandra Ward, was the president of the Business Hall and the town's mayor. With it being such a small town, she ran most of the picnics and activities held in Tree Heights. She really enjoyed being a helpful hand in the community, but she may have relished in the spotlight a bit too much. She held quite the successful stature in town, but what most people didn't realize was how hard she'd always been on Rikki, probably because she wanted her child to live up to her reputation. She forced her into numerous activities and after-school programs throughout her school years. She was expected to receive exceptional grades, although "exceptional" was an understatement. Bs were not allowed in Sandra's house; if you came home with a C on your report card, well, that was enough to give Sandra a heart attack. Sandra had given Rikki one choice after high school: go to college—but under her terms—or move out.

Rikki held quite a passion for art. Ever since elementary school, colors just spoke to her. She took some art electives in high school; during her last year, she'd fallen in love with watercolor painting. Sandra was never pleased with Rikki's "art obsession." She used to tell her that art wouldn't get her anywhere in the real world. When it came down to it, Rikki's initial choice of college was an art school a few hours away. This particular school required a deposit to hold one's spot, as long as the portfolio was accepted. However, the art portfolio wasn't the problem—the money was. When Sandra found Rikki's acceptance letter and portfolio while snooping in her bedroom one day, she told Rikki that she was insane if she thought she'd get any encouragement or support from her with such a ridiculous dream. So Rikki, feeling trapped between chasing her dream and wanting her mother's favorable reception, obliged and received an education in accounting at a school close by. Her only request was that she could still take some art classes. Sandra figured it was a phase she'd grow out of once she became an accountant, so she approved.

Four long, stressful years directly following high school, Rikki had obtained her bachelor's degree, but only with the sacrifice of time and, of course, her real ambition. The art classes she took during those college years were moderately fascinating, but nothing like she could have experienced at the other school. Rikki knew deep inside that she would have been capable of creating resplendent artwork, so ever since then, she held a silent grudge against her mother for crushing her dreams.

Sandra, who stood on this very warm day in her over-the-top outfit—a charcoal-gray professional pantsuit—glanced at Carson. "Carson, dear, thank you so much for helping my daughter out today. I want everything to go smoothly, and now I know it will," she stressed to her, but then casually glanced over in Rikki's direction. It was an intentional jab. Rikki glared at her mother. "Are you ladies ready to get started?" Sandra asked, looking back and forth between the two.

"Sure," Carson replied, and then looked at Rikki. "Why don't you start the grill, Rik? I've never been too great at it. I'm gonna get the table set up for customers, and I'll be over in a minute so you can teach me."

"Deal." Rikki, quenched by satisfaction, smiled at Carson as a silent *thank you.* Carson strolled off in the opposite direction. Rikki, about to wander off in the other direction, stopped when she felt her mother grab her arm.

"Honey, be careful. I know you have trouble in the kitchen at times." Sandra threw her daughter a *don't embarrass me* look that only further agitated her.

"Yes, Mother. Hopefully I can remember *something* from the six different Home Ec courses you made me take throughout my childhood." With that last snarky comment, Rikki stormed off without looking back, leaving Sandra desolate.

Once Rikki arrived at her grill station, she stood there silently and began to open the bag of charcoal. After dumping a sufficient amount inside for the abundance of food they'd be grilling that afternoon, she snagged the lighter fluid canister. She saturated the cone-shaped pile of coals and waited about thirty seconds before proceeding with igniting the lighter.

Once she flicked the button on the lighter, she lowered the small flame toward the heap of charcoal. Unfortunately, once she got close enough to the bottom, it blew out. She repeated the same operation three or four times, but still, the lighter would relentlessly blow out every time, and she couldn't understand why. It wasn't even very windy today.

Becoming slightly aggravated, Rikki decided to try the matches that sat on a nearby table instead. She went through about five or six before the seventh remained lit. Again, once her arm reached the bottom, the match blew out. She tried another time with the lighter, but this time the lighter wouldn't even cast a spark. *What am I doing wrong?* Rikki thought.

Rikki glanced over in her mother's direction; she refused to let her mother witness the expression of pure frustration that was obviously displayed on her face at that moment, especially to discover her defeat, so she tried another match. The last failing attempt, with a smokeless match still in her hand, was just enough to send her over the edge. Rikki slammed both hands down on each side of the grill and shouted, "Why won't you just start?!"

All of a sudden, the entire grill burst into flames, throwing Rikki backward a few steps. She glanced down at her hands. "What the hell?" Her hands were steaming. The weirdest part, though, was that they didn't hurt at all. No burn. No pain. Nothing.

Carson and Sandra, along with several other people, hurried over once they saw the fire. One of the men, a volunteer firefighter, held a fire extinguisher and quickly pulled the safety pin. He squeezed the handle to squelch the fire until it was entirely out. After he was done, he picked up several used matches. He stared at them, clearly exasperated. "Mayor Ward, you may want to teach your daughter how to use a charcoal grill for next time, or there would have never been a next time after what could've happened here today," he stated firmly before turning around and stomping away.

As everyone finally began clearing the area once the excitement was over, only Rikki, Sandra, and Carson remained.

Rikki stood silent for a moment and then peeked in her mother's direction. "It was an accident," she exclaimed, unable to come up with any possible reason for what happened.

Carson placed her hand on Rikki's shoulder for comfort.

Sandra, on the other hand, maintained her rigid demeanor with her arms crossed and a scowl of disappointment on her face as she studied the smoking grill. "One job, Rikki. You had *one* job. You could have injured someone here and, most importantly," Sandra paused for a long moment before finishing her sentence, "you could have hurt yourself." She finally glanced up at Rikki with a stern and riled expression.

"Mother, I'm sorry. I don't know what happened. At first, it wouldn't start, but then—"

"Rikki, I think you need to take the rest of the day off. Carson and I can finish." Anybody could have sensed the disgrace in Sandra's tone as she spoke to her one and only daughter.

"But, Mother, I'm fine. I can—"

"I don't have time to listen to this right now, Rikki. I have a picnic to run. Now just go home," she ordered blatantly, with obviously no desire to hear Rikki's excuses.

Outraged, Rikki spoke up. "Mother, I'm twenty-six years old. When are you going to stop treating me like I'm five?" she blurted out in utter frustration, unaware of all the eyes gawking in their direction.

Sandra, extremely embarrassed, waved them all off. "Everyone, she's just a little worked up still. Please proceed with your booths." She then faced Rikki. "When you start acting like an adult, I will treat you like one, but you have a lot of growing up to do." Sandra turned around, marched irately over to her booth, and began to rearrange supplies on the table.

"Don't worry about it, Rik. This is no big deal. I'll work the grill, and when I'm done, I can stop by your place to pick you up. You can stay at my apartment. Pack a bag. How about we have a girl's night?" Carson suggested.

Feeling grateful for the invitation, Rikki accepted. "That actually sounds like just what I need." She sighed and shook her head. "I'm sorry about this. I wish I could stay and help, but you're never given a second chance when it comes to Sandy Ward." She clenched her jaw in disgust.

"Rik, I want you to know you're a really great person," Carson said genuinely, "and if I had a grill, I'd gladly let you use it, or even accidentally blow it up any day." She winked, or at least attempted to wink; it turned into more of a blink-ing-twitching episode rather than a smooth gesture, and Rikki, of course, found this hysterical.

"Okay, Rik. You go home and relax, maybe paint or something. Get your mind off things. I'll pick you up later." Carson began to pivot her body back in the direction of the booth when Rikki got her attention again.

"Hey, Car?"

Carson turned around to face her again, eyebrows raised and attuned.

"Thank you."

This time, Carson heard the sincerity in Rikki's voice. She nodded softly. "You would and have *always* done the same for me."

CHAPTER 6

As Rikki shuffled toward the main parking lot, she forced herself to think of anything other than what had just happened at the picnic with the grill. She needed some time to relax, and took Carson's suggestion into consideration. Painting would calm her.

Rikki reminisced on a specific memory from just a few years ago—the main reason she began her current project in the first place.

Graham had thrown his hands up in a *freeze* motion, silently warning Rikki to halt; she stopped dead in her tracks. Carson tossed and turned a little, but remained in the same relaxed position on the couch. It was safe to say she'd finally fallen into a deep sleep. Rikki stood still in the middle of the living room, careful not to wake her up after the evening she'd had.

It had only been weeks since Evelyn left, and that night had been a rough one with sporadic episodes of tears, but Graham and Rikki were both off work, so they opted to spend the night with her. Carson was lying on the sectional opposite where Graham was sitting. He'd asked Rikki to sit next to him so they didn't have to shout across the room to one another as they finished the movie they had started before Carson fell asleep.

Rikki finally slouched down next to Graham on his side of the couch, with just a few feet separating them. She looked over at where Carson was resting peacefully for the time being.

"Do you think she's going to get better?" she had asked him.

Graham nodded in response, and then whispered, "She will eventually. It's just gonna take time. This was her first real relationship. She'll learn breakups are gonna happen through-out life, and it's okay to hurt. It's okay to miss them. But it's also okay to be alone, too."

"She's not really alone," Rikki argued and gestured back and forth between herself and Graham.

He smiled at her and nodded in agreement. They sat quietly for several minutes while watching the movie until Graham had broken the silence.

"Rikki?"

She turned her head to face him.

"Thank you."

"For what?" she asked, her eyebrows raised.

"This." He pointed at Carson. "Being here for my sister, especially now, when she needs you."

"She needs you too, Graham," she emphasized.

"Yeah, but I'm her brother. I have to be here for her. It's in my blood. You know, family," he joked.

"Trust me, I wish I had the relationship with my mother that you guys have with your parents, even the one you have with Carson. So blood doesn't always mean family."

He dropped his gaze down to the floor and a look of shame formed on his face. "Rikki, I'm sorry. I didn't mean it like that."

She smiled at him in assurance. "Don't be sorry. I've been dealing with Sandy Ward my whole life."

They had giggled together but quickly held their breath when Carson moved again, adjusting her position on the couch.

After Rikki was sure she was still asleep, she resumed their conversation. "Besides, your sister is my *real* family. She is the only person who gets me."

"*I* get you." Graham had spoken the words with distinct

sincerity, as if he had a point to prove. He then faltered a moment as though he was embarrassed and cleared his throat, adding, "We sort of grew up together. How long have we known each other now? Like, over ten years?"

Rikki nodded in accord. "Yeah, actually. Wow, I didn't realize it's been that long." She then became sidetracked, the commercial on the television her obvious distraction. She pointed to the screen. "You see that? That's a new reality show that aired a few months ago. It's about the so-called 'perfect' life of a famous sculptor. He's made millions through his work." She shook her head in disgust. "I've realized I don't really like reality shows."

Graham studied her in confusion. "Why?"

"I learned a lot about sculpting in one of my art classes," she explained, "and I did some research on that man. I mean, I *really* dug deep. He's a recovering drug addict." Putting her hands up in defense, she then exclaimed, "Not that that's the issue. It's just the fact that shows like that one make it seem like life is always perfect. And it's *not*. When he was struggling not to relapse, he'd sculpt. It distracted him, you know, kept him busy doing something he loved. I've been watching this show since it started and it never once mentions his background story. At least not yet."

"Maybe he's ashamed of his past?" Graham suggested.

She shook her head in disappointment. "He went through so much to get to where he is now. He shouldn't be ashamed. It was a part of what made him who he is now—a changed man, a better person." She sighed.

"That actually reminds me of something," Graham said, and Rikki turned to give him her undivided attention again. "Last year, when I went on a school trip to Italy, we discovered this large, wooden door on a hillside during the tour. And when I say door, I mean it was *just* a door. It was surrounded by pieces of broken brick that I'm assuming used to be part of an entire wall. It was as if the door, hinges, and frame were ripped from a building and placed on that hill. The door was aged and broken, and only hinged at the top. It was definitely in poor shape."

Rikki had watched him with intent as he explained.

"But when I opened it, I understood why it was there." He beamed, obviously reminiscing on the trip to Italy.

"What was it doing there?" Rikki asked him, intrigued.

"Well, it's a piece of art now," he gestured to her, "which you definitely would have loved. When you opened the door, you saw the horizon. The view was amazing, and it was rather symbolic. To me, it held an important meaning: Life looks rough sometimes, but you get through the hard parts because life has so much to offer. Every scar and imperfection can still lead to something beautiful. Something worth living for."

Rikki, who had been utterly lost in her thoughts, didn't quite make it to her vehicle before she heard a familiar voice call her name.

"Rikki, hey!"

She turned around to find Graham jogging over, sporting his usual everyday, gym-like attire. The white tank he wore clung tightly over his chest to reveal a well-defined torso underneath. His toned biceps and triceps were exposed and swelled, most likely from the heavy cases of canned goods that he volunteered to move and stack that late morning. His loose neon-blue gym shorts hung to about mid-knee in length, and his muscular calves bulged as he came to a halt in front of her. His topaz skin was predominantly highlighted by the sun. It was hard to believe she had watched him grow into this, although he was only two years younger than her.

"Hey, Graham." She smiled. It was nice to see a friendly face other than Carson's, especially after the rough encounter with her mother.

"You're leaving already?" he asked, a slight frown appearing on his face.

Speaking in a mirthful tone, she said, "Uh, well. You see, there's this thing called an egg donor and—"

"Sandy Ward trouble again?"

"Yup."

He grinned, obviously amused by her description of her mother. "I'm surprised. You usually last a bit longer before you finally decide to call it quits from her crap."

She shrugged. "Yeah, well, this time might actually be *my* fault to tell you the truth."

He shot her a look of confusion. "And how's that?"

She hesitated momentarily. "I almost burned the place down."

"Oh. That was you? But you're okay, right?" He walked a little closer, almost as if he wanted to inspect her.

"I'm good, yeah." She broke eye contact with him and looked in the direction of where she'd just come from. "But I have a feeling I might be grounded."

Graham smiled and shook his head at her sarcasm.

Rikki changed the subject. "So where's this new chick at? I haven't gotten to meet her yet."

His smile faded. "Oh, uh, she left. Said she had an emergency at work. But the good thing is that Car met her before she escaped."

Rikki nodded slightly. "She wasn't here very long. Must've been quite the emergency on a Saturday."

Graham glanced away from Rikki and squinted in the bright sunlight. He gazed out into the distance as if distracted in deep thought. "Yeah, well, duty calls, right?" He looked back at her with a vague smile, then quickly changed the subject. "So, Car told me you started a new painting. What's it of?" He watched as Rikki fiddled with her car keys in hesitation.

"Oh, um, it's just something I've been working on off and on for several months now."

He tilted his head. "Several months? Must be pretty important if it's taking you that long. It usually only takes you, what, less than a month to finish one? What's the theme this time?" he asked, keen with interest. He waited as she wavered on the subject. "Rik?"

"It's just a door," she answered diffidently. Her gaze remained on her keys for what seemed like minutes until she decided to take a peek in his direction again.

He didn't say a word. He just stared at her in question until his phone rang and it brought him back to reality. "Oh, hey, I gotta run. It's Amy. I'll, uh, talk to you later, Rik. Have a good rest of your day."

"You too, Graham." She smiled softly as they waved goodbye. He turned around and answered his phone. She listened to the sound of his gentle voice fading as he walked away, back in the direction of the town picnic.

After Rikki got home, she decided to take a warm bubble bath. She already felt drained from working late after Carson's party the night before, and the stressful event that occurred at the picnic just increased her exhaustion. Rikki thought back on the way the grill erupted in flames. She was almost sure neither the lighter nor the matches were lit long enough to even smolder the charcoal.

After Rikki got out of the bathtub, she put on some clothes and packed her bag to stay at Carson's. She sank down into her bed and then glimpsed the time on her phone: *2:37 p.m.* Carson wouldn't be done until seven-ish. She figured she might as well take a nap with how tired she felt. She lay in bed, fatigued and weary, but restless enough to burn holes through the ceiling.

Rikki awoke in an oppressive panic, her shirt saturated with sweat and her heartbeat pounding in her chest. She didn't remember dreaming, or even when she'd fallen asleep for that matter. She peeked at her phone, squinting from the strength of the bright light. *7:17 p.m.* Carson was probably cleaning up from the day.

Rikki lay there for a few moments, trying to remember what her dream was about, until she heard something peculiar—a crackling noise. She sat up and threw her legs over the side of the bed.

"Mother?" she shouted out her doorway. She sat there for several moments. *Nothing.* Rikki moved forward until she stood against the doorframe, just inside of her bedroom.

The sound resumed without interruption. She cautiously made her way out of her bedroom into the hallway. She heard nothing but quiet and that same *crack, sizzle, pop.*

"Is someone there? Car?" Rikki took more cautious steps forward until she finally made it to the living room. She surveyed the room. It was dark for the most part, with only a small lit lamp that disturbed the shadows. "Hello?" She continued to hear the crackling noises, which were incessantly getting louder. She finally stood in the middle of the living room and examined its entirety by turning in a complete circle.

That's when she saw the lights; bright lights reflected from a mirror on the wall facing the living room. Rikki looked around again. There was nothing in the room that would have caused such a disruption. She proceeded forth until she stood in front of the mirror.

Rikki gasped in utter disbelief. In the mirror, she watched as her entire living room seared under the engulfment of flames. The couch, the recliner, even the curtains were ablaze. She forcibly wiped her eyes in mental rejection. She turned around to face the fire at breakneck speed, but much to her surprise, the living room was the same standard room it had always been. There were no flames. No fire. It was absolutely *unremarkable.*

She looked back at the mirror. "What the..." Now she saw

nothing out of the ordinary. Everything was undisturbed.

Rikki took frantic steps backward, putting distance between herself and the mirror. "Ouch!" She stumbled right into something...or *someone*, rather. She spun around to find her best friend—and hero at that very second—up against the wall, completely boggled by the collision.

"Rikki? Are you okay? I thought I heard something inside while I was walking up your driveway, so I rushed in here. Why are you standing in the dark?"

Rikki, flustered and almost in tears, answered, "There was a fire! My living room was on fire!" She held onto Carson's arms, dragging her further inside the living room to witness.

Carson inspected the space and then walked over to flick a light switch on. She searched the room that Rikki claimed had just been in flames moments ago. "Um, Rik, are you sure? I don't see anything. I don't even smell anything burning." Carson shrugged.

Rikki marched straight over to the mirror on the wall. "Right here! I saw the fire in here! It was in the mirror!" She pointed to the mirror as if revealing cogent evidence, and then looked over to find the baffled expression locked on Carson's face.

Carson walked over to the mirror to investigate further. "What do you mean?" she asked, confused. "Like the mirror was on fire?"

Rikki shook her head. "No, no. I heard something when I woke up from a nap earlier. So I walked out here to find it, and I saw something bright in the mirror. When I got close enough to see what it was, I saw *everything* on fire," she sputtered impatiently, only pausing momentarily to take small, rapid breaths. "Except...when I turned around it wasn't there."

Carson looked at her skeptically. "Rik, maybe you had a bad dream. You said you took a nap. Maybe you were sleepwalking. Let's go to my place. I'll be there with you, and you can relax." But when Carson grabbed her arm to guide her away, she felt the heat of Rikki's skin on her hand. She was burning up. "Rik, you're really warm. Do you feel okay?"

Rikki snatched the fabric of her shirt from around her mid-torso, taking notice of the soppy material again. She was still drenched in sweat. "I don't know. I woke up this way, um, from a dream I had earlier—"

Carson arched an eyebrow at her.

Rikki threw her hands up in vindication. "No, Car, *this* was different. This didn't feel like a dream. I was wide awake before I walked out here."

Carson put the back of her hand on Rikki's forehead.

"Hey! I'm not five," Rikki whined.

Carson remained sensible. "I think you have a fever. You're warm to the touch, and you're sweating. And you could even be having..." She hesitated. "Um, hallucinations."

Rikki shook her head and rushed past her in the direction of her bedroom, where she ripped her shirt off and stood there in her sports bra. Carson followed and stood in the doorway with her arms crossed. Rikki opened her mouth to speak, but Carson held up a hand to keep her quiet so she could finish explaining.

"Just listen to me. All signs point to fever. I've seen this frequently working with the homeless. Fevers can be caused by infection. We should go to the E.R. This isn't normal."

Rikki flashed a disconcerted look at Carson and slipped a fresh shirt on. However, she did silently contemplate Carson's suggestion. Was it possible she was coming down with something? She *was* hot and definitely sweating more than usual, but the "seeing things" caused her to hesitate briefly. She just didn't want to appear insane. What would her mother think? "Okay. Let's go. I'm sure everything's fine, so whatever," she complied, "but can you do me a solid?"

Carson nodded and watched her with intent, waiting for a proper request.

"Don't call my mom. If everything turns out fine, she'll

treat me like a hypochondriac just for going."

Carson agreed but knew Rikki wasn't done talking because, well, she was never done without throwing in some sort of sardonic remark when it came to Sandra Ward.

As if right on cue, Rikki slapped her hands on her hips and tilted her body—mimicking her mother's usual stance—and said with a disciplinary tone of voice, "*Don't make excuses, Rikki. That only makes you look weak.*"

This, of course, caused Carson to burst out in laughter.

Still smiling in amusement, Carson finally managed a few words. "I promise not to call Sandy Ward if you just go and get checked out. You can come back to my apartment just as long as you're not on your deathbed," she explained lightheartedly.

Rikki grabbed her bag, and they both zoomed out the door.

The drive over to the hospital was quick with light traffic. The weather stayed warm and comfortable.

"Hey, Car?" Rikki gazed out the window as she spoke. "I don't want to tell anyone else about what I saw in the mirror. Um, I mean, because it sounds crazy. I *know* it sounds crazy." She glanced over at Carson. "I just want it to stay between us."

Carson nodded. "Okay, Rik. That part stays between us."

Once Rikki got registered and ushered into a room in the emergency department, Carson grabbed a pull-out chair and sat down beside her bed, a reassuring smile on her face. The nurse came in, took Rikki's blood pressure, and slipped the pulse oximeter on her finger.

"Honestly, I think I'm fine. I thought maybe I had a fever earlier, but I seem to be fine now. I'm probably wasting your time," Rikki explained to the nurse.

"Hey, better safe than sorry, I always say." The nurse smiled cordially at them both. "I'm Rita, by the way. I'll be the nurse taking care of you tonight alongside Doctor Wayne."

She ran a portable thermometer across Rikki's forehead to take her temperature.

Both girls were in mid-conversation about something picnic-related when Rita interrupted to speak to Rikki. "Ms. Ward, this thermometer is giving me an error," she explained as she stood up, "so I'm going to grab another one."

Rikki smiled casually. "Sure. No problem."

Rita walked over to one side of the room and opened a few cupboards and drawers in search of what she needed. "Aha." She pulled out another thermometer and then sat back down on the stool by Rikki's bed. Rita swiped the thermometer across her brow again. "Hm. This one is acting up, too. Excuse me a moment. I am just going to grab another. I'm sorry for the inconvenience."

Carson nodded and smiled humbly. Rikki shrugged.

Rita hurried out of the room. Only a few minutes passed before she came back with a few more tools. She ran another thermometer across Rikki's head once more. It beeped, and the girls watched Rita's eyes grow big when she saw the result.

"Is something wrong? What's it say?" Rikki asked, a little apprehensive now.

Carson sat quietly, but inwardly she also felt anxious as she waited for Rita's answer.

"I think there has to be something going on with these particular thermometers. They're just giving me some issues. I'm going to try a few others. Is that okay?" Rita asked politely.

The delays without a significant answer were beginning to feel detrimental, but Rikki nodded anyway. "Okay."

"It'll be all right, honey. I am sorry for the trouble. Technology and electronics these days just don't do it the way they used to in the old days." Rita flashed a faint but consoling smile. She rummaged through another drawer close by and yanked out a few more tools. "Right here I have a digital ear thermometer and your good ol' oral thermometer. You've probably used this one when you were younger." She held up the oral thermometer to Rikki, who nodded slightly in accordance. "I'm going to use both of them since my other ones aren't working. You just sit back and relax."

"Uh, okay," Rikki agreed, but with ostensible reluctance in her voice.

Rita started with the ear. She placed a sterile cover over the tip of the thermometer, pulled Rikki's ear slightly upward and back, and then carefully positioned the tip inside. She pressed a button.

Rita studied the numbers on the thermometer with a frown on her face. She took it out and set it aside, then snatched the other thermometer and placed another sterile cover over the tip. "Last one. This one goes underneath your tongue, so open up real wide." Rikki did as she was told, and Rita stuck it under her tongue and then had her close her mouth. The time it took for Rita to take these readings felt interminably long to both Carson and Rikki, and it had only been a few minutes.

A few more beeps sounded, so Rita pulled it out. Gaping at the result, her eyes betraying her disbelief, she managed to keep a calm tone of voice. "Ms. Ward, you say at this very moment you feel fine. Is that correct?"

"Yes. I don't have any of the problems I had just an hour or so ago." Rikki's eyes narrowed quizzically. "Why?"

"Well, I've used various thermometers, and they are all giving me the same reading on you. I'm going to get the doctor. He'll be in the room in just a second." Rita zoomed out of the room before Rikki or Carson could get in another word.

The girls heard talking outside the room. The voices were just low enough that they couldn't make out what they were saying.

An older man with gray hair and a white lab coat entered with Rita by his side. "Hello, Rikki. I'm Doctor Wayne. Rita here was explaining to me what has been going on with you this evening." He held a chart in front of him, looking down at it intermittently. "You say you felt a little warm and also complained of diaphoresis, which is some sweats, right?"

"Yes, sir, but I feel fine now."

He nodded in understanding. "Well, Rita took your temperature several times. The result was just about the same for all. Sixty-five degrees Celsius. That's nearly 150 degrees Fahrenheit."

Rikki and Carson stared at the doctor in amazement.

"How? There's gotta be a mistake," Rikki exclaimed.

"Honestly, Ms. Ward, I don't understand it myself. Normal body temperature ranges from ninety-seven to ninety-nine degrees Fahrenheit, and yours exceeds any logical explanation. Realistically speaking, a fever higher than 107 degrees Fahrenheit is high enough to cause brain damage in an adult if left untreated."

"Well, I feel fine. I'm not even warm anymore." She placed the back of her hand on her forehead to substantiate herself to him. Everyone in the room could tell she was agitated. "I'm not sweating. I doubt I have a fever anymore."

Carson squeezed her arm in an attempt to comfort her.

"Now, if we're done here, I'm gonna go." Rikki commenced leaving by shifting her body forward to get off the bed.

"Just a minute, Ms. Ward." He gestured for her to sit back. "Frankly, I don't think you have a temperature that high either. It's unlikely, especially because you're not showing any other symptoms concerning a fever, besides the warmth and the sweats, which you say have both been resolved. The assessment Rita did on you otherwise was all perfect. Your blood pressure is good, along with your oxygen levels and even your heart rate. You appear to be in good health for your age," he moved his hands enthusiastically as he spoke, "so I'm hoping to find some sort of rational excuse why we are getting a tremendously high temperature reading on you. I've never seen one that exceeds over 110 degrees in the past thirty-two years I've practiced, and even that particular patient wasn't as lucky as you seem to be now."

Rikki chimed in immediately, because she knew where the doctor was going with this, and she just wasn't having it. "Listen, I honestly feel like I've just wasted your time. Like I already mentioned, I feel *fine* now."

Doctor Wayne smiled briefly at her. "Although you feel all right now, you did come here with the intention of being treated for a fever. So, with your best interest in mind, we'd like to keep you overnight. Run a few more tests. Do some blood work, a CAT scan, an MRI and such. Just keep you for observation."

"I don't think that's necessary. Why can't we do some tests and then you can let me leave?" She felt the hassle of an inconvenient hospital stay slowly creeping up on her.

"Well, as long as you have a temperature that persists in being that high, it would be ill-advised to let you leave without complete and proper treatment. I would be neglecting the situation at hand, whether the readings actually are errors or not. Now, it is of course your choice, but we are merely here to help *you*. We can't do that if you decide to leave."

Carson intervened, glancing at Doctor Wayne. "Can you guys give me a few minutes in private, so I can speak with her? We just need to discuss everything, and she may even need to call her mother."

"Fuck *that*," Rikki exclaimed blatantly, her eyes big with disapproval once she heard the last sentence escape Carson's mouth.

Carson literally slapped her hand over Rikki's mouth to keep her from speaking another word. Rita and Doctor Wayne appeared a little taken aback by Rikki's choice of words.

"Just a minute is all we need, please." Carson smiled politely.

"Sure. Take all the time you need. We will get the admission papers ready, just in case." Doctor Wayne forced a smile and then left abruptly, followed closely by Rita.

Carson turned back to look at Rikki. "Rik, look. They're only asking you to stay for the night. You heard the doctor.

He said he doesn't honestly think there's anything wrong. Just stay to get some peace of mind. And I hate to say it, but you should probably call your mom, so she knows you're okay."

Rikki sighed. "I'll stay. But you're crazy if you expect me to put on one of those hospital gowns. And I'm not calling my mother. I can dodge her calls until I get out of here."

Carson crossed her arms and repositioned herself in her chair. "Then I guess I'm staying here for the night."

Rikki's eyes lit up with shame. "What? No, Car. You go home."

Carson shook her head in disapproval. "Don't 'you go home' *me*. Someone's gotta stay here and make sure you live through this."

Rikki arched an eyebrow. "Um, isn't that what the doctors and nurses are for?"

Carson shrugged both shoulders and nodded. "Good point. But who's going to make sure the doctors and nurses live through this?"

Rikki smirked in amusement. "Not even *you* can save them," she laughed.

Carson giggled and then began to yawn. "Well, I do think maybe I should stay for a few hours," she insisted, "just to make sure you get settled in."

It was Rikki's turn to shake her head in disapproval. "Car, I'm fine. Don't worry about me. I have to get all these tests done anyway. It would be pointless for you to sit in my room all night. Besides, I'm probably getting out early. I'll text you bright and early. 5 a.m." Rikki flashed a wide, witty smile. "You can pick me up and we'll go get breakfast."

"That sounds good. But text me as soon as you find out your test results. I don't care what time it is, all right?"

Rikki smiled and nodded in agreement.

As Carson walked through the sliding glass doors and out of the hospital, she pulled out her cell phone to look at her messages. She had one from Graham:

Hey Car, I'm coming over. I wanted to ask you something.

It had been sent at 8:30 p.m. and it was now going on nine, so he was probably at her apartment waiting impatiently and wondering where she was. As she proceeded to walk to her vehicle and text Graham back, she paused halfway through, taking notice of a figure in the corner of her eye. She looked up to find a strange man leaning on her car.

"Um, hello. Can I help you?" she asked him, providing enough space between both of them just to be on the safe side. The stranger's head was down, and he appeared to be mumbling to himself. "Um, sir, do you need some help? Are you all right?"

"I've waited years to speak with you again," he confessed as he raised his head to face her. Two bloodshot eyeballs each embodied a glowing, dark orange iris. Those eyes were familiar. That cold, disgruntled face was one she'd seen before. She couldn't forget a grimace like that.

Carson realized this was the same man who had sat beside her on the bench outside the Business Hall four years ago.

"Uh, I'm sorry. I don't think we've ever met." She made a play for pretending she didn't remember who he was, but her voice quivered with fear. Four years had gone by, and this same person had obviously been following her. How else did he know where she was at this very second? And why did he show up now all of a sudden?

She backed away from him, forcing some more distance between them. She wanted to make a run for it. She turned around quickly to see if anyone was in sight, but she saw no one. The parking lot was desolate and quiet. She heard only the sound of the wind whistling through the leaves of the trees.

The man's harsh, heavy breathing interrupted her train of thought. "You've been marked," he barked in an exasperated tone, "by the Light One." He leaned near her, his brow furrowed. His eyes glowed brighter, similar to the way blazing embers in a campfire brighten when the wind hits them. Carson then thought she was hallucinating, because she was sure they transformed into a bloodred color, and no average, ordinary person has eyes that look like that.

All of a sudden, Carson became unreasonably dizzy. She felt herself wobble as she took another step back in the direction of the hospital. Her gait was unsteady. "Wh-what's this? He-help!" she shouted for someone, anyone to save her.

She heard the man snigger wickedly. "Go ahead and try to fight it." She noted the saturnine tone in his voice. "It's so much more enjoyable when you do." His fiery eyes began to seep some sort of black discharge. He lifted his arms slightly, and Carson noted the skin of his arms possessed a scorched appearance. His fingertips were black, the color of soot. She saw the veins on his arms become prominent and darken as if there was a dark fluid flowing directly beneath his skin, ready to burst out at any second.

In her semi-paralytic state, she watched as the stranger slowly moved closer to her, almost as if things were in slow motion. She finally forced herself to turn around and make a run for it, but that's when he appeared directly in front of her within the blink of an eye.

He smiled at her devilishly. "Ah, ah, ah." He wagged his finger at her in disapproval. "You don't want to leave just yet. You'll miss the best part."

Carson's heart thumped rapidly and heavily with fright. At that moment, the man tightened both of his hands around her shoulders. Carson felt the heat from his hands as he singed her skin, burning atrociously past the first degree. She saw the smoke rise from where his fingers squeezed. Carson screamed in pain and struggled to free herself from his deathly grip, but it was no use. No one was around to hear her. Only the two of them proceeded to stand alone outside together, and Carson felt helplessly doomed.

"You know the thing about ether," he scoffed villainously as he let go of her and backed up a few strides. He raised both of his hands, palms upward. "Is that it's highly flammable."

Carson witnessed flames physically appear on both palms of the stranger's hands. And that was the last image she saw clearly.

The man threw both hands forcefully in her direction. It all happened so fast. She flew backward into her car, smashing the windows and hitting her head as she fell onto the ground. Shattered glass coated the blacktop.

She managed to bring herself somewhat upright, just enough to lean her back and head against the car. Besides the pain, the first thing she felt was something dripping down the side of her head. She struggled as she ran her hand across her left temple and held it out in front of her face, squinting and trying to focus. It was blurry, but she knew it was her blood.

"If only Eleanor was here to see this," he spat out mockingly.

Wincing in pain, Carson looked straight ahead. She could hardly keep her eyes open as syncope almost set in, but she did see the man's silhouette inch nearer. She voluntarily closed her spent eyelids, because she knew this was it. *This was the end.*

Then something happened. Carson heard the man scream in agony. A bright light interrupted her last few seconds of peace, so she weakly fluttered her eyes open to try to see what was going on in front of her. It was still blurry, and she couldn't make everything out, but she did see a bright, luminous light.

The light moved inhumanly fast, winding around the man in all directions. *Is that moving through him?* Carson wasn't sure. There was another noise that drowned out the man's screams; an abnormally loud buzzing sound. It was so intense, it caused her eardrums to ache. *What is that?* She flinched in more pain as she squinted to get a better look, but still, the event taking place in front of her was just a mix of shapeless blurs.

Shortly thereafter, an unpleasant, sulfurous odor wafted through the air near Carson, filling her nostrils and consequently turning her stomach. Her dizziness increased. She watched the outline of the man finally drop to his knees, but when he did, Carson saw a figure standing close behind him. The glary figure, wholly consumed by light, stood still for a few moments. Carson's impaired vision wasn't doing her any favors. She peered as hard as she could, studying the bright fluorescence in front of her, but couldn't manage to identify the stranger.

Suddenly, the effulgent light eased. All sounds subsided. The man's body fell over onto the ground and lay there, motionless. Seconds later, the mysterious person took a few soft steps in Carson's direction. She could hear the boots of her hero clicking on the pavement as she neared. Among all the smells, this stranger's scent was the strongest. She *knew* that fragrance; it was evocatively familiar and comforting.

The stranger bent down, reached out, and gently placed their hands on her shoulders. Carson flinched in more pain from the sudden touch. That was where the man had scorched her—and with his bare hands, nonetheless! But then...the pain began to fade. She felt a soothing sensation take over; a calm, safe feeling that made her relax. Her eyelids heavy from exhaustion, she fought to stay awake. Before she finally passed out, she heard voices. Many *shouting* voices. People running, panicking. And then Carson was out.

Carson slowly allowed her eyelids to rise as she listened to the soft mumbling of voices around her. Her head was throbbing and the bright lights in the room weren't helping matters at all.

"Carson, honey! Oh my God! Just lie still. You're in the hospital." Carson's mother, Jan, who looked as though she'd been recently crying due to the tear stains on her cheeks, rushed to the side of Carson's bed.

Carson's eyes widened a little more as she took in her surroundings. She found her mother, father, Graham, and Rikki all gathered in the room.

"Hey, champ. How ya feeling?" Gregory, Carson's father, asked as he placed his hand on top of Carson's.

"My head hurts. What happened?" Carson didn't remember a thing.

"Greg, could you go find the doctor? And tell him she's awake right away!" Jan exclaimed as she faced her husband. He nodded, turned around, and rushed out of the room as if he was on a time-sensitive mission.

Carson's gaze flickered over to Graham and Rikki, who were standing side by side on the side of the bed opposite her mother. Rikki placed a hand on Carson's arm.

"Seriously, what happened?" Carson asked her. Her head was foggy, and she didn't know whether that feeling derived from the violent migraine she was suffering from at the time or whatever the doctors were pumping through her IV.

Graham interjected, "They're saying someone hit your car. Probably right after you got into it to leave. You didn't see it coming and you hit your head. The docs say you most likely have a mild concussion. They found you passed out in your car outside the E.R. here." Peering over his sister and speaking through gritted teeth, he said, "Your car is dented on the passenger side. Bastard must have taken off right after it happened." His glowering eyes softened. "Do you remember any of it, Car?"

"What? No. The last thing I remember is being here with Rikki." Carson struggled to sit up. In doing so, she discovered she was prisoner to more than just the IV. There were also wires snaking out from the front pocket of her gown and thick tubing under her nose releasing uncomfortably frigid air into her nostrils. "Isn't this a little excessive?" she asked her mother sarcastically, but Jan maintained the same grievous demeanor Carson had woken up to.

At that moment, the doctor walked into the room, followed by her father. "Hello, Carson. Long time no see. Remember me? Doctor Wayne." He smiled a warm, welcoming smile.

She smiled back and nodded, squinting through the pain from her headache and feeling as though she could vomit at any minute. She tried to focus on what he was saying.

"Can you tell me what happened? Remember anything? You have quite the goose egg on the side of your head."

Carson hesitated before answering because she really couldn't remember anything that had happened. She looked out the window beside her bed at the dark midnight sky. Ironically enough, that was what she saw when she attempted any recollection of the past few hours; just darkness. Nothing but blank, empty space. She glanced back over to see everyone in the room, including the doctor, awaiting her reply as if their lives depended on it. "I can't really remember, but my head is pounding."

Doctor Wayne nodded. "That's normal, especially after bumping your head so hard. I'm going to get a CAT scan ordered just to be on the safe side. I think you'll be just fine, but we want to make sure there is no hemorrhaging. I've examined the rest of you, and I only see a few minor scrapes and bruises. With the amount of damage to your car that was initially reported, I'm surprised you survived with only that bump on your head. Does anything else hurt?" he asked her.

Carson shook her head in silent response.

"Okay then. After we do the CAT scan and get the results back, and as long as they're normal, you'll be free to go. Having some slight memory loss is typical. Your memories should come back around, though, and when they do, be sure to reach out to the police department to let them know what you remember. Like I mentioned earlier, a report has been filed with what we know so far, but you aren't able to make much of a statement right now with your condition. I also recommend somebody drive you around. Take a few days off before you get behind the wheel again. Use Tylenol for the head and body aches. You'll be sore the next couple days. Side effects from whiplash."

After her family expressed their appreciation with a long, drawn-out thank-you, he hurried out of the room.

"Honey, your father and I are going to make a few calls, and we will be right back, okay? It'll just be a few minutes," her mother reassured her, caressing Carson's forehead with her hand. "I'm so glad you are all right. Your guardian angel must have been watching over you tonight." Jan bent over to kiss her on the head, and her father squeezed her hand before finally exiting the room.

Carson shifted her head back to look at Rikki, eventually noticing her blue hospital gown. "That's not really your color, is it?" Carson asked as she giggled in amusement, but then stopped instantly when she became aware of how much it worsened her headache.

Rikki sat down, crossed her arms and legs, and blurted, "Laugh it up, Car, because it's not yours either," with a sardonic expression on her face.

Carson lowered her gaze to see her own new fashion attire. She had the same type of hospital gown on. As if on cue, both girls sprang into laughter.

"Hey, Car?" Graham interrupted. "Are you sure you don't remember anything? You don't even remember walking to your car? No bystanders?"

Carson shook her head in disappointment. "It's a huge blur." She could tell he was curious about something, though. "Why?"

Graham glanced over at Rikki and then back at Carson, hesitating to let the words spill from his lips. "You know how I am your emergency contact?" Carson nodded. "Well I got here before anyone else. I called Mom, Dad, and Rikki. I spoke to the man that found you before anyone got here. He said that when he found you, you kept mumbling something. He thought it was someone's name." His gaze dropped to the floor, and he appeared anxious, as though whatever he was thinking really bothered him.

Carson's brow furrowed. "What was it?" she asked him, gripping the back of her head as if that would numb the pain for a few moments.

"Evelyn." His gaze shot back up to meet hers as he spoke. "He said you kept calling for Evelyn."

CHAPTER 7

"Babe, it'll only take me a minute to finish this," Carson exclaimed in between chuckles as she attempted to squirm out of Evelyn's grip.

Evelyn wrapped her arms securely around Carson's body and finally carried her away from her desk.

"Rayna needs me to send files on the new shelters for this year. I'm almost done. What's so important that it can't wait three more minutes?" Carson asked, tilting her head but grinning with admiration at the woman she loved.

Evelyn offered a faint smile back, but it was definitely more along the lines of a pensive expression. Her smile eventually faded altogether, and she let go of Carson's hand. She walked over to the window and gazed outside as if in deep thought. Moments passed by as Evelyn stood quietly by the window, just staring out into the early spring weather.

The deafening silence was beginning to make Carson feel uncomfortable, so she stepped in close enough until she stood right behind her girlfriend. "Ev?"

Evelyn finally proceeded to turn and face Carson, but she was unable to look her in the eyes.

Carson slipped both of her hands into Evelyn's. "Ev, what's wrong?"

It was as if Carson's touch triggered Evelyn to focus back on the present moment. She reached into her right jacket pocket and pulled something out. Something that dangled. It was a necklace. A *beautiful* necklace.

"I have to give you something. It's been passed down from my ancestors for decades," Evelyn claimed. "And now I want you to have it," she whispered, presenting the necklace to Carson.

The black neckband was made of some sort of very durable material, like leather, in a braided design, which made it all the more lovely. The pendant that hung from it was actually that of an intricately shaped crystal, which possessed an assortment of bright colors. Carson saw a bold mixture of red, blue, and green. A small metal clip held the band and the pendant together.

Evelyn unclipped the back of the necklace and placed it gently around Carson's neck. Although it had appeared heavy, it felt just the opposite; light and natural, almost as if she was already accustomed to wearing it.

Carson was nonetheless speechless, but she managed to force out a few words. "Evelyn, I don't even know what to say. This is the most wonderful gift anyone has ever given me. I honestly don't know how I can accept this."

As if startled by the words Carson had spoken, Evelyn slipped her hands back into Carson's and squeezed softly. "Please take it. You're the most important person in my entire life. I've never met anyone like you. It would mean so much to me if you would wear it," she said as she inched closer to Carson and brushed a strand of hair behind her ear. "It holds a lot of history, and it's been around for a long time," she explained. "There are mythological stories behind it, stories indicating the necklace's owner will endure great protection. If you keep it on, I'll know you'll always be safe. You know, peace of mind."

Carson smiled lightheartedly. "Like a guardian angel, right?"

"Exactly." Evelyn nodded. "I love you, Carson," she whispered and leaned in, closing the distance between the two of them, and gently placed her lips against Carson's.

But this wasn't just *any* kiss. There was a significance behind this kiss that Evelyn only hoped Carson wouldn't sense, and *that* was deep sorrow. Evelyn was sorry because this time, she knew she was kissing Carson goodbye.

67

CHAPTER 8

A few days passed after the accident. Doctor Wayne suggested Carson take it easy for about a week due to the concussion. She was instructed to go straight back to the emergency department if her symptoms worsened.

Rikki was released from the hospital the morning after Carson's accident, finally receiving normal results. She called her best friend to check up on her and fill her in on her current situation. Rikki still believed her unreasonable temperature readings had been a fluke, especially since the doctor never did conclude why they'd been so outrageous. He'd even apologized for the inconvenience of her stay, but explained that he was just keeping her best interest in mind and that his observation was the best thing for her.

Graham greatly aided in Carson's recovery by running all her errands while she was off work. He even dropped off a doctor's note at the shelter, although it wasn't exactly necessary. Carson's assistant, Rayna, who was just as qualified as Carson to run all the homeless programs, gladly accepted and welcomed the extra work after Carson called and spilled the news about her recent hit-and-run. For as much hard work as Carson put in, Rayna had literally begged her for umpteen months to take some time off for herself.

"You're always here. You and Miss Red need to book a vacay somewhere extremely hot with sand and mimosas," she'd say.

Carson got in touch with the police like she'd been told and provided a statement about the accident as best as she possibly could. Unfortunately, she still didn't remember much about it, and she was starting to wonder if she would ever conjure up anything from that night.

Friday evening rolled in; it had been almost a week since the accident. It seemed as though each day dragged by slowly, taking its merry time, and Carson could only muster up feelings of curiosity regarding what Graham mentioned that first night. Had she really been mumbling Evelyn's name in an unconscious state?

After the breakup, Carson still dreamed of Evelyn constantly. She would wake up in tears, mourning in pain from the illusion that time had been reversed and she was back in Evelyn's arms again. Carson would just sink into her bed and helplessly let herself fall apart once the truth of reality returned. Fortunately, nothing like that had happened in months. Her thoughts, her feelings, and even her dreams had improved, but then again a dream is fundamentally different than getting knocked out cold and randomly calling out for your ex-girlfriend in front of a stranger.

That evening, Carson's parents joined her for dinner, along with Graham, who had been slightly late. Of course, his reason was that he had an argument with Amy, but he emphasized the fact that they were doing better than ever—as if Carson really believed that. She still wasn't incredibly fond of Amy, but she refused to butt heads with Graham over his relationship and wasn't going to invade his business.

That same night, Carson tossed and turned in bed, her body feeling exhausted but her mind running chaotically. Graham's words repeated in her head, and she couldn't focus on anything else. Her mind slipped into thoughts about the past four years. She thought about the first time she met Evelyn; how vibrantly beautiful she was, and how easy it had been to fall in love with her. She wondered just when that feeling of being in love had captured her; when she actually knew she loved Evelyn unconditionally—but that was just it. She couldn't remember a time when she didn't. Although it sounded horribly cliché and unrealistic, she'd loved her since day one. But with the happy and joyful memories came the dark and gloomy ones, too. She thought about the day she found that note in her apartment. A tear escaped her eye and ran down her cheek. She closed her eyes forcefully as if that would push the heart-wrenching memory away, but the words written in Evelyn's handwriting appeared clearly on the back of her eyelids anyway.

I have to leave. Forgive me.

Carson opened her eyes. She wasn't in her apartment. As a matter of fact, she had no idea where she was. It was dark, unfamiliar. She pushed herself up onto her feet. She searched the area, perplexed and completely baffled. *How did I even get here?*

She realized she was somewhere outside, and as her eyes wandered, she noticed that the land stretched on for miles with leafless trees scattered in all directions. The ground was covered in something white. Snow? No, not snow. It wasn't even cold. They were ashes...ashes that masked the entire ground. She glanced up and watched them sprinkle down, dusting the trees and the path she was walking on. It was as if the sky was a large campfire, dispensing its particles all over the earth. The sky exuded reds and purples, unlike anything she'd ever seen before. There was no sun or moon, which was strange. She continued to walk. It was quiet, so she could only hear her footsteps crunching in the debris on the ground.

Carson eventually came across a large mirror resting on the ground in the middle of nowhere. The mirror itself was round with a strong, complex frame that kept it sitting upright, like an easel. There were fine, intricate details on the bronze frame, and it looked to be distressed as if very old. In the mirror, she wasn't alone; a woman stood close by, her back facing Carson. She didn't know how long this woman had been standing there. *Did she just appear?*

The stranger was garbed in tight, black, warrior-like apparel that hugged her feminine curves fiercely. Intrigued, Carson cast her gaze over the rest of the woman. Long blonde curls fell down the woman's back, and she wore black combat boots that reached mid-calf.

At that very second, the woman spoke. "The necklace. Carson, you need to get that necklace. Put it on."

That voice. That warm, familiar voice. Carson *knew* that voice.

The woman slowly turned around. *Evelyn.* "There's so much I need to tell you." Her bright blue eyes watched Carson as she continued, "But for now, you need to wear it, please."

Carson was consumed with so many emotions. Shock, because she hadn't seen Evelyn in so long. Anger, because Evelyn had just up and left with only a small, pathetic note to serve her justice. But also a strong urge to just throw her arms around her because she was standing right there in front of her, staring into her eyes once again. Carson was confused. *What's she even talking about?*

Suddenly, the emotion Carson was feeling was interrupted by a loud, evil scream; an almost hiss-like screech. Angry bloodred eyes with streams of black tears appeared inside the mirror, accompanied by wisps of black smoke that floated aggressively in her direction. The emotions that once consumed her were now replaced with one thing—fear. But she couldn't move, and she couldn't even speak. Carson felt almost...paralyzed.

"Carson, you need to go. Please, don't forget about the necklace!" Evelyn pointed behind her in the direction Carson had come from. Carson heard a familiar buzzing sound and with that, Evelyn's eyes glowed and shimmered brightly, letting off a strong fluorescence. *What the hell? Is that electricity?* Thunder echoed in the distance, getting closer and growing louder. Then Carson saw only pitch-black darkness.

Carson woke up in a sweat. Thunder boomed, causing the glass in her windows to shake violently. She heard trickling sounds outside, and when she glanced over, she realized it was storming. Raindrops smacked the window ferociously, and her bedroom lit up as lightning flashed outside. *What a dream*, she thought to herself. She was drenched. She sat up in bed and reached down to grab the bottom of her shirt, attempting to pull it up over her head. When she did, she discovered something in her hand. It was hard. *A rock?* She opened her hand to find the necklace Evelyn had given her, right there in the palm of her trembling hand.

Carson was beyond rattled. *How did this get here?* It had been in a box in her closet, packed away since shortly after Evelyn left. She set it on her bed as she jumped up, turned the light on, and scrambled over to her closet to investigate.

Carson ripped boxes, clothes, and items she didn't even remember having out of the way as she rummaged through in search of one specific shoebox. She finally came across the one she knew she had left the necklace in. She set it in front of her, took a deep breath, and opened it. The necklace was inside the box, sitting right there in front of her.

Carson turned back to her bed. She saw no sign of the necklace she had left there. "Am I imagining things? I have to be going crazy, or my mind is playing tricks on me," Carson said aloud.

Then Evelyn's words invaded her mind again. *The necklace. Carson, you need to get that necklace. Put it on.* Her warning echoed, and Carson sat there with the box in front of her. Minutes passed until she finally grabbed it. She unclipped the back of the necklace, placed it around her neck, and clipped it on.

All of a sudden, Carson remembered *everything* from her accident the week before. She remembered the dangerous man in the hospital parking lot. The disorientation she felt when he got close. The burning pain when he touched her. His unexplained force that threw her into her car. The inhumane look of fury in his eyes—his red, soot-dripping eyes, like the eyes in her dream. And...*the figure*. Carson recalled the mysterious person who had saved her life. The man's screams of agony. She remembered all the smells, but one familiar scent in particular that belonged to the other person when she'd gotten close. The way her touch took all the pain away before Carson passed out. There were buzzing sounds too, the same ones from her dream. *Was that...electricity?*

And then it *clicked*. That familiar scent. That person in her dream was the same person who rescued her the night in the hospital parking lot. *And* the same person who had spontaneously showed up out of nowhere when this man appeared four years ago. *Evelyn*.

CHAPTER 9

Evelyn traipsed through the grassy field, wondering where it could be. The Dharo Dagger, which was rumored to be the one sacred weapon that could possibly put her out of the eternal misery that was cast upon her, was speculated to be hidden here in Nepal. It was said to be engraved with a powerful incantation that would reverse the hold on her as the Light One. She would die as a human, and she couldn't think of any better way to go.

But what would happen to the dagger once she was destroyed? Would it fall into the wrong hands? Who would then be the Light One? At this point, she didn't care. She'd continue to search for the Dharo Dagger until she was forced to depart again. Her only motive was to find a way out of this life, which really wasn't a life at all, and whether it be the dagger that did the deed or some other means, the final conclusion was this: she'd be at peace with actual death soon enough. Of course, the Elemental Elders would be irate, but then again, did she ever listen to them with any regard to the rules?

Then Evelyn heard something. The cries were soft at first, but then grew intense and deafening. She sensed fear from within someone, and this person wasn't human. She knew a distraction was the last thing she needed right now, especially when she was on limited time, but this shook her. Evelyn could smell *blood*. She moved nearer the weeping, eventually coming across a cave. The overbearing odor had become more potent, and the cries were ear-splitting at that point. There wasn't a way inside; it appeared as though someone had buried the entryway with a vast amount of rock, so no one could get in... or out. It took Evelyn only a matter of seconds to remove the large chunks of stone.

Once inside, it didn't take her long to discover the source of the distraction. A young child, who'd been beaten and battered, lay on the cold, dirty ground, gasping for air. Her face was bloody and bruised, and her clothes were torn and soiled with bloody grime. She could barely move, let alone speak. The only sounds that she could manage to let out were the soft groans and gurgling noises that only Evelyn could have heard so easily from miles away.

Evelyn rushed over to the young girl and crouched down, inspecting her injuries. She gently placed her hands upon her and began healing her significantly. While doing so, Evelyn could feel just how damaged she really was. The young stranger had several broken bones, one a rib that pierced her left lung, causing her to nearly drown in her own blood. Her skull and face were also fractured, and she struggled to open her swollen eyes. She'd been beaten so badly, she was even blind in one. She was only ten years old. Sure, Evelyn made mistakes, which then caused catastrophic effects, but whoever could do this to a child...they were the real monsters.

Once restored, the small lungs that previously crackled with blood while battling for oxygen now expanded with fresh air comfortably. The child opened her eyes to find Evelyn hovering. She spoke in another language, but Evelyn could easily translate, an advantage of her superhuman power. "Light One," the girl breathed quietly, "you came."

At that point, Evelyn knew exactly who she was. Unquestionably, she was one of the elementals; the powerful beings Evelyn was entitled to protect as the Light One. So instead of fleeing after reviving her, Evelyn carefully sat the young girl upright. "Who did this to you?" she asked.

"The group of humans who have been hunting our kind

for decades. Our kind, well, these humans suspect things about us. They don't like how we're, say, '*different*,'" she explained.

Evelyn furrowed her eyebrows in question. "Why did they choose to come after *you*?"

"I'm the youngest, most vulnerable. They believed killing me off first would destroy any chance for more of us since I'm, well, not fully developed yet." Her eyes browsed the cave a bit, then her gaze fell back upon Evelyn. "I was dying in here," she admitted, "but you heard me." The young child lightly placed her hand on Evelyn's. "I don't believe the things they say about you. You aren't an abomination."

The child's sincere words struck Evelyn somewhere deep inside. She hadn't heard anything positive about herself in such a long time, let alone a compliment. *Does this child not realize what I have done in the past or the pain I've caused?* Evelyn thought to herself. She'd basically abandoned all her duties as the Light One and selfishly spiraled off into a path of destruction.

Evelyn smiled warmly with appreciation. "Thank you. These men you speak of...do you know where I can find them?"

The young girl nodded. "They own a shop in town. *Rugart's.* We believe it's just a cover-up, so they can keep a close eye on us here in our country of origin." The child turned her head, breaking eye contact with Evelyn, and discovered the open entrance. "I fear they may come after my family soon."

Evelyn carefully picked the child up and carried her out of the cave. "Let me get you back to your family. What's your name?"

"I'm Bhumika."

"Hello, Bhumika. Call me Evelyn. I won't let what happened to you ever happen again. To any of you. I promise."

Chapter 10

Carson was on a mission. It didn't matter that it was two-thirty in the morning—she needed to figure out what was going on. *Was it only just a dream I had? What I actually thought I remembered from the accident, was it all even real?*

Carson zoomed out of her bedroom and into the room around the corner. She pulled the chair out from her desk, took a seat, and logged into her computer. She didn't even bother turning on a light. Who had time for that when you've been attacked by some demonic-looking man-thing?

Carson decided the only way she could find some answers without having to physically ask someone was that handy-dandy thing called the World Wide Web. Besides, she'd only get one reaction out of an actual person if she told them what she thought happened to her. She'd be given suspicious looks as if she needed to be thrown into a straightjacket and locked in an insane asylum.

Carson felt the chill of the cool plastic keys underneath the pads of her fingertips as she began to type out her first question, fumbling for the right words. She was without a doubt completely intrigued by her dream, but intimidated at the same time. She wondered what the electricity in Evelyn's eyes was supposed to signify. Starting with a dream search, she clicked a link on the screen in front of her and read aloud, *"When you experience the visualization of electricity and/or lightning in your dreams, it may symbolize an unexpected change in your life, or one that is about to happen."*

Okay, maybe this broad dream search isn't the easiest route.

Carson decided to narrow her search a little. Feeling a bit

silly for doing so, she typed in *"lightning powers"* and hit the image-search button. She skimmed numerous pictures and icons that appeared across the page, noting that most were male gods she'd learned about as a child. She saw Zeus, Indra, and Perun, who all had their own unique mythological background stories. She even spotted the name Thor a few times. *This is getting me nowhere*, Carson thought impatiently. She was beginning to feel a bit discouraged.

Carson had gone through several pages, but it wasn't until she found a particular picture that really piqued her curiosity. A painting—no, it was a *photo* someone had taken of a painting. This specific framed work of art was mounted on a wall, and someone had snapped a photo of it and posted it here online.

The actual painting was that of a woman wearing a white and blue dress, standing in the middle of a field. Her arms extended straight up into the air, and lightning bolts shot out from each of her hands, striking up into the stormy sky. Carson couldn't make out her real eyes; they were so bright and powerful, and completely overcome by refulgent beams of chaos. They ignited electric sparks, which seemed to follow the same wave of electricity that guided her hands up into these massive bolts of danger. Her blonde hair was blowing in the wind wildly except for the right side; it was pinned back with a blue and silver hair comb. What the woman was feeling was remarkably evident by the expression on her face—*pain*. The painter really captured the emotion. It was as if Carson could actually feel the agony and suffering the woman was experiencing just by looking at her.

Then Carson noticed something else. A red, blue, and green crystal bound in a silver spiraled wire and linked to a silver chain fell loosely around the neckline of the woman in the painting. "Is that..."

In a scramble, Carson quickly unclipped the back of her own necklace and held it out in front of her, comparing it to the woman's. She looked down at the colorful rock in her own hand and up at the screen what must have been a million times in disbelief.

"How's this even possible?" Carson asked, hoping she would find an answer by saying the words out loud. She scrolled down impatiently, searching for the painting's owner.

Down in the lower right-hand corner of the painting, it was signed "*B.M. 1925.*" Carson raised her eyebrows in shock once again. "This was painted in 1925? That would have been..." She paused, thinking deliberately for a few seconds. "Ninety-five years ago." She shook her head, astonished. Although the woman's eyes were basically disguised and the crystal had a much different chain than the one she was wearing now, Carson couldn't help but wonder two things: was that really the same crystal as the one she had now, and was that...*Evelyn?*

"There's no way. It's not possible. Okay, now I'm positive I've gone crazy. Just *great*," Carson mumbled.

Below the image, the caption read, "*Beloved art created by our very own family adorn the walls of each of our buildings.*" Carson clicked on the link and was immediately directed to another website. *Avani & Bhumika Natural Creations.* It was a small nature gift shop, and much to her surprise, it was only three hours away.

So that was it. It was time for a spontaneous road trip. She printed the picture of the painting and decided to call the one person that she knew would believe the very illogical situation in which she was now trapped.

Rikki Ward sat at her desk at Blaine's Accounting late that Friday night. It was actually going on 3 a.m., so technically it was Saturday morning. She had a lot of work to get done but could barely focus. The last three hours, she'd only completed charting on one, maybe two documents. She didn't know what was going on with herself lately. Almost a week had passed since her hospital visit, and had experienced no more hallucinations—well, none while she was awake. But she was having odd dreams every night since the picnic, and she couldn't come up with any reasonable explanation as to why.

Each night, once Rikki fell into a deep sleep, she'd find herself confined as overbearing and boisterous crimson flames surrounded her, cornering her until she could barely move. They'd hover over her, crackling with threat until she'd just curl up in a ball and shut her eyes, praying for the nightmare to stop. Sometimes she awoke in a sweat with her heart racing as if she'd really been standing there in front of them; as if it were actually real. The dreams persisted for hours, or at least it seemed that way—hours of just watching the blazing tips flicker back and forth, taunting her while she felt the scorching heat upon her face.

Rikki was so consumed in her own thoughts that she didn't notice her cell phone light up right away. She glanced down at a text message from her mother:

Blaine informed me that you had almost next to no errors on this year's completed customer tax return forms compared to last year's. Still, next to no errors means you made some. Remember, Rikki, we learn from our mistakes the first time, we don't repeat.

Glaring at her phone, Rikki couldn't control the rage she felt inside. Nothing was ever good enough for that woman, and she was constantly reprimanded for it. She thought back to all the times her mother told her she could have been better or tried harder. She replayed her childhood memories in her mind. *"I don't care if it's just a spelling bee, third place isn't first,"* and *"losing isn't winning."* She heard her mother's words repeat themselves in her mind, attempting to pull her down into a pit of self-failure. And, of course, Sandra always reminded Rikki of her own accomplishments by firing antagonizing, unjust remarks in her face. This only made the despise she held against her mother worsen with every gripping thought.

Sitting there in nothing but feelings of absolute fury, she almost forgot to breathe.

Rikki was forced back to reality by an odd smell. She looked down in realization that she'd been death-gripping the arm of her desk chair so aggressively that her knuckles had turned white. It was only then that she saw the smoke rising from that hand, and when she let go, she saw the perfect outline of her handprint in melted plastic. Frantic, she flipped her hand upward and examined it closely, but there was no indication of a burn. There wasn't anything there at all, for that matter.

"What's happening to me?"

Just then, her cell phone rang, and when she saw Carson's name on the screen, she felt some relief. *But why would Carson be calling at this time of the night?* Clicking the green button, she answered the phone, "Hello? Car?"

Rikki listened to the fluster of Carson's voice as it ran a million miles a minute on the other end, but she couldn't make out what she was saying or even talking about.

"Whoa, whoa, wait a sec. Calm down, Car. Take a breath! Now, what did you say is going on?"

This time, it was a little more comprehensible. As she listened to her best friend explain her situation, Rikki knew she looked like a deer in the headlights. She quickly logged off her computer and got up to collect her things. "Carson, give me fifteen minutes. I'll be right there to pick you up. I have something to tell you too, and you're not going to believe me."

Once Rikki arrived at Carson's, she helped her pack a few things because they were, in fact, going on a road trip. Rikki asked questions while sitting on Carson's bed, and Carson filled her in on the details as she stuffed some clothes into her suitcase. She explained what she remembered really happened the night of the accident, and how she'd come face-to-face with this same man four years ago, the very day she met Evelyn. She described the mysterious figure she saw, and the photo she found online. Finally, she told her about her dream and how she woke up with Evelyn's necklace in her hand.

Carson pulled the picture out of an envelope and held it inches from Rikki's face.

Rikki's eyes probed the picture quickly before speaking. "Judging by the amount of lightning in the sky, I'd say there's a good chance of rai—"

"The woman, Rik. Look at the woman," Carson interjected, setting the picture on Rikki's lap and crossing her arms.

Rikki threw her hands up in defense. "What? It was a joke. Come on, it's Saturday." She watched the lines of Carson's mouth quirk up. Just because they were attempting to justify some crazy, paranormal theory that other people might find completely nuts didn't mean they couldn't still act like best friends. "Okay, but how do you even know that it is Evelyn in the picture?" Rikki asked in earnest.

"Look at her necklace." Carson pointed to the woman's neck in the painting. Rikki inspected the photo carefully, her eyes looking it up and down, eventually focusing on the necklace. "Now look at mine," Carson demanded, grabbing her friend's arm to get her attention. Rikki's shifted her gaze to Carson's necklace. She looked from Carson's neck to the photo and back again several times before Rikki finally voiced her opinion.

"This photo was painted in 1925. Plus, the chain is different. And this could just be some made-up superhero someone randomly decided to paint."

Carson nodded, agreeing with her friend. "I know, but that pendant looks just like mine. Is it really a coincidence? Back when Evelyn gave it to me, she mentioned something about a myth. She said that whoever wears the necklace is protected." Carson paused and placed her fingers around the rock. She gently yanked it outward and held it far enough away from her body that she could glance down at it briefly, then she looked back up at Rikki and continued, "After I put it on, I remembered everything that happened to me, clear as day.

This man, or whatever he is, has attacked me twice now. I want to know why. The dream, the necklace, this painting, all of it. That's why we're going to find the person who painted this. I need answers!"

"Or we go and find out it was some twelve-year-old kid who likes Storm from *X-Men*," Rikki muttered sardonically.

Carson crossed her arms again and glared at Rikki. "Okay then. Tell me this. Do you really believe ninety-nine years ago, someone decided to just randomly paint a picture of the exact same crystal as mine? Oh, and not to mention the fact that this woman here looks exactly like Ev. And what about the electricity, Rik? Can you explain that and why the same thing happened in my dream?" Carson stood there firmly, peering down at Rikki.

Rikki formed a thin line with her lips. "Point taken."

Carson calmly sat down on the bed beside Rikki and sighed. "The day she and I met, Ev had just magically appeared out of nowhere. I used to wonder what would have happened if I had never met her that day, and now I think I know." Carson turned to face her best friend. "I think she saved my life, Rik, that night at the hospital. I know it was her. I could *feel* her."

Rikki nodded. "Then let's go find her. But Graham isn't going to be happy about this."

"He doesn't have to know."

The girls switched the lights off and Carson locked her door. She followed Rikki out of her apartment. Rikki tossed her things in the back seat as they both piled in the car. Carson typed the address in her GPS, and Rikki started up the car. At last, they pulled out of the apartment complex.

Once on the road, Carson turned her head to face Rikki. "Rik, you mentioned on the phone you needed to tell me something, too. What is it?"

Rikki froze up. "Um...it's kind of hard to explain," she said, quickly glancing over at Carson and then back at the road. "And you might not believe me."

Carson's hickory eyes grew wide as if she was offended by Rikki's response. "Did you listen to anything I just told you back at the apartment? Do you think any of it really sounds believable? Please tell me what's going on, Rik."

Rikki admitted Carson had a good point. What she'd told her was anything but ordinary. On the other hand, though, Carson was her best friend and she vowed to understand regardless, no matter how absurd it sounded. Rikki hesitated, feeling uneasy and struggling to find the right words to say. "I think there's something wrong with me," she finally murmured.

"What do you mean?" Carson asked. "I thought the doctors cleared you on everything last wee—"

"I'm burning things with my bare hands," Rikki blurted out. She winced as if preparing herself to feel rejection and glanced over at Carson, who, in fact, looked stunned. "See? I told you. It's too crazy to expl—"

"Hang on, it's not that I don't believe you. I just don't understand. Tell me exactly what you mean," Carson urged, adjusting her body to a more comfortable position in the passenger seat.

Now it was Rikki's turn to explain. She filled Carson in on what happened the day of the picnic; how the grill just exploded spontaneously when she touched it, and the hallucination in the mirror the same day. She even emphasized that there really was no logical explanation for her high temperature results at the hospital. She told Carson about her unusual dreams, elaborating every detail about how the flames haunted her each night and the boiling heat she felt that constantly woke her up in a panic. Rikki concluded with the strange incident that had taken place hours ago.

Carson brought her hand up to her chin, her pointer finger and thumb holding it softly. She placed her other arm underneath her elbow for stability. Her brow furrowed and her penetrating gaze shot from one side to the other as if she was determined to find something. Finally, she asked, "What do all of these things have in common?"

It wasn't an open-ended question that Rikki needed to solve. She'd been thinking about the same thing for days now. She didn't want to say it out loud, but did ultimately allow the words to escape her mouth. "Fire." In her peripheral vision, Rikki noted the slight nod that Carson provided. "What if there's no logical explanation for this, either?"

"Rik, we'll figure this out." Carson smiled meekly at her friend. "I promise."

The conversation during the rest of the drive was normal. They talked about work, their families, and their everyday activities. Rikki vented about her mother's insulting text, and Carson expressed her shrewd suspicion when it came to Graham's girlfriend, Amy, whom she didn't trust in the least. Rikki mentioned she was almost finished with the production of her newest watercolor painting, which was a living room engulfed in flames—go figure. Carson informed her friend that her charity may be adding a new location, as well as an assistance program for the disabled homeless. The conversation went every which way as both girls talked, laughed, and enjoyed their time together, neither thinking about their current problem at hand.

Although Tree Heights had tall trees and lovely sights, it was nothing like the thick, deciduous forests they discovered around them as they drove. A vast variety of plants and wildflowers that covered the ground were guarded by humongous trees with leafy branches that sprawled out in all directions, sheltering the forest floors. Dispersed rays of sunlight broke through the canopy of trees, skimming the ground's surface. Carson and Rikki rolled their windows down, allowing the crisp, fresh aroma of nature to flow through the car.

"In a quarter of a mile, your destination will be on the left," the disembodied female voice from the GPS stated loudly, interrupting their unwavering gazes.

As promised, they pulled onto a short dirt road on the left that led them into a clearing surrounded by three wooden buildings. Rikki eyed up a spot on the side nearest the woods and desperately pulled over. She jerked the gear into park, and as if on cue, both girls sighed with immediate relief.

Carson and Rikki sluggishly removed themselves from the car and stood up to stretch. Once they were no longer stiff from being cramped for hours, they scoped out the area. Carson, taking a few steps away from the car, let her gaze roam. Her body quickly followed where her eyes guided her and she found herself standing in front of the three buildings, with Rikki following closely behind.

The buildings were centered in the middle of the clearing, spaced perfectly apart as if they were placed there like LEGO bricks on a LEGO board. All three were reasonably small and had cabin-like structures. The gift shop, which Carson noticed was the smallest of the three, sat in the middle. "*Avani & Bhumika Natural Creations*" was displayed on a large, darkly stained wood sign that hung above the main doorway of the shop.

The other two cabins joined the middle one on both sides but at forty-five-degree angles. The exterior of all three cabins possessed a majestic, polished oak finish. The exterior beauty of the log buildings was riveting to the eye, but what was really spectacular was the dense foliage of harmonious-colored plants that climbed the walls and cascaded over the entrances of all three.

Thick, vigorous bushes were distributed sporadically among the grassy surface of the ground. Trailing plants and vines wrapped around a large wood fence that outlined the clearing. Creeping shrubs, ferns, and other small plants sprouted from the ground near the fence. Oddly enough, it was only May, and all the plants here appeared as if they were already in full bloom.

Carson discovered that the cabin on the right was actually

a small motel, so she suggested staying there for the night. Rikki, already profoundly exhausted from being up the entire night before, agreed before Carson even finished asking her.

The cabin on the left was a restaurant, petite in size, but what it didn't offer in size, it surely made up for with the savoring smells of homemade food. Carson and Rikki welcomed the mouthwatering aroma of freshly baked apple pie and a rich assortment of herbs and spices ranging from roasted pumpkin to smoked paprika.

As Rikki and Carson began to make their way up to the middle cabin, a group of adults barged out of the doors, laughing and conversing loudly. Once the group realized they weren't alone, they quickly contained themselves. Two couples, a young man and woman in each, darted down the steps of the middle cabin with enough space in between that they didn't run into one another. Carson made an attempt to study them as nonchalantly as she could.

The first young man had reddish-brown hair. It was moderately wavy and layered with longer strands on top, making it droop slightly over his forehead. He had a pair of brick-colored eyes that gleamed in the sunlight, and bushy brown eyebrows that were pinched together in an unfriendly slant. The light stubble on his face traced the outline of his jaw, which he clenched with relentless force. He narrowed his eyes as he inquisitively scanned Carson and Rikki up and down.

He was extremely in shape. His white T-shirt clung desperately to his overly defined chest and arms, but hung loosely over the waistline of his tan, form-fitted jeans. His pants hugged his brawny legs, except for the very bottoms that appeared ruffled around the rugged, mud-brown boots he was wearing.

His eyes continued to flicker back and forth between the two girls, and he arched an eyebrow questioningly. Once he caught sight of Carson's necklace, though, the corner of his mouth shot up slightly, forming a sly smirk. Carson wasn't sure what to make of his unusual behavior.

The man had his arm draped around the neck of the young woman beside him. She, on the other hand, wasn't hard to read. A poor attitude was evident on her face, and she wasn't hiding it. The woman glanced at Carson for a few seconds, but then her gaze fell upon Rikki, whom she glared at in sheer vehemence. Her long, auburn hair fell flawlessly around her shoulders and down her back in waves. A thick strand swooped over her forehead and was pinned tightly in place with a black and gold hair comb on the side of her head. Her dark, elegant eyebrows accommodated her coppery eyes; eyes that still glowered at Rikki as she walked past. She had fine cheekbones, which thus exposed the dimples in each cheek. Unlike her boyfriend, her complexion was a little pale, but immaculate nonetheless. She wore red lipstick, a hint of blush, and some black mascara that complimented her long, delicate eyelashes. Her ruby-colored lips were full, but pressed into a thin, displeased line.

The young woman flaunted a scarlet-red and black dress that reached about mid-thigh. Two larger straps of the dress gripped both her shoulders, and two smaller straps plunged across her chest, attaching themselves to the décolleté neckline, directly meeting at a point between two voluptuous breasts. Four red buttons lined the middle of her dress, with the top two already undone, further exposing her cleavage. The large black belt that was bound around her torso hugged her tightly enough to reveal her curves. The belt buckle was gold, shiny, and circular, and well-coordinated with the outfit. She wore black combat boots that were slightly unlaced up the front and buckled down the back, completing the outfit.

Although only seconds passed by as Rikki and this unwelcoming stranger took part in an uncomfortable stare-down, they certainly dragged it out. Eventually, the woman offered a snobby eye roll as she turned her head and ambled on with her boyfriend.

Unlike her female comrade's unneighborly demeanor, the

other woman appeared calm and cordial. Her vibrant, caramel skin was unblemished and impeccable, and she had long, mocha-colored hair that fell around her face, reaching down past her shoulder blades. Her beaming, cornflower-blue eyes studied the girls curiously, but still, she offered an amiable nod and flashed a cordial smile as she walked on by the two of them. This woman looked oddly familiar, as if Carson had seen her before.

The woman possessed a small nose, high cheekbones, and a dimple in her chin. She had prominent pink lips that made her smile radiant. Carson caught sight of a threaded band that hung loosely around her neck, with some sort of unfamiliar symbol on the tarnished gold patina-like pendant. Her pastel-blue crop top halted right above her belly button, and a long white skirt ceased just above her ankles. Carson noticed a small tattoo on her left hip bone, but it was partially hidden by the elastic low-cut waistband of her skirt, so she couldn't tell what it was.

The woman glided with ease in a pair of fawn-colored flip-flops that showed off Curacao-blue-painted toenails. Her gait was far livelier and more buoyant than the other two's as she held onto her boyfriend's arm mirthfully, following her friends.

As for the boyfriend, he displayed much of the nonchalant attitude that his girlfriend showed. He was the tallest, maybe a few inches taller than the other man. His wavy, naturally blond hair remained in perfect position, styled and slightly combed back without looking greasy or slick. Unlike his friend, this man didn't possess any facial hair, but his fair-complexioned skin glowed. He was in good physical shape with a solid body and wore a steel-colored sweater and dark denim jeans that fit snugly around his long legs.

His eyes also wandered down to Carson's necklace, but eventually made their way back up to her face. He beamed, his face secure with courtesy, but he became distracted when his girlfriend grabbed ahold of his hand and dragged him in her direction a bit faster. She giggled playfully and that made his smile widen, exposing his perfect white teeth as he caught up with her. There was a particular aura that this couple released that was so completely different from the other one. This one was pleasant and tranquil. The other, smug and impetuous.

Carson peeked over her shoulder at the group as she hiked up the steps to the entrance. *Was everyone here that beautiful?*

Chapter 11

"So what's the next plan, boss?" Henry asked Arnold nonchalantly as they stood in the back room of their cigar shop. "When do we take out the next one?"

It was nine o'clock on the dot, and Arnold Jones took a long, unrestrained puff of the enormous Cuban cigar between his small, pursed lips. "Smith, I told you. We'll be making another move very soon, which actually reminds me. What's taking Ryan so long?"

Henry Smith snatched the hat off the top of his head and held it in one hand as he spoke. "He's on his way back. Had to take care of some—well, unfinished business, as you can imagine."

Arnold turned his body around to face his old colleague. "Ah, yes. The big sleep. Details, please?"

"You know the cave in the fields? We left her there. Blocked the entrance. No one'll ever find her, at least not for a long while. And when they do, the body will be quite past the decomposition stage by then. We're out of the clear, that's for sure."

Arnold revealed a wicked grin. "Ducky. Things are falling into place just as I planned. Now that the youngest is taken care of, we can surely move on up the line."

At that moment, the bell on the entrance door of the shop sounded, so Arnold shot a look over to Henry as if to warn him. "Okay, enough chat. We'll speak more later when we have absolute privacy."

Henry nodded in silent agreement. Then Arnold, followed

closely behind by Henry, made his way out into the core of the shop, taking in the delightful appearance of a young blonde woman who meandered near the shelves of cigars hanging on the walls. She hummed as she roamed the room.

"Ahem, um, can I be of some assistance to you, miss?"

The young woman continued to wander impassively, humming a pleasant song while her back faced the both of them. Though her voice was a bit muffled, she did in fact reply to Arnold's question. "I'm in search of something very specific for someone special. You see, I've been a bit on the wild side these days. Untamed. Relentless. Unforgiving, perhaps."

Arnold nodded his head, pondering what to say next. It was clear to him that women desired a man who spoke as though he was always in control, and he was just that man. He took a smooth but risky shot in the dark, guessing at her current situation. "So you presume a costly cigar for your husband could subdue some of his anger for your behaviors?"

The woman turned around to face both men, but locked her eyes on the man in charge, who happened to be Arnold. She smiled as if he had read her mind, and that of course pleased him. "Do you think that could work? Do you think I can be forgiven for what I've done?" she asked.

Arnold took a few steps toward the young woman, his eyes darting up and down her body greedily before he came to a halt. She was absolutely stunning, almost *surreal*. "Depends. Quite the bearcat, eh? Want to know a secret? Well, the only real way to a stubborn man's heart is through a fat Cuban cigar, and you happen to be at the right place for the perfect occasion," he chimed, smirking conceitedly.

The young beauty smiled. "That's quite the secret, but I do believe I have a few secrets of my own, as you can imagine." She winked at him.

At that moment, another middle-aged man burst through the door. "Jones, it's don—"

"Ryan, we have a guest. This is Ms....?" Arnold waited

patiently for the woman to offer her name.

"Light."

Arnold nodded in welcome. "Ms. Light. She is interested in a cigar for her husband. Could you please show her our variety, Ryan?"

Ryan removed his hat so as not to be rude. "Certainly. It's a pleasure to meet you, Ms. Light. I apologize for my unmannerly entrance. Please allow me to give you a tour of the finest cigars in the area." He smiled politely.

"Thank you, Ryan," she said appreciatively, and followed him over to the first wall, but turned around briefly, capturing Arnold's attention again. "I didn't catch your names."

"Arnold Jones." Arnold smiled egotistically and pointed to the man beside him. "And this is Henry Smith. And you met Ryan there. Ryan Williams. The three of us own the shop here in Nepal. Pleased to meet you, miss."

"Charmed, I'm sure." The woman nodded as if impressed and then turned back around to face Ryan, fully distracted by the first shelf of cigars.

Arnold and Henry stood in the corner of the room, speaking softly, careful to avoid any eavesdropping.

Arnold spoke directly to Henry, but gazed longingly at this new, beautiful stranger. "Magnificent, ain't she? I've never seen her in the area before. She must be a tourist."

Henry nodded, also gawking at the woman. "She's *something*, that's for sure."

"Smith, we've had a brilliant day. Why not celebrate by insisting our guest stay a while?" Arnold's perverse grin widened.

Henry nodded, portraying the same expression on his face. "I like the way you think, boss."

Arnold ambled over to where Ms. Light and Ryan were standing, catching the last bit of a "fun fact" Ryan was explaining to her about one of their cigars. "Excuse me, Ms. Light? Would you be interested in our finest giggle water? Made in the United States, of course."

Ms. Light smiled in pleasure. "Wow, you boys are discreet. How in the world were you capable of getting that here?"

"Contacts, of course," Arnold boasted, smiling in vain. "It's your lucky night. We don't usually offer such things to customers, but I'm feeling especially generous this fine evening." Arnold spoke ceremoniously, as though the offer was extremely rare. He became quite satisfied once he saw the slight smirk on the young woman's face transmute into an expression of gratitude. "Perhaps your husband wouldn't mind if you joined us?"

Ms. Light turned around and walked leisurely over to their check-out counter, and then spoke in a low, sober tone. "Can I let you in on a little secret of my own, boys?" she asked, still facing the counter. The lights began to flicker. "I haven't been completely honest, but then again, neither have you."

Arnold, Henry, and Ryan looked at each other in confusion.

Suddenly, light bulbs began to burst all around the room. The lights on the ceiling went out in a domino effect until darkness finally dominated.

"What the hell? What's this rubbish?" Arnold asked, dumbfounded by what just happened.

There were bright lights, loud sounds, but worst of all, lots of pain.

Arnold eventually came to and realized he was lying on cold, hard ground. He coughed from the over-inhalation of dust in his lungs, and his body ached with sharp pain as he struggled to sit upright. He could smell dirt and mildew, but had no idea where he was. He saw some candles burning around him and realized Henry and Ryan were also there, limp on the ground beside him. "Smith! Williams! Wake up!"

Ryan and Henry both groaned as they arose.

"What is going on? What happened?" Henry mumbled as he battled the weakened state of his arms to push up off the ground. "I can barely move. Where are we?"

They all looked around, stupefied. Despite the lit candles, darkness engulfed them.

"I don't believe it," Ryan exclaimed. "This...this is where I hid the body, but I don't see it." He whipped around and around while peering into the darkness, searching for what he knew he had left behind. "I don't see her anywhere!"

Arnold shifted his body impatiently to face Ryan and grabbed him by the shoulders. "What? What do you mean you don't *see* her? Is this some sort of prank? Williams, don't fool around with me!"

"Oh, Arnold. You're so uptight."

All three men turned their heads in the direction of the voice that had spoken before them. They watched as the young woman who'd been shopping for a cigar in their shop stood calmly in front of them, surrounded by candlelight.

"He's right. The body isn't here anymore. She's safe and sound with her family again."

"How did... You...you brought us here?" Arnold stared at her in utter puzzlement until he finally realized something. "Ah, I understand now. You must have overheard our conversation earlier. Well, let me assure you that it'd be well-advised you look the other way, miss, and we can actually forget about this whole misunderstanding. You're a pretty thing. What would your husband think if you disappeared?"

The young woman snickered. "Oh, Arnold. I never said I had a husband." She then crossed her arms. "And you call this a misunderstanding? Beating a young, innocent girl to death is a misunderstanding?" She shook her head. "I don't think so."

Arnold glared at her. "Trust me, I'm warning you. You don't want to make enemies with us." His voice shook with anger, and his chest rose and fell violently with every breath of air that he forced in. "If you have any wits at all, you'd realize you're stuck in an abandoned cave with three very wealthy men who have a reputation to uphold and a business to run. Do you think we'd put that on the line for a woman? Do you realize how stupid you are, girl?"

"You silly, materialistic man," she chuckled. "Can't you see what actually matters at this point is how many of you so-called *reputable* men are going to leave this cave tonight?" She held her hand up as if to count. "It's looking pretty slim to none."

Arnold's body began to shake with rage. A woman—a person who was obviously degraded in his eyes and much lower than a man, especially one of his stature—was actually threatening him. "I'm going to bury you alive!" he shouted as he lunged toward her. With two tightened fists full of wrath and both of his colleagues by his side, Arnold rushed to attack the young woman, but stopped dead in his tracks once he saw what she'd done.

Bright, effulgent electrical sparks spiraled around her entire body and even made their way inside her eyes; they scintillated and sparkled intensely past the now-roiled expression upon her face. She held a finger up to Arnold as if to warn him from taking another foolish step. "I wouldn't. You're already in too deep, so don't push it. You don't want to sink."

"Who...who are you?" Arnold asked while all three men stood in shock at the ever-so-real image in front of them.

"The...the lightning..." Henry Smith spoke as though he'd just placed the last piece of a very complex puzzle. "Ms.... *Light*... I get it now." His glance shifted between Arnold and Ryan before finally settling back on the young woman. "Don't either of you remember the stories we'd been told as boys about the immortal who was sworn to protect the elements? The-they're true," Henry stuttered nervously as he watched the woman smile in satisfaction. "Y-you...you're the *Light One*."

"I prefer Evelyn," the woman clarified.

"If...if you're the Light One, then that means that you're the same cursed and destructive revenant my grandfather told me about," Ryan interjected.

"You've done your homework," Evelyn replied.

"Ah, I guess we are no different after all," Arnold said smugly, and crossed his bulky arms. He sneered at Evelyn. "I do in fact take the lives of those who get in my way, but then again, so do you, Light One. We're the same, but the only thing that separates us is that you failed to protect the elementals... especially from me." He laughed in pleasure at his diabolical remark.

Evelyn glared in hatred as the bright sparks surrounding her dissipated. "Don't assume you know anything about me."

Arnold nodded, but kept the smirk on his face. "You and I...we would work well together. You don't like rules, and, well, neither do I. Join us."

Evelyn crossed her arms, mimicking Arnold. Her eyes wandered the room as she appeared to contemplate. "You and your boys are right about one thing." She flashed an evil grin as the sparks began to consume her eyes and entwine her arms once more. "No one will ever find a body in here."

After a few weeks, it was reported that Arnold Jones, Henry Smith, and Ryan Williams were missing. Months went by, years, but they never turned up again.

Chapter 12

Once Carson and Rikki made their way inside, pushing through the large wooden doors of the middle cabin, the strong aromatic scent of burning incense smacked them both in the face. The smells of sweet jasmine and damp leaves teased their nostrils as they wafted through the air. It reminded Carson of the way the air smells after a heavy rain.

Carson glanced around the shop briefly. Much like the outside, she saw a diverse collection of plants, but mostly vibrant-colored flowers in vases scattered about on stands, shelves, and tables. She heard water dripping and drizzling. The atmosphere of the shop was calming, to say the least. Her eyes wandered about, absorbing the elaborate paintings and earthy décor. Her gaze landed on the back counter, which appeared to be vacant.

Carson strolled through the shop with Rikki directly behind her until she stood in front of the counter.

Rikki sighed as she shifted her body into a more casual position, setting her elbows on the desk and placing her head in her hands. "Maybe they're not open, Car."

"But that wouldn't make any sense. It's early yet, and you saw those people. They just came out of here."

Rikki rolled her eyes. "Oh, I saw them, *especially* Ms. 'I-forgot-my-crown-at-home-but-don't-forget-I'm-a-queen,'" she quipped with a sarcastic tone as she bobbed her head from side to side mockingly.

Carson watched Rikki with amusement and couldn't help but let out a slight giggle once Rikki's eyes eventually met hers. "Her behavior *was* strange. Wonder why she glared at you like that."

"Who knows? She was probably Daddy's spoiled little girl but also her high school's popular female bully. For girls like that, they don't need a reason. Like, okay, Victoria, we get that you like to torment other women because you feel threatened and are incapable of normal human behavior, but not all women in this world are spineless, antagonizing bitches like—"

"Can I help you girls?" a woman's conspicuously authoritative voice asked from behind them, cutting Rikki short from finishing her so-called accurate presumption. The woman placed her hand on her hip with an irritated expression on her face. She was dark-complexioned and looked to be of mixed ethnicity. She was also young, probably in her twenties, and had emerald eyes that reminded Carson of a rainforest. She wore light makeup that fit her extremely well. Her physical natural beauty was the most attractive thing about her, considering her unfriendly demeanor. She was clothed in a royal-green sheer sari laced in gold and a shawl around her head of the same color.

Embarrassed, Carson's first instinct was to apologize. "Um, I'm sorry. My friend likes to reminisce back on her college years."

The woman's eyes shot over to Rikki, who'd already shrugged it off. After a few seconds of obvious silent shaming, the young woman walked around the counter to face the girls directly.

Carson continued, "My name is Carson, and this is Rikki. We're from out of town."

The woman stared at her, unimpressed. "Many people who visit the shop here are travelers passing through. Is there something I can help you with?"

"Um, this isn't exactly an unplanned stop." Carson carefully pulled the picture out of the envelope and set it on the counter in front of the woman. "I saw a painting online that you have here. I was wondering if you still have it."

The woman glanced at the photo, a neutral expression on her face. "That one is actually not for sale," she said, possessing a hint of an accent Carson hadn't noticed at first. "We do, however, have many others available. What do you like? Waterfalls, sunsets? Ah, I know. I think we have some realistic paintings of thunderstorms."

"Actually, I'm more interested in who painted it." Carson pointed at the initials in the corner of the painting. "Who is B.M.?"

The woman hesitated, but ultimately gave in and answered, "My grandmother, Bhumika. She painted it a long time ago, along with many others that line the walls of our building complex." Her hands rose and she motioned to either side of her. "You can find them throughout this shop as well as the restaurant and the motel on each side of us. But, they're just for show. She was an amazing artist back in the day with quite the imagination, as you can see, and we're very proud of her. They're her personal paintings she created throughout her life." The woman set her hands back down on the counter.

"They're beautiful, I agree. Is your grandmother around? Maybe I could speak to her? I just have a few questions about this one." Carson placed her hand on the picture.

"Unfortunately, she's unavailable at the moment."

"That's okay," Rikki interjected. "We can wait around until she is."

"You'll be waiting for quite some time, then. She isn't here."

Glancing over at Carson and then back at the woman, Rikki flashed a bold-faced smirk. "We have all day, actually. Oh, and you mentioned a motel, right? We might as well get a room since we'll be waiting a while."

Clearly annoyed now, the woman shot back, "I told you she's out of town and I don't know when she'll be back."

Before Rikki could lash out again, Carson placed her hand on her shoulder, reassuring her that she could handle it. Determined to get back on the woman's good side, she spoke in a respectful but desperate tone. "Listen, we aren't trying to cause any trouble. We drove three hours just to speak to someone about this painting. If she isn't here, that's okay. Maybe you can answer my questions." Carson offered a hopeful smile. "This necklace right here," she pointed at the necklace in the painting, "looks like the same one I have, despite the chain. Do you know anything about it? Or how about who this woman is?"

It was obvious the woman was uncomfortable with Carson's questions by the way she was acting. She was stubborn. *Extremely* stubborn. She clenched her jaw. "I'm sorry. I can't help you—I don't know anything about the painting. Like I said before, she had quite the imagination back in the day. Now, if there's nothing else I can do for you, I think you both need to leave."

"*Avani*," a firm, empowering voice thundered from behind them, alarming everyone in the room. Carson and Rikki turned around to find another woman standing several feet away. "You don't treat guests that way. You may leave. I'll accommodate our guests."

"But Mother, they were just lea—"

"Go check on your brothers. They're probably doing something dangerously foolish as we speak." She didn't leave room for Avani to argue.

"Yes, Mother." Avani nodded and turned the corner behind the counter, disappearing from sight completely.

The other woman glided over and Carson immediately realized where Avani had acquired her beauty from. She was just a younger version of the woman standing in front of them. The woman's green eyes twinkled in delight. She too wore a sari, but this one was a gorgeous, metallic blue with silver trim. She had a few wrinkles at the corner of each eye from what the middle stages of life had given her, and the laugh lines on her face likely originated from that very welcoming, buoyant smile that she seemed to display often.

"I'm so sorry, girls. Please forgive my daughter. She has been working in this shop for hours. I think she's just tired. I apologize for her behavior," the woman said sincerely. "Anyway, my name is Prakruti, but please spare me the sad attempt of trying to pronounce it. Call me Rudy for short." Like Avani, she possessed an accent, but hers was a bit stronger than her daughter's.

"I'm Carson, and this is Rikki. We're visiting from Tree Heights." Carson offered a friendly smile.

"It's a pleasure and an honor to meet the both of you," Rudy replied as though she was actually pleased to be formally introduced. "So," she continued, "what can I do for you girls?"

Carson pointed at the picture. "Your daughter said her grandmother painted this, but she told us that she isn't available today. I just had a few questions. Would you be willing to tell me about this painting?"

Rudy glanced down at the counter, spotting the picture. "Ah, 'Prakash Ek.' What a beautiful soul."

Carson and Rikki glanced at each other in confusion.

Rudy picked the picture up with both hands and held it out in front of her. "This painting is magnificent. It reminds me of my childhood when we lived back in Nepal. My mother Bhumika and I are originally from South Asia. We moved to this country years ago, but we do get to visit very often."

Still puzzled, Carson drove for answers. "You said Nepal? Is the woman in the painting from Nepal?"

Rudy shook her head. "Oh, no, no. I believe my mother told me she was a visitor the day they met. You see, when my mother was just a child, this woman saved her life. So, she wanted to create something memorable in honor of the person who gave her a second chance." She set the picture back down on the counter.

"What do you mean she saved her life?"

"When my mother was about ten, she got bullied for being

what others perceived as different. A few American men who owned a local shop severely beat her and left her in a cave to die, and she almost *did* die. But," Rudy pointed at the woman in the picture again, "this woman just happened to be around at the right time to find her before it was too late."

Carson's eyes widened in awe. "Wow, I'm so sorry to hear that happened to your mother. How traumatic."

"What happened to the men? Did they get into any trouble for what they did to your mother?" Rikki blurted out, interrupting.

Rudy narrowed her eyes, looking up toward an empty space in the air between them as if she was thinking back. "Oh yes, big trouble," she emphasized, and focused her eyes back on the two girls. "They happened to get just what they deserved."

"Did Bhumika keep in contact with this woman after that?" Carson studied Rudy with a level gaze.

"She did, of course. This woman would visit often to check up on her."

"Is she still around?"

"Well, my mother is now in her nineties, so you do the math." Rudy winked and smiled.

"Right," Rikki said, "makes sense. That would make the woman well over a hundred years old." She shot Carson a distinct look, silently encouraging Carson to continue.

"What was her name? The, uh, woman in the painting?"

"Hmm. Well, now. Her name has slipped my mind but I'm sure it'll come back to me soon enough. Forgive me, age has done its worst to my memory." She laughed lightheartedly. "Anyway, are you girls interested in staying? We provide the utmost satisfying breakfast, lunch, and dinner here." Her eyes twinkled. "Catered by none other than yours truly."

"Yes, we'd like to stay for the night. We drove for quite some time to get here," Carson explained. "Can I ask you one more thing? The necklace in the picture." She tapped her pointer finger on the image in front of her. "Does your mother know anything about it? I have a crystal just like it. It really caught my attention when I saw this online. They look exactly the same—well, except for the chain."

Rudy looked at the picture again and then at Carson's neckline, where the crystal lay along her collarbone. "Yes, indeed. They do have quite similar features. From what I've been told, the one in the picture was rumored to hold great power. A source of eternal protection."

Carson arched an eyebrow and glanced at Rikki. "Hm, where have I heard that before?" She looked back at Rudy. "Protection from what?"

"Oh, there have been stories passed down about individuals who have influential speed, strength, and power over the elements."

Once again, Rikki interrupted. "Um, elements? You mean like fire, for instance?"

Rudy's eyes danced as she laughed. "Sure. The story has probably changed so many times through the years, so tell it however you want." She winked at them. "Now, you girls must be hungry. Please, come over to my restaurant. I'll cook something delicious for you. And it's on me."

By the time the girls left the shop, grabbed their things from the car, and checked into a room, it was past noon. The name of the small motel was *Kshitij ka Rahasy Inn*. It was named after Rudy's oldest son, Kshitij, or Teek for short, who also happened to be out of town. The inn's interior was just as spectacular as the shop's. Their eyes feasted upon a chromatic scale of art and remarkably large, healthy plants distributed throughout the hallways. Rudy helped them get settled into their room, but before she left, she informed them she'd have lunch prepared at the restaurant when they were ready to eat.

Starving, the girls threw their bags on their beds and sprinted out of the room.

As Carson and Rikki sauntered along toward *Dine at Divine Dishes*, the name of the small restaurant obviously owned by Rudy, uncontrollable laughter captured their attention. Eyes wide in surprise, they watched as two boys hooted and hollered as they leapt from tree to tree and branch to branch by the forest's edge. These boys were nothing less than fearless, having an ecstatic time dozens of feet up in the air. Carson wasn't close enough to make out their faces, but she could tell they were shirtless and barefoot with only a pair of cut-off sweats on each of their lower halves.

"Who are those guys? That's so dangerous," Carson exclaimed, shooting a glance over at Rikki, whose jaw had also been stuck in a temporary dropped position.

As Rikki and Carson watched in stunned disbelief without as much as a blink, neither one realized Rudy had joined them.

"Oh my, I've told them a million times to stop doing this. You'd think they'd grow out of this dauntless phase by their age, but it seems just like yesterday I was growling at them for climbing out of their cribs." She shook her head in displeasure. "Those are my twin boys. Come." She waved her hand for Carson and Rikki to follow her. "Please let me introduce you."

The boys stopped jumping once they noticed their mother's arrival.

"Boys! Get down from there. You know what I told you about this game. Come down here. I want to introduce you to someone." She motioned for them to come down, and as if they were toddlers listening to their mother demand that they spit out that hard piece of candy, they climbed down, slipped on their sandals, and followed her. Rudy was muttering something to them on their way back, but Carson didn't know what; she was speaking in another language.

As they drew closer, it became apparent that the boys were twins. They appeared identical, with even the same length of hair. What separated them from each other was the unique tattoos displayed on their bodies. They were both blessed with silky, chestnut-colored hair that they constantly brushed back out of their faces. Again, Carson couldn't overlook the two pairs of viridescent eyes that marveled back at her and Rikki, as though they were just as fascinated with the two of them.

"Carson, Rikki." Rudy looked at both girls. "I'd like you to meet my sons, Mayank and Aarush."

One of the boys stepped forward. "Welcome. Call me Mayo. It's nice to meet you." He smiled. His eyes twinkled with friendliness. Carson noted the tattoos that started on his chest and made their way down his abdomen. They were the different stages of the moon.

"And you can call me Rush," the other twin added as he cut in front of his brother. "The superior twin always gets to shake the hand of a beautiful lady first," he giggled as his brother shoved him jokingly. His tattoo was on his left shoulder. It looked like a symbol of a sun, but much more complex and intricate.

Their eyes sparkled with every durably vivid hue of a rainforest, just like Avani and Rudy's. The twins were physically toned and dark-complexioned, which exposed their muscle definition significantly.

Carson and Rikki shook their hands.

"How do you guys do that?" Rikki asked blatantly. She motioned toward the trees.

The boys followed her finger, but when they focused back on her, they both appeared confused.

"Do what?" Mayo tilted his head to the side.

"Jump from tree to tree like that. And you're so high up. That's crazy!"

The boys snickered at one another.

Rudy replied for them, "This is exactly what I keep telling them. It is foolish. But they continue to roam around up on the treetops."

This comment caused the boys to chuckle.

"You guys realize how high up you are, don't you?" Carson asked them.

"Not high enough," Rush teased.

"Don't get any ideas!" Rudy warned them.

Finding their mother's warnings humorous, they both giggled again.

"When you discover what you can be capable of, there's no such thing as fear. The feeling of invincibility consumes you," Rush explained.

"But aren't you afraid of falling? You know, getting hurt?" Rikki asked.

"Well, sure," Mayo looked profoundly into Rikki's eyes as he spoke, "but it can be more frightening to live with constant fear than attempt to overcome it. We all fear something, but we also control what we fear. It's okay to be afraid, but you can't let fear run your life."

After the introduction, the boys disappeared back into the woods and Carson and Rikki followed Rudy into Divine's. They stuffed themselves with stew, fresh bread, and even a fruit pie, all of which was prepared by Rudy herself. Carson practically begged Rudy to take her money, but she would not accept it. Once she was out of sight, Carson left a gracious tip on the table. Carson didn't know her well at all, but she could tell each lifeline on her face was one she earned with time, labor, and being a hard-working mother. Carson felt comfortable around her.

Once back outside, Carson and Rikki longed to explore, so they scanned the perimeter and discovered a dirt path leading into the woods. They followed the path, admiring the engaging scenic display of nature surrounding them. They saw no sign of the twins. Every now and again a gusty wind whirled around the girls. The air was crisp, and it smelled just as refreshing outside as it did in the shop. The path looped through the tall trees and finally concluded at a wooden bench.

Much to their surprise, the bench was adjacent to a cliff that overlooked a massive lake. The girls hadn't noticed the large body of water as they drove through due to the drop in elevation; it was much lower than the land they were standing on. Plus, it was hard to see anything through the dense trees.

Afraid of heights, Carson inched a few steps backward. "Uh, Rik, I'm gonna stay back here. This is too close to the edge for me." She took a seat on the bench.

Rikki, whose eyes were still locked on the water, sat down beside Carson, but held a distant expression on her face.

Carson immediately sensed her uneasiness and placed her hand on Rikki's arm. "Hey, what's up? You look lost all of a sudden."

Rikki was silent for a few minutes. "Is that what's wrong with me, then?" she finally asked.

Carson didn't understand what she meant. "Is *what* wrong with you?"

"Rudy claims that the necklace protects from elemental beings. Fire beings. You know what an elemental being is, don't you, Car? The fake stuff you see in movies. Superheroes. Villains. Magic powers. It's just not possible. So I'm just a freak." She stood up suddenly. "I'm a freak, aren't I?"

"Rikki." Carson took a deep breath in and turned her body to face her friend. She pulled her back down on the bench so their knees were almost touching. "Remember when I told you in the car that I promised we'd figure this out? I meant that. Besides, Rik, if you're a freak, then so am I. And we're the best kind, because we're in this together. I don't care if it all sounds crazy. I wouldn't let you go through this alone. You never left my side when Evelyn left. It was hard for me. And you're still here after everything. Whatever is going on, I know it's hard for you, too. So I'll never leave your side either." Carson wrapped her arms around her best friend in a long, consoling hug.

Rikki didn't say anything back, but she didn't have to. Carson knew what she was thinking when she felt Rikki wipe a tear from her face.

CHAPTER 13

Carson roamed her apartment in search of her missing girl-friend. It was strange—Evelyn usually met her at the door when she got home from work, but today she wasn't there. Carson eventually entered her office, where she saw the window was open, and when she walked over to shut it, she found Evelyn sitting outside on the roof.

Evelyn looked back to greet her. "Hey, you."

"Ev, what are you doing out here?" Carson asked, wedging half of her body out of the window. "Babe, come back in here. You could fall."

Evelyn smiled and then faced the sky. "I'm admiring the view. It's amazing how big such a small town appears. Come out here with me. Come look." She patted a spot beside her, motioning for Carson to join her on the roof.

"Uh…" Carson, reluctant to move due to her drastic fear of heights, hesitated before answering, "I don't know, Ev."

"I won't let you fall, Car. You can hold onto me. Trust me," Evelyn insisted.

Carson bit her lip, silently contemplating. She finally decided to climb out and sit down next to Evelyn. Once she realized how high up she was, though, she closed her eyes tightly while secretly regretting her decision.

Evelyn chuckled as she looked down to find Carson death-gripping her leg. She gently slipped her hand under Carson's, lacing their fingers together. "Relax. It's okay. See?"

Carson, who was barely peeking through one eye, snuck a

glimpse of the horizon in front of her. She felt Evelyn's thumb caress her hand, and that seemed to calm her nerves. Slowly, she widened her eyes to take in the view. She finally allowed herself to look around. "Wow. You're right. It does look big, and it's beautiful up here."

Evelyn nodded in agreement.

"But how do you do this?" Carson asked.

Evelyn turned her head to face Carson, a puzzled expression on her face. "What's that?"

Carson pointed down. "This. You're not afraid of how high up we are or how dangerous this is. You are fearless." She shook her head in disbelief. "And now that I really think about it, I don't think I've ever seen you get scared of anything."

The corners of Evelyn's mouth turned slightly downward. "Everyone is afraid of something. Even me," she whispered, returning her gaze to the sky. "I used to be afraid of heights as well, actually. Well, years ago."

"Really? What did you do to get over it?" Carson questioned, her brown eyes centered on Evelyn.

"I just used to think about how much higher off the ground I could really be. I was never at the highest point, and I knew that, so it made me feel better. Less afraid."

Carson glanced at Evelyn with a look of disarray, so Evelyn continued to explain, "For instance, your apartment is on the second floor," she held up two fingers, "but there are five in this building, which means the fifth is higher than the second, and therefore, you realize how much higher you could actually be. We could be on the fifth or the very top of the building. That's higher than where we are now. Know what I mean?"

"But what if we're at the highest point of something?" Carson asked.

Evelyn pointed up to the sky. "There's always somewhere higher."

It made sense. Carson had to admit it; it made a whole lot of sense.

They sat like that for several long moments, marveling at the sights surrounding them. The warm wind blew, cooling their skin from the sun's intense rays, when Evelyn finally broke the silence.

"Carson, do you believe there is a fine line between good and bad people?"

Carson looked at Evelyn, confused. "I think that's a very open-ended question, babe."

"Do you think we should be judged by the things we've done in our pasts, even if we're no longer that same person?"

Carson shook her head. "You never know someone's full story."

Evelyn waited a few seconds before replying. She pointed straight ahead in the direction of the town. "You see all those cars racing around? All of those houses? Well, I can bet there isn't one person there who doesn't have a secret they aren't ashamed of," she explained, glancing at Carson. "We all have something that haunts us."

Carson's brow furrowed again. "You mean like skeletons in the closet?"

Evelyn nodded. "Unfortunately, no matter what it is, people are so quick to judge. They simply judge without ever really knowing the situation."

"I don't believe other people's opinions define who someone is as a person. Just because somebody says you're a bad person doesn't make you a bad person," Carson offered.

Evelyn agreed. "And yet we're all criticized for the mistakes we make every day."

"We're only human. We're bound to make mistakes. That doesn't make you a bad person, no matter how many you make."

Evelyn nodded but appeared unsatisfied. Her light blue eyes were pinned to a point straight ahead as if she was distracted by her own thoughts.

Carson softly placed her hand on Evelyn's. "Ev, you possess a lot of depth. Do you know what that means?" she asked.

Evelyn shook her head. "Tell me."

"It means you feel things deeply," Carson explained. "You dig down to the most profound parts, especially when you believe in something. I feel like you'd really fight for something you love."

"Not everyone appreciates the good hearts in this world," Evelyn stated, to which Carson replied, "I do, because I see one in you." Carson squeezed Evelyn's hand, and for a brief second, Evelyn smiled.

"Do you think that evil people have depth, too?"

Carson nodded. "Absolutely. Even the people in this world who do bad things, they still have depth. There's a heart in there somewhere. Sometimes it's just hard to see."

"What about the ones who have wronged others?" Evelyn's eyes narrowed curiously, awaiting Carson's reply.

Carson paused, deciding how she wanted to word her answer. "I think people usually have reasons for what they do, and situations are easily misunderstood. Evil isn't always what you think it is. They could have experienced some sort of trauma that may have caused them to end up that way, but I also believe in forgiveness. Anybody has the potential to become a better person, and I honestly think even those who are misguided can turn around and be the best person they know how to be."

Evelyn grew silent for a moment. "You believe evil can be forgiven?"

"That's the thing, Ev. All it takes is forgiveness to change a person completely."

Chapter 14

Carson let the hot water from the shower spray down onto her skin as she leaned on the wall, deep in thought. Memories of Evelyn occupied her mind. She thought back to the conversation they'd had on the rooftop outside her apartment window.

Carson used to get lost in the way Evelyn spoke; it was as if she'd been through all the good and bad situations in life, but she never portrayed herself as a genius or an egotist. It was more like she was just full of wisdom, and it drew Carson in like a magnet the more time they spent together.

They could talk together for hours, and that was one of the most important things to Carson when it came to their relationship. Evelyn had a way of making Carson not only feel, but *know* that she was the most important thing to her. She didn't consider Evelyn a surface-level person; there was so much inside her. She was complex, and Carson had never met another person who rendered that much depth.

After the walk back from the bench, Carson and Rikki decided to rest for the remainder of the evening. They'd planned on waking up early enough to catch the woman who had painted that picture. Carson was set on finding answers, and she wasn't leaving without some.

Once Carson got out of the shower, she glanced down at the vanity counter where her crystal now lay. She grabbed it, settling the crystal in the middle of her palm. *What's it about this thing that seems so special? Why was it so important to Evelyn that I wear it?* She thought about putting it back on, but didn't. She'd just slip it back on in the morning.

Carson rounded the corner and grinned with amusement when she saw her best friend sprawled out on her bed, drooling on the pillow. Carson couldn't blame her; the girl had literally been up the entire night before. And aside from that, she knew Rikki had some overwhelming things going on in her life too, so no wonder she was exhausted. Carson got into bed quietly and shut the light off.

An hour or so went by as Carson shifted in bed every which way, trying to get comfortable enough to fall asleep, but her mind was too distracted. Using her cell phone's flashlight to guide her, she threw the covers over her and sat on the edge of the bed. She grabbed a jacket close by and slipped it on. She gazed across the dark room to see Rikki still fast asleep, now sprawled in a different position across the bed. Carson shook her head and smiled.

It was almost past midnight, so only serene moonlight squeezed through the curtains in their room. She got up, walked over to the door, and without making too much noise, opened and closed it gently behind her. She looked around, searching the premises. The moon was vibrant and shone radiantly over the clearing. Even as the darkness cast itself over most of the domain, the view was still exquisite. Carson made her way across the clearing and toward the path. If she couldn't sleep, she may as well go for a walk to think. Who knows, maybe she'd be tired by the time she got back.

As she strode on, Carson realized she hadn't noticed the solar lights that lined the entire path during the day. Although the moon was bright, these lights made it much easier to see. Eventually she made it to the bench, but she didn't sit down. She just gazed out at the lake. The moon's large reflection glimmered on it, dancing around as the water stirred from the wind.

She thought about that day when she and Evelyn sat on the roof together. She'd ended up so absorbed in their conversation that she'd forgotten all about her fear of heights, especially after the point Evelyn made.

She pondered for a minute, then wandered over to the edge of the cliff, getting just close enough to peer down and take a look at the bottom. *Too close.* She turned around, but just as she did, she thought again about what Evelyn said that day. *There's always somewhere higher.* The words repeated themselves in her mind. She turned back around to face the water, a few feet from the edge.

Carson closed her eyes, trying to picture something higher, but what was taller than this cliff? *Think. Think. Ah, I got it! A mountain!* Carson imagined the outline of the peak, and then she envisioned the drop below, the whole way to the bottom of the valley. She opened her eyes and looked back down at the bottom where the water was splashing into the rocks. Much to her relief, it became clear to her that it *wasn't* nearly as high as the mountain she'd just imagined. *It worked!* She smiled, proud of her accomplishment.

As Carson beamed with pride, she experienced an alarming sense of lightheadedness that struck her out of nowhere. *Okay, time to get away from the edge.* Carson attempted to turn around, but she only wobbled and stumbled more as the dizziness grew stronger. She could smell something sweet in the air, and the more she inhaled, the worse it got. Carson felt as if she was drunk.

Struggling to catch her footing, she staggered back a few steps. She was still so close to the edge, and everything around her was spinning. Then, all of a sudden, Carson tripped over a large tree root and fell forward.

Catching onto a root jutting out from the side of the cliff, Carson gripped the grubby piece of earth strenuously, winding her arms tightly around it. Moments passed as she hung there, hovering high above the sharp rocks at the bottom. "HELP! HELP! SOMEONE HELP ME!"

"Carson..." someone whispered. She heard it several times, echoing all around her. She looked down below, watching as some sort of substance rose in the air. It was either smoke or fog, and she wasn't sure which, but it continued to float up in her direction.

"The Marked One..." the voices chanted. There was someone down there!

As Carson's arms suffered from fatigue and her grip weakened, she began to slip. Eventually she was hanging on by only her hands. She knew she wasn't strong enough to hold her body up for much longer.

Eyes burning as she squinted through the thick haze in the air, Carson watched in astonishment as many pairs of blazing, scarlet-red eyes began to appear down below.

"Wh-who are you?" Carson called out into the darkness. She heard only giggling in return. Her suspicion was right; there *was* someone down there—more than one person—and they appeared to be moving closer as they continued to torment her with evil laughter and creepy whispers. Although her adrenaline was at its peak and her heart was racing, her arms grew more and more tired and her fingers became numb. A few fingers started to slip. She pinched them tighter.

"Carson..." The figures were even closer now, climbing up the rocks with such swift movements that it was just humanly impossible.

Am I hallucinating? At long last, Carson's strength finally gave in, and her fingers slipped. She felt gravity pull downward.

She didn't fall, though, because at that very second, *somebody* caught her. She could feel the warmth of someone's hand as strong fingers wrapped themselves around her own. Carson jerked her head up to face the person.

Squinting from the extraordinary light emitting from the person's eyes, she finally felt herself being yanked up. The figure with the luminous, light blue eyes wrapped one of their arms around her waist, pulling her up to safety effortlessly and dragging her backward onto the ground. That's when she could make out the face. *Evelyn.*

"Carson, stay here. Don't move." Evelyn's eyes sparked ferociously with electricity. She turned around to find the figures who were climbing up the side of the slope at the very edge now, their hands digging into the ground as they lunged forward at her. Carson watched as Evelyn's entire body became engulfed in sparks. *Another dream. This has to be another dream.*

"What the—" Carson, at a complete loss for words, watched lightning bolts soar rapidly in all directions. Loud zaps pierced her ears. Bone-rattling booms of thunder shook the ground without interruption. The way Evelyn moved made it seem like a *Matrix* movie. She twisted and flipped with ease, striking the figures and electrocuting them until their bodies fell over the edge.

Carson thought for a second that maybe she really *was* dreaming—until she realized she was having trouble breathing. The cloying odor was greater and much more potent in the air now. Carson coughed violently as she struggled for fresh air. Her throat felt extremely hoarse and her eyes were irritated as if she'd been standing in a confined room full of dense smoke.

Finished with the intruders within seconds, Evelyn looked back to find Carson choking. The sparks surrounding Evelyn's body attenuated and then faded altogether. In a split second, she was crouching down by Carson's side. "Car, I'm so sorry about all of this." Lightning streaks darted across the sky and thunder bellowed in the distance.

Disoriented, Carson could barely focus. She opened her eyes slightly, forcing herself to speak. "Evelyn, what was—" She fumbled for words, but painful coughs broke through instead. She could vaguely hear something in the distance. Were those footsteps running toward them? Leaves crunched, and she was sure it was multiple people. As the sound became more prominent, it was obvious they were getting closer. Carson wasn't ready for more. She wanted a break. She could hardly breathe or open her eyes as it was.

The wind grew powerful, cool gusts swirling around them, and Evelyn's hair blew wildly in the air. Carson heard loud splashes coming from below the cliff as if giant waves were crashing below. *Oh no, they're coming back,* she thought. She felt raindrops pelt against her overheated skin. There was a crackling noise, like the sound a campfire makes, and she swore she could actually feel the heat from it. Through blurred vision, she watched as more figures surrounded them, all of their eyes glowing effulgently. This time Carson saw not only red eyes, but green and blue also.

Carson wheezed and coughed. Her chest felt tight.

"Here, I can help you," Evelyn implored, placing one of her hands on the left upper side of Carson's chest, directly over her heart.

Carson saw the figures close in on them. "Ev…" she tried to warn her, but it was no use. She waited for them to attack, but much to her surprise, they never did. Instead, they only observed. Carson could hear them talking, but she only made out a few words.

"She's not wearing the necklace." That voice in particular sounded oddly familiar. *Was that Rudy?*

Gradually, the burn in Carson's throat and the pain in her chest alleviated. The sting in her eyes even started to subside, and what was left was a feeling of only pure calmness, a state of comfort. Carson felt drowsy, but not in the same way as earlier. She felt tranquil and safe, and this led her to fall asleep peacefully. Before she did, though, she managed to whisper a few more words.

"You left me."

Carson woke up in her bed inside the small motel room. At first she didn't realize where she was, but then she heard Rikki's voice and looked over to find Rikki on her cell phone, arguing with someone. It didn't take Carson long to figure out who was on the other end of the phone.

"I don't know, Mother. It was just a last-minute road trip with Car. I don't know when we'll be home. Why does it matter?" Once Rikki noticed that Carson was awake, she hopped at the chance to get off the phone. "Oh, what's that, Car? You need help with the grill? I don't have time to talk, Mother. I have important things to do."

Carson heard the beep of the phone, which abruptly ended the call. Sandy Ward wasn't going to be very happy.

"What time did I go to bed? I don't even remember falling asleep," Carson mumbled.

"I don't either. I passed out. I woke up about an hour ago. It's almost nine," Rikki informed her, glancing down at her phone.

Carson yawned and wiped her eyes. She stretched momentarily, suddenly feeling the heaviness of something solid lying on her chest. *The crystal.* The necklace was fastened around her neck. She thought she'd taken it off before her shower. No—she *knew* she did. *What happened last night?* She backtracked her night silently while Rikki fiddled with her phone.

Glowing eyes. Electricity. Another dream? No...it wasn't a dream at all.

It all hit her at once. *Evelyn.*

Carson jumped out of bed and zoomed straight for the door.

"Car? Car, what's wrong?" Rikki called after her friend, only to become more confused as she watched her race out the door. "Car! Hang on, dude! I need to put a bra on!" She grabbed a hoodie and followed Carson.

Carson, not easing up at all, dashed straight over to the gift shop. With her hand on the door, she took a deep breath and pushed it open.

"Car, can you please tell me what's going on?" Carson stopped dead in her tracks so Rikki blindly bumped right into her. "Ouch! What the frickity frack, Car?"

She finally noticed several people in the shop encircling them, including her recent death-stare competition.

Carson saw all familiar faces; the couples from the day before, Avani, and her twin brothers were all present. But no Rudy, and no Evelyn.

Carson stepped forward in Avani's direction. "You!" She pointed at Avani. "You acted like you didn't have a clue why we came here. Just a few girls asking silly questions, right? I've been attacked twice now. The first time was a week ago, and then again last night. You are going to answer my questions this time. Where's Rudy?" Carson glared.

"What? Who attacked you?" Rikki asked, completely thrown off by what had just come out of her friend's mouth.

"I'm sorry, but Rudy isn't here at the moment," Avani countered.

"Oh, here we go again. Just like your grandmother was 'conveniently' out of town when we arrived. Let's all act oblivious to what's really going on here. The same way you acted when you saw the picture of Evelyn. I want to talk to her."

Confused to no end, Rikki interjected once again, "What? Evelyn is here?"

Carson turned around to face her friend. "Oh yeah, Rik. You'll love this. They've all been lying. They knew who she was the entire time. Even their mother." She motioned to Avani and the twins. "I heard her voice last night. She was there with Evelyn."

"What the hell? Why didn't you just tell us she was here?" Rikki glowered at Avani.

"You're all hiding something. I'm done playing this game," Carson spat out.

Fuming with disgust, Rikki took a few raging steps toward Avani but didn't get far. The same woman who had given her the death glare yesterday stepped in front of her, blocking her way.

"I think you need to take a step back before this turns out the opposite of how you expect it to, darling."

Rikki sneered and stepped to the side slightly, peering around the woman's body to lock eyes with Avani. "Oh, I get it now," she said and nodded her head toward the woman in front of her. "She's your puppet."

The woman stepped closer to Rikki. "I'm warning you. Back off."

Rikki closed the space between them, building tension. Neither one blinked. It didn't even look as though they were breathing.

The friendly dark-complexioned woman finally chimed in, "Abellona, let this go."

Carson, fully aware of Rikki's temper, didn't want any more problems than she already had. "Yeah, Rik. Come on, relax."

"Chiraz, let them be. I like watching women with a bit of fire in them." Carson wasn't surprised to hear this come out of Abellona's boyfriend's mouth. He snickered, instigating the situation.

"Don't worry, Chiraz. I'm only testing her," Abellona gibed, taunting Rikki more.

"Bad idea." Rikki clenched her jaw and tightened her fist.

"ABELLONA," Rudy shouted as she joined the group, appearing out of nowhere. "That's enough."

Abellona, still staring at Rikki, finally backed away. A sly grin spread over her face. "It's comical. You know the rage you've been feeling over any little thing? The heat you know is flaring and rising inside you as if you could explode any second? Let it out. You don't even know what you're capable of because you're so in denial. It's adorable."

Rikki, obviously baffled by Abellona's statement, stepped back beside her best friend. Carson knew Rikki wouldn't let someone else get the last word either way. "In this case, you surely don't want to find out."

Carson, relieved once she realized Abellona wasn't going to reply, turned to face Rudy. She walked over impatiently until she stood an arm's length in front of her. "Rudy, please tell me where she is. I just want to talk to her. She saved my life last night."

Rudy, with a genuine expression on her face, opened her mouth like she was going to respond but was instantly distracted by something over Carson's shoulder. Everyone grew quiet, even Rikki.

"Car."

Carson turned around to find Evelyn standing there. It wasn't how she imagined it; she figured Evelyn would look a bit older, maybe have a new haircut, possibly a new style of clothing. But nothing changed. And she was still just as flawlessly radiant as ever. Her tight-fitted jeans were dark denim and slid into black combat boots. A long-sleeved black shirt fit securely over her upper body. Her long blonde hair fell perfectly over her shoulders. She was still just as irresistible as always.

Carson gazed at Evelyn, just taking in her appearance. It had been two whole years since she last spoke to her—well, in a sober and normal state of mind, at any rate. The last few occurrences surely didn't count, did they?

Carson was flustered. "Uh…" She searched for the right words to say. "Last night?"

Evelyn nodded. "That was me."

"And the night at the hospital?"

Evelyn nodded silently.

"How many times have you come around without me knowing?" Carson's voice began to shake with frustration.

"Just twice, Car. Those times specifically. I was away for two years."

For a minute, Carson forgot all about everyone else standing around them and focused just on Evelyn's words, which made her feel even more deceived. "Oh, that's right. Seeing you just now almost made me actually forget how you ended our relationship."

"Carson, I know you're angry with me, but you don't understand. I—"

"No, Evelyn, YOU don't understand. You don't understand the pain you put me through. For a while, I thought you were in trouble. But you're here, alive and well. I wouldn't wish what I went through to get over you on my worst enemy!" Carson, raising her voice, began to feel tears swell behind her eyes. She didn't want these people to see her break down, especially Evelyn. She didn't want to give her the satisfaction. But she'd rehearsed this moment in her mind many, many times; she knew exactly what she'd say to Evelyn if she ever saw her again, and she needed to say it now.

"A note, Ev." She shook her head in disbelief and choked on her words as she continued, "You left a note, and you never showed up in my life again. Did I mean that little to you?" A single tear escaped and rolled down her cheek as she watched Evelyn in utter disappointment.

Evelyn took a few steps closer, but Carson warned her to stay put with just the motion of her hand. Evelyn spoke from a small distance across the room. "Carson, you're the most important person in the world to me. I know you don't understand it now, but I didn't have a choice."

"Bullshit, Ev. There's always a choice." Carson stared at her indignantly.

"I don't deserve you, Carson. You're a remarkable person, and the day I met you was beyond luck for me. I've met millions of people throughout my life, and I've never come across anyone like you. There's a lot about me you don't know, and you may not understand."

Evelyn's words evoked more questions than answers, but they also reminded Carson of the main reason she and Rikki had driven three hours to get there in the first place. She glanced over at Rudy, who stared back at her with a look of nothing less than guilt.

"That painting." Carson glared at Evelyn as she spoke. "You know which one I'm talking about. The woman with the lightning bolts…" She swallowed the lump in her throat. "That's you, isn't it?"

Hesitating, Evelyn finally nodded in infamy.

"How old are you? Don't you dare say twenty-eight. Don't lie to me anymore."

Evelyn paused for another moment before she spoke. "I was born in 1720."

Carson's brows furrowed and there was a long, painful silence before she responded, "That would mean you're…300 hundred years old. How's that even possible?" she asked, incredulous. "You look the same now as you do in that picture. Like you haven't grown at all."

Evelyn nodded. "Things are not always how they appear in this world. Please, let me show you who I really am." She gestured to the others in the room. "Who *we* really are. You deserve to know the absolute truth. I won't blame you if you never want to speak to me again."

Carson watched her, silently contemplating.

"You once told me you were a firm believer in forgiveness. I don't expect forgiveness, but maybe just the opportunity to explain."

"Fine," Carson agreed impassively. Inwardly, she hoped no one had seen her trembling.

Evelyn smiled faintly then turned to lock eyes with Rikki. "Rikki, please join us. This is going to make a lot more sense for you than it is for her."

CHAPTER 15

Carson and Rikki agreed to meet Evelyn and the others after they showered and got dressed within the hour. Carson still couldn't wrap her head around everything that was going on. So her ageless ex-girlfriend could spawn electricity through-out her body. Big deal, right?

Rikki's voice pulled her out of her thoughts and back to reality. "This is crazy. What she is saying is *crazy*," she blurted out, staring at herself in the mirror, smothering her face in makeup. At a time like this, the girl was still worried about the way she looked. "But it sorta makes sense with Evelyn. You know, the mysterious, brooding woman that she was when you met her." She smirked as though her comment was a clever one. "But what about her past? You never questioned her past, Car?"

Carson, who was sitting on her bed, grew silent for a moment before responding. "I never thought past what she told me. She never gave me a reason to wonder. She claims her parents died and left her with an inheritance. She was debating on whether to go back to school or not. Four years ago, I was fine believing just that."

Rikki paused and turned her gaze to Carson. "Do you think you'd have questioned things this late in the game if she'd have never left?"

"I think some truth would have come to the surface at some point," Carson answered. "But that's just it. She's acting like she didn't have a choice over leaving me. I don't under-stand that part, and those are the answers I want most."

Rikki went back to finishing her makeup. "If you get answers, can you forgive her?"

Carson pondered how to answer that question. *Would I be able to forgive Evelyn after all was said and done?* It depended on so many things. "Although I want to hate her for leaving, the last thing she said was right. I told her I believed in forgiveness, and forgiveness means second chances. I'm sticking to that, but not for her. This is for me. That's the person I am, Rik."

Rikki nodded.

"Besides," Carson continued as she stood up to throw a jacket on, "she keeps saving my life."

After they were dressed and Rikki considered herself moderately acceptable in appearance, the hour had flown by. Carson opened her door to find Evelyn standing outside of it.

"Um, hello." Evelyn flashed a warm smile at Carson, but her movements articulated nervousness.

"Uh, hi," Carson replied, her body language mirroring Evelyn's.

They stood uncomfortably like this for countless seconds until Rikki snapped them both out of whatever trance of awkwardness they'd fallen into. Walking in between them, she spat, "God, for 300 years old, you're still socially inept. Congrats."

"I've only been working on it for 200," Evelyn retorted.

Although it wasn't the time for jokes, Carson couldn't help but giggle. It reminded her of the past; Evelyn and Rikki would battle constantly. It was never serious, and it always made Carson laugh. That was another reason it had been so hard to let Evelyn go. Carson's best friend got along with her so well. *Everyone* did.

Rikki refused to let up. "So where are we going, grandma?"

"Does this stuff just come to you spontaneously?" Carson asked Rikki, following her out the door.

"Not always. Sometimes it takes me a few minutes," Rikki replied with a large grin on her face.

Evelyn led them to a large tree in the forest where everyone else had been waiting patiently; everyone except for Avani.

Rudy was the first to greet them. She scurried over with a smile on her face. "Girls, I'm so pleased you decided to come!"

Carson watched as Rudy placed a gentle hand on Evelyn's cheek, as if she was blessed to have her there as well. The gratitude was obvious in her eyes.

Carson surveyed the rest of the area. She noted the twins, each sitting on a branch of the tree in front of her.

"Carson and Rikki, dears, I want to introduce you to everyone!" Rudy exclaimed, stepping in between them and wrapping her arms around their waists. She happily guided them toward the tree and first motioned to Abellona and her boyfriend, who stood side by side silently. "You've met Abellona. This is her boyfriend, Leo."

Leo shot them a narcissistic smirk, but Abellona just rolled her eyes. This didn't surprise Carson in the least.

Rudy shook her head and pointed to the other couple. "This is Chiraz and Paxton. They're a little more well-mannered than the other two, as you can see." She cast a look of displeasure in Abellona and Leo's direction.

Leo shrugged his shoulders. It was clear this was their usual behavior.

Chiraz moved forward to greet both girls, her hand locked with Paxton's, pulling him to follow her. "Lovely to meet the both of you. I apologize for the way my friends act. You know, when people usually make the excuse 'it's just the way they are'? Well, in this case, I honestly have to admit it's the way they are." She chuckled.

Paxton settled beside Chriaz. "Hello. It's an honor." He smiled handsomely and held out his hands. Once Carson and Rikki each placed one of their hands in one of his, he kissed the back of both of them, one right after the other.

Although it was upmost genteel and quite charming, Rikki found it comical and thus triggered a witty remark that apparently she couldn't suppress. "You guys must be from the 1700s, too."

They both chuckled lightly at her presumption.

"We age differently than Evelyn does. We grow and get older, and our age does eventually show, but it's not as fast as somebody, well...*human*," Chiraz explained.

"What do you mean?" Rikki asked.

Carson tilted her head in confusion and turned to face Evelyn. "Do they have the same ability as you?"

"Not exactly," Evelyn answered. "Chiraz and Paxton are 'hydrogracers.' They have influential power over water," she informed them.

At that moment, Paxton held his hand slightly above a large puddle of water on the ground in front of him. His eyes began to glimmer like bright blue lights. Gobs of water surged into the air. He guided the water—without even touching it— and directed it further up to Chiraz.

Carson blinked her eyes forcibly, as though she wasn't seeing clearly. *Was this an illusion?*

Once the floating fluid reached Chiraz, she joined in, her eyes becoming the same majestic brightness as Paxton's. "Almost three-fourths of the earth's surface is occupied by water. In fact, it's the largest thing in the world. It's a wonder how something so beautiful and so calm can be so dangerous," she emphasized.

After ascending the water above everyone and causing it to flow miraculously in the air, they guided the water back down to the puddle. It moved gracefully.

Wow. Carson understood why they were given the name "hydrogracers." She shot a glance over to Rikki, who looked just as taken aback.

"Is this too much?" Evelyn asked Carson, studying their reactions.

Carson immediately shook her head.

"Okay then. Rudy, would you like to officially introduce your boys?"

"Oh, we met them the other day," Rikki informed Evelyn.

"To a certain degree, yes. But you only saw one side of them," Rudy corrected. "Were you not curious how they could jump from tree to tree so easily?"

Rikki nodded.

"Aarush." Rudy motioned to the tree. "Aarush means 'sun' in Hindi."

Rush sat peacefully on the left branch. He smiled at both girls.

"And Mayank," she glanced at her other boy, "means 'moon.'"

Mayo fell backward and hung on the branch by his legs. He then reached his right hand up and grasped onto the branch tightly. He flipped himself backward and hung by that arm as if it was a natural, everyday movement and had taken no energy at all.

"And as for myself—"

Carson and Rikki looked back at Rudy.

"Prakruti means 'nature.'" Rudy's eyes illuminated vibrantly, now shining like two neon-green iridescent beams. "It's a pleasure to properly meet the both of you." She raised her hand and opened it, revealing a dandelion. Just like the water had, it floated upward into the air and over to her boys.

The twins joined her and opened their hands. As if on cue, endless dandelions and leaves levitated up into the air, swirling around all of them.

"My daughter, who chose not to join us today, is the same. And her grandmother, my mother, Bhumika. Both of their names mean 'earth.' We've been given the name 'terradescendants.' We're one with Mother Nature. We possess the ability to levitate forest life, as well as ourselves. We understand and communicate with the animal mind. We can strengthen the sun and intensify the gravitational pull of the moon. We can even influence the weather."

"You guys give tree hugger a whole new meaning," Rikki interjected.

Carson gave her a look that implied she should stop talking.

"What? It's not a bad thing," Rikki countered.

Rudy busted out in laughter.

Rikki glanced toward Abellona, who had her arms crossed with a displeased expression on her face. "So what do you do? Oh wait, let me guess. You can fly? Actually, that makes sense. All witches can fly. Where's your broomstick?" Rikki sneered at her.

Abellona sneered back. "Oh! You mean like that show where she wiggles her nose and snaps her fingers?" She arched an eyebrow at Leo, who smiled in admiration at his girlfriend.

"Not quite," Leo revealed, shaking his head.

At that very second, Abellona snapped her fingers. A ring of fire outlined the ground around the couple. It was as if they lit a trail of gasoline and watched it ignite. Leo chuckled at his girlfriend's doing.

Flames appeared on Abellona's fingertips. Her hair was ablaze and her eyes flickered like burning embers. The look on her face was nonetheless *I-told-you-so*. Leo's eyes replicated hers, and the hair that hung down in front of his face blazed brightly as well. He held his hands in a position as if he was holding a ball. A sphere-shaped source of fire appeared between his palms and grew larger as the motion of his hands expanded. It emitted a bright fluorescence.

"They're pyrobanants, Rikki. They have control over fire," Evelyn informed her. "And *you* are one of them."

Surprise was far from the expression that took over both Carson and Rikki's faces.

Eyes wide with disbelief, Rikki slowly backed away from the group. "Huh? Me?"

"You've had quite the temper lately, right?" Leo asked her.

"Well, yeah. But I've always been that way," Rikki countered. "That doesn't mean I can shoot flames out of my hands and burn bright like Hades."

Leo glanced at Abellona with a look of befuddlement, then shot his gaze back at Rikki. "Was that supposed to be an insult?"

Rikki opened her mouth to answer, but Evelyn interjected. "You've never had a temper like the one you're dealing with now, and you know that. You have all this pent-up energy inside you. It usually starts to come through when you hit adulthood, you know, eighteen years or so. You're a late bloomer. Although you've probably been capable since an earlier age, you haven't shown signs until now." She took a deep breath and a step toward Rikki. "Which leads me to believe you've had a lot of experience holding back your feelings. You've had a lot of practice keeping things bottled up."

Rikki arched a daring eyebrow at Evelyn's audacious use of vocabulary, then she crossed her arms as if guarding her emotions. Evelyn was describing Rikki's only means of appeasing her mother's behavior throughout her life, without actually saying the words, and Carson understood that—and by Rikki's obvious reaction, she did, too.

"The most dangerous thing you can do to a new pyro is push her buttons, but you've somehow always managed. That is quite impressive."

Rikki tilted her head, confused by Evelyn's choice of words. "Wait a second. Ev, did you always know this about me? Even four years ago?"

Evelyn nodded and dropped her gaze to the ground. "I always sensed it. And I waited for something to show. But you always held back. Even when I saw you at your angriest, I think you just got used to keeping things in. You have so much potential to be a great pyro. You already have so much control over it."

Rikki glared and shook her head in disagreement. "No." She motioned toward Abellona and Leo. "Whatever they just did, that's never happened to me."

"You and I both know the things that *have* been happening to you are unexplainable, other than what I'm telling you now. We can help you control this. You just need to trust us."

Rikki scoffed and looked at Abellona. She was averse to the idea of Abellona helping her. "Trust *her*? How am I supposed to do that? This is probably an excuse so she can set me on fire herself."

Abellona's mouth quirked up in amusement, but she didn't say anything.

Rikki shook her head in disbelief. "How did this even happen to me?"

"It's genetic. But you didn't get it from your mother. Believe it or not, she's human. It was your father," Evelyn replied.

Rikki shook her head again. "I never met my father. He died before I was born."

"Rikki." Carson, who'd kept silent for most of the conversation, finally voiced her opinion. "This makes sense. All of those things that were going on with you. It makes sense. They could help you."

"I don't know. Can't it just stay inside? I got by just fine before."

Evelyn offered a small smile. "I know that's what you feel like you want, but it's inevitable. It's already starting to break free, and you don't have to go through this alone."

Rikki cast her a look of apprehension. "What if someone gets hurt?"

Carson knew Rikki was referring to the incident at the picnic, when the grill just about exploded.

Evelyn gestured to the hydrogracers. "We have Chiraz and Paxton. Do you realize what they're capable of?" She then pointed in Abellona and Leo's direction. "Anytime these two let their temper get the best of them," she pointed back at Chiraz and Paxton, "those two are there to cool them off. They can protect you and everyone else."

Abellona rolled her eyes again. It was beginning to be her trademark expression.

"We promise to only help you, Ms. Rikki Ward." Paxton shot her a convivial smile. Chiraz offered the same pleasant expression of reassurance.

Rikki stood there, deep in thought for a few moments. "You mean because water can put out a fire." She glanced at the hydrogracers, then back at the pyrobanants, and finally at the twins. "If water destroys fire, then that means fire destroys earth." She squinted her eyes as if that would aid her in comprehension. "You can all destroy each other. How does this work?"

"I'd never harm another elemental. Only a victrolic," Abellona exclaimed, finally joining the conversation. "And only if I had to."

"She means we are family," Rudy translated, "and we work well together. But there are others who don't work well with us."

"You mean a victrolic? What's that?" Rikki asked, her brows furrowed.

Carson didn't have to put two and two together. "I know," she replied before anyone else could answer. She turned to face her best friend. "I've seen them. The things that attacked me." She then shifted to stand in front of Evelyn. "Whatever fume they released...it made me dizzy, almost like I was drunk. The stronger it got, the harder it was for me to breathe or to move. It was like I was paralyzed."

"It's ether," Evelyn stated. "The chemical compound they used as a sedation drug over a hundred and fifty years ago. It's highly flammable and it can irritate your eyes and throat. It can even cause severe frostbite when enough is exposed to the skin. It can be fatal in high doses and it runs through their veins."

Rikki frowned. "I remember hearing about it in my chemistry class in college. Isn't it colorless and transparent?"

"You can't see the gas in the air, but they emit smoke to terrorize. That's what she saw," Rudy said.

"What about his eyes? There was this...black discharge

seeping out of them. And the scorched look on his arms. I could even see his veins. They were dark, and definitely not normal like, well...*mine*," Carson explained.

"Ether can come in the form of a liquid or gas. Victrolics can ignite flames similar to pyros. That's why you saw him cast flames off his bare hands. They've been confused with pyros in that aspect, but they have distinct physical features that separate them, despite the chemical itself." Evelyn held up her hands to demonstrate. "You probably noticed the black fingertips along with the scorched skin. That's the frostbite appearance. What you saw coming out of their eyes and trailing up the veins of their arms is their blood."

Carson listened to Evelyn's explanation with intent, but became confused by the last fact. "Um, but it's black?"

Evelyn nodded. "That's what ether has made them. Their appearances have steps. When they want to attack, their eyes become bloodshot, and then they become a complete bloodred. Their veins become prominent with their thickened blood, ready to be released to their victim. This all happens when they get close to an enemy, like us, or purposefully to a victim. And when they get close to an elemental, their eyes usually give themselves up."

"They can't really control it around us. It's like the anger inside them boils until it finally erupts," Leo chimed in. "Relatable."

Carson nodded. "I noticed that. The closer he got to me, and the angrier he got, and the worse he looked."

"Their surface appearance expresses exactly what they can do to someone. They feed on fear." Evelyn put her hands behind her back and took a few steps in another direction, then turned around to speak directly to Carson. "What was the first thing you thought of when you saw him change that night at the hospital?"

Carson hesitated. One word came to mind. "Death."

Evelyn nodded. *Point proven.*

"It felt like he burned me when he grabbed me that night before you, uh, saved me," Carson stuttered.

"They can melt skin upon physical contact, so the burning sensation you felt was just that. They give pyros a bad reputation."

"Psshh. You mean worse than the one they already have?" Rikki flashed a wry smile, but then straightened up in a more serious manner when everyone shot a critical look at her.

"No elemental beings get along with them lately for that matter. When ether is in liquid form, its density is much greater than that of water." Evelyn pointed to Chriaz and Paxton. "Water and oil don't mix. The two substances separate instead. The same goes for hydrogracers and victrolics."

"Where did they come up with the name 'victrolic,' anyway?" Rikki questioned.

"Now that you mentioned it, a scientist many years ago named the substance 'The Sweet Oil of Victroli' because of its pleasant scent. They have the ability to cause you to experience euphoria. After that, you're trapped."

Carson crossed her arms as though she was cold, but it wasn't the wind that made her shiver. "It's starting to sound like they're ruthless. Are they unstoppable?" she asked Evelyn.

"No. Although fire beats nature and water beats fire, theoretically speaking, it's a bit more complex in our case. It's determined through one's strength of ability." Evelyn squatted and scooped up a small handful of water with her right hand from the puddle Chiraz and Paxton had used. She snatched up a pile of leaves in her left. "Now, pragmatically, a bucket of water can put out a campfire, right? But that fire first has the chance of spreading into something large, like a forest fire, and of course a bucket of water is not going to extinguish an entire forest fire. But it can be contained until it stops. This is similar to what humans—firefighters—do." She opened her right hand to let the water dribble back down onto the earth's surface. "So how do firefighters stop forest fires?" she queried as if she was a teacher quizzing students in a classroom.

Rikki was the first to speak up. "Only YOU can prevent forest—"

Clearing her throat, Evelyn shot Rikki an unamused look.

Rikki raised her hand as though she needed permission to speak after that. "Well, there are three main sources for the combustion process of fire. The heat, the fuel, and an oxidizing agent. A fire can stay lit on its own from the heat that it emits to itself. It keeps the fuel at ignition temperature. So, forest fires are only contained by removing the fuel around them. That includes the trees and the grass. You can't remove oxygen from the air or the heat to stop a forest fire. It's impossible," she stated.

They all looked at her bemusedly, blinking in mild astonishment.

Rikki shrugged defensively. "What? I've been doing a lot of research on fire lately, okay?"

Evelyn's smile widened. "Yes, Rikki, you're correct. For the most part, anyways." She motioned for Abellona to join her. The fiery deity ambled over in Evelyn's direction until she stood right in front of her. Evelyn then opened her left hand to reveal the leaves in her palm. Abellona held her hand over Evelyn's, palm down, and cast a small flame that eventually caught the bundle of leaves afire.

Evelyn glanced at Rudy, who spoke next. "It is true that humans can't remove oxygen from fire." Rudy positioned her hand over the tiny fire in Evelyn's hand and, just like that, the flame began to attenuate. Eventually, the small flame completely died.

Carson took a step forward to get a better look at the once-ablaze clump of remnants in Evelyn's hand. She looked at Rudy. "I get it. You aren't human. *Terradescendants* aren't human, so they can remove oxygen," Carson said.

Everyone glanced at Rudy and then at the twins, who were still sitting peacefully on the branches of the tree, listening to their conversation.

"Exactly," Evelyn agreed. "Fire needs oxygen to ignite. What happens to a fire without oxygen, even if it has something to burn?"

"If there's no oxygen present, the flame goes out. Even if it has something to burn, it still needs oxygen for the burning process. It's like putting a glass over the top of a candle. You watch it diminish slowly but surely," Rikki answered.

"And then it's contained." Evelyn's point was clearly understood. It was dependent on the strength of the element.

Chapter 16

"Hey, Ev, now that we got the boring part out the way, can Abe and I borrow Rikki?" Leo asked while throwing a curious glance Evelyn's way.

"Excuse me?" Rikki swung her head in his direction so fast that Carson was shocked it didn't crack right off her body. "You must've huffed too much gasoline if you think I'm coming with you two."

"Oh, relax. He only wants to give you your first lesson," Abellona explained. The twins giggled loudly above their heads, which made Rikki all the more suspicious of Abellona and Leo's plans. "Besides, Chiraz and Paxton will be with us. We can't get away with *that* much."

Carson interjected before Evelyn could give Leo a proper answer between the bickering. "Um, actually, I think that's a great idea. I wanted to, um, ask Ev something in private anyway, Rik," she turned to look at her best friend, "if that's okay. I'll catch up with you in a few minutes."

Rikki's eyes widened. "What? Car, I just met them. What can they really teach me in a day?"

Obnoxious chuckles echoed above everyone again.

Carson wrapped her hand around Rikki's wrist, dragging her away from the group purposely out of earshot. Grasping her necklace to attest, she resumed a private conversation with her best friend. "Listen, I need to ask her about this. I want to talk to her in private about it." She turned her head to face the group, but caught only Evelyn's locked-in gaze. "Uh, and a few other things, I guess."

Rikki turned to face the group as well, but *her* gaze fell

upon Leo and Abellona, who both wore droll expressions on their faces. "This is such a bad idea," she whined. Abellona sardonically blew a kiss her way, which made Rikki roll her eyes. "This is a *really* bad idea."

"But apparently they've been ready and willing to teach you. You heard Ev," Carson said distractedly as her eyes lingered a little too long on Evelyn.

Rikki watched as Leo winked at her this time. "Car, are you even *seeing* this? They're setting me up here."

Carson finally joined Rikki in observation, heeding Abellona and Leo, but all she witnessed were two polite smiles and friendly waves. "Like I said, they seem ready and willing to teach you." She teasingly nudged her best friend.

Rikki sighed. "Okay, but I have one more thing I have to tell you, and I *promise* I'm not just trying to procrastinate."

"What's that, Rik?"

"I just saved a ton of money on my car insurance by switching to Gei—"

Carson rolled her eyes, smirking, and blatantly walked away from her best friend mid-sentence. Some things were never going to change.

Leo and Abellona ultimately led a not-so-happy Rikki to the shore adjacent to the cliff. Paxton and Chiraz agreed to join them for the tutorial. Rudy and her boys hurried back to her restaurant, where she'd told everyone she would have lunch prepared within the hour. This left Carson and Evelyn alone for the next sixty minutes.

Evelyn eased down onto a large tree stump while Carson attempted to gather her thoughts. She wasn't really sure what the best way to start a conversation was at this point. *Do I start with the necklace? Do I bring up the note? Should I ask to see what she can do?* Her jumbled thoughts finally became spoken, audible words.

"So, uh, you never showed us what you can do. Um, I mean, you know…your powers."

Evelyn looked at her as though she was confused. "I think you saw enough last night."

Carson gave her a knowing look. "I was under the influence."

The sides of Evelyn's mouth turned upward slightly at Carson's joke, but then she frowned once she glanced down and caught sight of her necklace. "You won't be in any more danger again. As long as you have that on, no one can hurt you. Not them and not *me*, either."

Carson arched an eyebrow. "You?"

"It's just a precaution."

Carson pursed her lips in a fine line before she spoke. "You're not going to show me, are you?"

Evelyn crossed her arms. "I only use it when I have to." Her gaze dropped to the ground, and Carson sensed she was uncomfortable, so she didn't push the subject.

Carson clutched the crystal in her hand. "Okay, let's start with this, then. What's this, Ev, really, and what does it do?"

Evelyn stared at her, contemplating for a few long moments before finally standing up. She left her arms in a crossed position and turned away from Carson, facing the shore. She didn't speak right away, but Carson assumed she was gathering her thoughts.

"It was a gift given to me many, many years ago," Evelyn explained. "It protects from elemental beings, including me." She swiveled her body to face Carson again. "I guess it's like a safeguard when you wear it." Evelyn began to walk in Carson's direction until she stood directly in front of her, proceeding to explain the rest up close. She pointed to the crystal. "The red provides protection against pyrobanants, the blue against hydrogracers, and the green against terradescendants. You can't see it, but there's ether, the gas, inside it too. That, most importantly, provides you safety against victrolics."

"You said it protects me from you, too, though," Carson mentioned.

Evelyn nodded. "The black band around your neck...that's actually an enchanted rubber. You know how rubber is an insulator when it comes to electricity? It's sort of the same thing in this case. I added it after I met you."

Carson nodded, able to comprehend everything Evelyn told her, but unremitting questions still pelted her mind, and one specifically that included the dream she'd had a few nights ago. Carson unclasped the necklace and held it in front of her, noting the slight look of uneasiness on Evelyn's face while doing so.

"I had a dream about you Friday night. You told me to keep this on. It was like you were warning me, and it all felt so...real. That was really you there, wasn't it?"

Evelyn moved her head down slightly in a way that Carson could only assume was a nervous nod. "I can teleport into dreams, but I, um, never did that to you before, just so you know. I'd never invade your privacy. But victrolics...they can pollute your mind, like a hallucination."

Carson shook her head in puzzlement. "Wait, are you saying there was a victrolic in my dream, too?"

Evelyn shook her head. "Not in the same way I was, but there was one in Tree Heights. I don't know who it is, but I sensed them, and whoever it is was close enough to turn your dream into a nightmare." She locked eyes with Carson. "But Carson, if you wear this necklace, no elemental being can hurt you. They won't invade your thoughts. They can't touch you."

"I did, Ev. For a while, I mean. I wore it just up until the last six months. So why wasn't I attacked then?" Carson asked.

Evelyn looked over in the direction of the cabins. "Bhumika and Prakruti know how important you are to me. They kept you safe. They're very powerful when they need to be. When it comes to protecting family." She turned back to the shore once again. "Actually, everyone you met today has watched over you, even Avani. They've all watched over you for me."

Carson's brows furrowed and she gestured to the shore. "Abellona, Leo, Paxton, and Chiraz have all been to Tree Heights?"

"Yes. There was always someone there. They made a promise to keep you safe. It's all I wanted."

Carson's mouth dropped open. "Every day for two years?"

"Well, yes, but as long as you had the necklace on, you were safe. We can sense when it's on you, and so can the victrolics."

"Now that I think about it, I am sure I saw Chiraz the day my family threw me a surprise party," Carson said.

Evelyn smiled. "You did."

Carson shook her head in bemusement. "Okay, but why them? Why couldn't you watch over me?"

"Because I just couldn't at that time."

"You can generate electricity throughout your body. You have relentless strength. And you can teleport into dreams. I'm just going to assume there's more you aren't telling me. What are you, Ev? And why couldn't you protect me yourself if I was that important to you?" Carson demanded, now glaring at Evelyn. She got the gist that this conversation was just as nerve-wracking for Evelyn as it was for her, because Evelyn took in a deep breath and let it out slowly, as though it was draining every ounce of her energy to elaborate. She walked back over and stood directly in front of Carson again.

"I've been given the name 'Light One.' It's similar to the titles given to the others. The only difference is that there's only one of me, but there are countless elemental beings like them in this world." Evelyn reached out and gently grasped the necklace out of Carson's hands. "I actually didn't get this necklace through my family. I've just had it since I became the 'Light One,' and before you, it had been with me for hundreds of years."

Evelyn took a step inward, which ultimately put her just

inches away from Carson, and clasped the necklace around Carson's neck where it previously hung.

The momentary contact between Evelyn's hand and Carson's skin was just enough to send Carson's body into a panic, and she realized she hadn't been this close to Evelyn in two years, at least not voluntarily. The close proximity to Evelyn during the most recent encounters hadn't quite registered in her mind yet, Carson being drugged by the ether and all.

Nevertheless, at this very moment Carson knew she was fundamentally sober, and the limited amount of distance between their bodies wasn't allowing her to think clearly. She felt dizzy, but it wasn't in the same way as when she had been attacked by the victrolics the night before. This particular feeling was similar to the rush you get when all the blood goes to your head, and when your body provokes you to act but your mind tells you to stay put; the way you feel when you're about to fall, but you know you need to quickly catch yourself before you do. Carson's mouth felt dry, so she swallowed. That part, though, must have been distinctly visible because Evelyn took a step back, enabling some space between them.

Once Carson had the chance to breathe again, she immediately felt angry and disappointed in herself for letting Evelyn have such an effect on her. The woman had only been back in Carson's life for a few hours, and it wasn't fair that she brought those emotions back to the surface, even if they were familiar. Yes, Evelyn had a complex history that was hard to understand, and she wasn't human, which was even *harder* to understand, but those things surely didn't explain why she had left in the first place, and Evelyn was purposely deflecting the most important question.

So Carson, discomfited for obviously letting her feelings get the best of her, reacted defensively by blurting out a few spiteful remarks so she could regain her pride. "So when are you planning on running away again? Tomorrow? I guess you have two years to figure it out." *Ouch.* Carson instantly felt something heavy, like a brick, in the pit of her stomach as she watched the hurtful expression seize Evelyn's face in slow motion.

"I'd have never left if I had a choice, Carson. I want you to know if I really had that choice, it would've been you. Only you. You don't understand."

"Then *make* me understand," Carson demanded. She stepped backward and motioned to her surroundings. "Because even all of this—your powers, this necklace—it still doesn't justify you leaving." She crossed her arms, impatiently waiting for a good enough explanation.

"It's complicated and *really* hard to explain," was all Evelyn could muster up.

Carson glared again. "You just told me you were an ageless immortal being living with other immortal beings who battle *other* immortal beings. You gave me a magical necklace for protection against God knows what. You didn't have trouble telling me those things. I think I can handle a little more. You said you'd give me answers, Ev, and I expect them."

Evelyn nodded guiltily and turned her back to Carson again, slowly walking a few steps away. The frown remained on her face as she gazed out into the distance. Carson heard her take a deep breath before she spoke at last. "I die every two years."

Carson froze. *Did she just say she dies?* The thought of Evelyn actually *dying* and being ripped away forever made Carson feel even more nauseous than seeing the hurtful expression on Evelyn's face moments ago. "Wait, what do you mean you *die?*"

Evelyn shifted back around to look Carson in the eyes formally, and she answered her patiently, as though the question was an expected one. "Every two years I die, and then two years later I come back. That's why I left you, Carson. It was my time to go, and there was nothing I could do to change it."

Carson's brows furrowed. "But I thought you said you've been alive since 1720?" she questioned.

"See what I mean when I said it's complicated?"

"Well, where do you go, then? And why does this happen?"

Evelyn fumbled for words. "Uh, it, um, has to do with being the Light One. And it's almost like I'm in a lifeless coma for two years. My body stays just like this," she pointed to herself, "but it feels like I'm not actually inside it." She shifted on her feet for a moment. "Can we maybe not—"

"No, that's not right. That doesn't make sense. You can't just die because you're *something* or *someone*." Carson shook her head skeptically. "That sounds like punishment."

Evelyn shrugged. "I've gotten used to it."

"What about your body, then? If it stays just like that, where does it go?"

"Prakruti and Bhumika have a place underneath the cabins that they keep secured. They take my body there and watch over me while I'm gone. It's kind of become a routine."

"I don't understand. How do you, um...I mean, is it painful?"

Evelyn hesitated. "Car, can we maybe finish the rest of this lat—"

"Tell me. Please."

Evelyn glanced down at the ground again in shame. "Yes. Every time."

Carson felt the brick that had originally been in the pit of her stomach transform into several bricks. Her chest felt heavy. She sensed that Evelyn didn't want to tell her anymore, but she yearned to know more. "How does it happen?"

"Car, can we—"

"How?" Carson was determined to get answers, and wasn't giving any chances for procrastination.

"Electrocution."

"What? But you're basically *made* of electricity. I just assumed it couldn't hurt you."

"I never said it doesn't."

Carson, still shaking her head, felt a sudden sense of overwhelming guilt strike hard inside of her. The ache in her chest when Evelyn had left a few years back didn't compare to the present gut-wrenching despair she was experiencing at finally knowing the truth. "I, uh, I didn't know. I didn't know this, Ev." Her eyes swelled with tears but she didn't even attempt to hide them.

"Listen, Car." Evelyn hurried over to stand in front of Carson once again. "Of course you didn't know. I never gave you the option. I just *couldn't* tell you. Nothing about my situation is normal. I couldn't just bombard you with all this and then disappear. It was better to let you live your life without me because, Car, I'm...not good for you."

Carson swallowed the large and painful lump in her throat. "All this time I thought you left because you didn't want to be with me. You left because you..." She couldn't finish her sentence. She turned around and placed her hand tightly over her mouth, trying to hold back a sob. She took some deep breaths as hot tears pooled down her cheeks. "Evelyn, I was so angry at you." Carson bent slightly over, holding her other hand over her stomach, wincing through tears. She felt sick.

Eventually, Carson heard the rustle of Evelyn's jacket and the crunch of leaves on the ground, realizing she'd moved closer to her. She could feel her right behind her.

"Carson, you're hurting. You don't have to hurt. I can take it away. Let me help you."

"No one can help me! I was angry for so long and I had no right to be, because you didn't leave. It was so much worse. You were *dead!*" Hearing the words come out of her own mouth made her feel all the more terrible, and she could barely stand now. She'd spent the past two years in bitterness, feeling betrayed by Evelyn, whom she just found out had been basically tortured until she was no longer in living condition. How was she ever supposed to cope with that?

All of a sudden, Carson felt a light touch on her arm. The godawful ache in her chest began to subside, along with the heavy feeling of guilt that had consumed her. It all completely alleviated, replaced by nothing less than a feeling of pure tranquility. Carson realized it was a familiar feeling, like she'd experienced it in the past.

Carson wiped away her tears, took some deep breaths, and turned back around. She searched Evelyn's eyes. "You've done that to me before, haven't you?"

Evelyn offered her a warm smile. "I could never bear to see you grieve."

Carson inhaled again deeply. "I just figured my sadness always went away because being with you made me feel better." She moved closer to Evelyn. "Ev, if you'd have never used that on me, you wouldn't have seen any difference either way. Just being with you made me happy. I was always okay when I was with you."

Evelyn tilted her head. "You're describing the same way it feels to be with *you*."

They stared at each other for a long while before Carson finally remembered something. "Oh no, I forgot about Rik!" She'd told Rikki they'd meet her shortly, and that must have been half an hour ago.

The smile Evelyn flashed was not exactly the same as the warm one she offered prior; this one had amusement written all over it. Evelyn knew something that Carson didn't, thanks to her overactive senses, but that was becoming quite obvious to Carson.

"Ev? What's going on? Is Rikki okay?"

"She's fine. Beginner's course."

"So why are you grinning like that?"

"Because it's Rikki," Evelyn laughed. "If only you could hear her right now. Come on, we'll go join them."

CHAPTER 17

"You do realize why I can't just 'flame-on,' right? I mean, seriously, it's 'cause I'm human. You're confusing my bad attitude with your fire power problem," Rikki muttered.

"The more you make excuses, the more difficult it is to let it out," Leo proclaimed. "Stop denying this. You just need to find it inside. You can feel it in your core. It's right there—"

"Pretty sure that's where my liver is," Rikki responded, palpating her abdomen. "Oh, wait!" She felt around on her belly as if discovering something for the first time, but then shot them a sly grin. "Nope, just my liver."

"We've been at this for almost forty minutes. We're wasting our time, babe," Abellona insisted to her similarly irritated boyfriend while performing her infamous eye-roll.

Leo peered down at her, then peeked over at Paxton and Chiraz, who looked comfortably distracted as they threw one another playful looks and flirted heedlessly. Every now and again they'd flick their eyes over diligently to make sure they weren't needed. Leo then shot a glance at Rikki as she stood on the other end of the shore, fidgeting with her manicured nails. "Let's not waste any more, then," he whispered. He and Abellona exchanged a smug smile as if reading each other's thoughts.

Rikki sighed in thought as she glanced down at her nails. *I'm not one of them. I can't be one of them. Something like this doesn't happen to people like me.* She wondered when Carson would rescue her from this ridiculous situation, but she knew her friend had a lot to discuss with Evelyn. Her thoughts were cut short drastically once she caught a glimpse of a bright light in the corner of her eye. She jerked her eyes up to find Abellona and Leo cornering her with actual fireballs in their hands, and the worst part was the expression on their faces. "Um, hey, what are you guys doing?"

"We said we'd teach you, but you insist on ignoring everything we say," Leo growled.

"Therefore, we have to do this the hard way," Abellona interjected. "Don't take it personal, darling, but pucker up."

Before anyone could react, they both threw the fireballs at Rikki's body.

Rikki screamed in agony as she found herself completely engulfed in flames. She patted her body forcefully as if trying to remove a million bugs, but the fire didn't let up. She rolled around on the ground, but that didn't work either. It was inevitable: she was going to burn alive.

"What's going on?" Evelyn hurried over with Carson by her side.

Carson, immediately terrorized by the sight of her best friend on fire, shrieked with panic. "Rikki! Oh my God! Someone help her!"

Leo and Abellona cackled and snorted through laughter as they watched Rikki race around aimlessly, ablaze.

Chiraz and Paxton began to move until Evelyn halted them. "Car, she's not in pain. She's just in shock. Look." Evelyn pointed to Rikki. "You see how fast she's moving? It's surreal. No normal person can move that fast. She's not going to die. She's a pyrobanant who, in her own words, 'flamed-on' for the first time in her life. Well, with the shaming help of these two." Evelyn shook her head and pointed to Abellona and Leo, who were still laughing. "I hope the both of you remember this when you request another one-on-one because it will be supervised by me next time." She glanced back at Carson. "Rikki just needs to calm down. Look, I'll go help her."

Carson observed Rikki carefully. Evelyn was right; Rikki moved so fast that she actually left streaks of light behind her, almost as if the flames couldn't catch up to her speed, and Rikki didn't even realize it. She was completely inundated by fire, but she wasn't dying, or even slowing down for that matter. She was only panicking by what she thought was supposed to be harmful.

"She's headed for the water!" Leo spat out through chuckles.

Evelyn fled just as fast across the shore to stand in front of the new pyrobanant, blocking her way. "Rikki, relax! Relax! Look, you're alive, listen, you're oka—"

"I'm on fucking fire! I'm burning! Get out of my—*ouch!*" Evelyn had reached out and zapped Rikki mildly. She stood still, rubbing her arm where Evelyn jolted her. "What the hell, Ev?"

"I'm trying to show you what pain actually feels like. Now...look at yourself."

Rikki glanced down at her hands, and even at her legs. She was still on fire, but it didn't hurt—at all. "I'm...I'm...I'm okay?"

Evelyn nodded with a proud smile on her face. "You're okay."

Carson rushed over to stand beside Evelyn. "Rik, are you all right? Wow! You look amazing!" She now had an up-close view of Rikki's pyrobanant side. Her entire body was ferociously dazzled in smoldering flames, the same colors as the hottest burning coals at the bottom of a firepit. Her ginger hair was now blazing in all directions, the tips flickering the same way a campfire does. She no longer possessed the rust-colored eyes Carson was used to looking into; bright orange embers replaced them.

"Yeah, I mean, I think so. I feel good, surprisingly," Rikki stammered in astonishment. "Um, but how do I turn this off?"

Chiraz, Paxton, Abellona, and Leo finally made their way over.

"If you need assistance, we shall help you," Paxton insisted.

"One sec, Pax. I want Rikki to try this herself," Evelyn

explained, "and *without* anyone else's help this time. Rik, take a deep breath. You can even close your eyes. Calm yourself down enough to feel nothing but repose. Think of something that makes you happy, or lets you feel at peace with yourself. It's easier to 'flame-off' than 'flame-on.'"

"You know, when I mentioned the 'flame-on' thing, that was a joke. Haven't you ever watched *Fantastic Four*?"

"Rik, just try," Carson persisted.

Rikki sighed ambivalently, but eventually closed her eyes. She took a long, slow breath in through her nose and exhaled out through her mouth. A few minutes passed by and she didn't feel any different. "I don't think this is—"

"Rik," Carson said in loud excitement, "you did it! Look!"

Rikki opened her eyes and looked down at her body, noting that she was back to her normal *human* self again. She looked back up at Carson, who was smiling, and rushed in to give her a hug.

"You did awesome!"

"Amateur," Leo chuckled.

Rikki turned to face the other pyrobanants. "You two!" She stormed over to Abellona and Leo and fired a ferocious glare back and forth between them. "You ever try that again, and I can promise—"

"Promise what?" Abellona asked, moving just a bit closer to her. "Should we expect something nice?"

Rikki's jaw tightened.

"Guys, come on. Can't this be enough for today?" Carson asked, suggesting an unspoken compromise. "She learned what she is now. Please, let's not push it."

"Oh no, Car. If this is what I am, I might as well put it to good use now." Rikki scowled.

Abellona snickered, taunting her. "Is that so? I bet you can't do it again, then—you know, by yourself this time."

Rikki only grew more furious, which was evident by the rapid rise and fall of her chest and, of course, her clenched fists.

Carson attempted to interject again. "Abellona, please. Just let this—" She felt Evelyn's hand on her arm and glanced over to find a reassuring expression on Evelyn's face.

"Mommy's little girl, right?" Abellona jeered. "I wonder what your mother would say if she knew how little effort you put into trying today. And that Leo and I had to actually do everything ourselves."

Rikki began to shake. "Don't bring my mother into this. I'm warning you to stop right now!"

"Or what? You're gonna call her? Actually, let me save you the trouble." Abellona pulled out her phone and held it in front of Rikki. "Mayor Ward should be in her office today, right? I'm sure she'd be thrilled to hear about your epic fail today. We shall see."

"I said stop!" And just like that, Rikki exploded into the same fiery goddess she'd been minutes ago, lunging forward and striking Abellona, who flew several feet into the air until finally landing on both feet.

Carson's mouth dropped open in shock. *What a day,* she thought.

Abellona tilted her head and smiled self-righteously. "Not bad, Ward. I suppose we can call it a day now."

"Way to go, Ward! You're a feisty thing!" Leo chimed in, patting her on the back.

Even through Rikki's red-hot transformation, Carson could still see the confusion on her face as she stumbled over what to say next. "Huh?"

"Rudy is probably ready for us, guys. We wouldn't want to be rude, now would we?" Leo hollered back as he hurried over to Abellona. They both zoomed off at lightning speed with Chiraz and Paxton close behind them, each one leaving sudden flashes of reds and blues.

"Am I missing something?" Rikki asked, dumbfounded.

Carson noticed she'd returned to her human appearance. "Hey, look. You didn't even have to try this time."

Rikki held up her hands, observing them carefully. "Huh, look at that. I guess confusion works the best."

Once everyone was together and they'd all gathered at a table in Rudy's small restaurant, Chiraz stood and gently tapped a spoon on the side of her glass, requesting everyone's attention.

"It's been quite a day," she said, glancing in Carson's direction. "But I just wanted to say how thankful I am to have finally met you, Carson, and you as well, Rikki. We've all heard so many good things about you both. To Carson and Rikki."

Carson smiled in appreciation as most raised their glasses around her, even Abellona and Leo.

"To Carson and Rikki!" they all repeated in harmony.

Avani, on the other hand, sat silently with nothing but a frown upon her face. Carson wondered what was going through the girl's mind. *Why does she dislike me so much?*

"Evelyn, dear." A mysterious voice Carson wasn't familiar with spoke delicately beside her.

Carson turned her head to find a dark-complexioned elderly woman standing at the end of the table. She wore an orange and red sari and held a long wooden cane that appeared to have intricate details carved into it.

"She's more beautiful than I can remember. It's a pleasure to finally see her up close now." The woman's voice held a pleasant and warm tone.

Evelyn quickly stood from her seat beside Carson, walked over to the older woman, and patiently guided her to the seat that she herself had just been sitting in moments before. "Carson, I'd like for you to meet someone that I've known for a very long time. After my parents passed away, I didn't know what family was until I met this woman. This is Bhumika."

So this was the woman who had created that enthralling

picture of Evelyn; the one who hadn't been around yester-day when most of the excitement took place. Carson held out her hand in cordial friendliness, but to her surprise, Bhumika didn't take it. Instead, Bhumika softly placed her hand on Carson's cheek as if she'd known her for years and the fact that they were practically strangers didn't count for anything at all. Oddly enough, it felt natural, like she was a long-lost friend. Evelyn had mentioned that Bhumika was one of the ones who kept an eye on Carson for the past few years.

"You hold so much more than you know." Bhumika gently spoke while staring into Carson's eyes, almost marveling in amazement. Her gaze flickered down briefly at the crystal that hung loosely between Carson's collarbones.

Those weren't the words Carson expected during an introduction. "What do you mean?" she asked.

"I understand that this has been an overwhelming day for both of you," Bhumika replied, glancing at both Carson and Rikki, "but in each and every day there's always going to be some sort of struggle. You just have to figure out how to make the best of it. Just remember, where there's darkness, there will be light. You hold the power to change any situation."

Of course Bhumika would say something extremely wise that was enough to raise Carson's spirits after the day she'd had, but she couldn't help but wonder if it was an analogy for something completely different.

Carson offered an easy smile, acting as though things weren't that complicated. "I never imagined something like what happened in the last twenty-four hours would ever take place in my life, but I've always believed everything happens for a reason," she explained, glancing up at Evelyn. "Whether it be good or bad, everything that happens shapes you as a person. Before, when I was angry with you, Ev, I think I just had the wrong reasons."

"Are you kidding me?" And there it was at last: Avani's input. "She doesn't know the half of it, Evelyn. And you're putting *all* of us in danger. You're putting *her* in danger!" The table shook as Avani's fist crashed down onto it, and she glared in resentment at Evelyn.

The room grew uncomfortably silent, and even Mayo and Rush could offer no more than a mortified expression each. Evelyn also stood quietly with her arms crossed.

Avani rose from her chair and looked around the table. "You're all honestly sitting here celebrating when you know the truth. Now that the Marked One is reunited with the Light One again, the victrolics don't have any reason to not attack us."

Rudy, who had heard the blowout from the kitchen, came rushing out in an effort to stop Avani while she was ahead. "Avani, how dare you! This isn't your business to discu—"

"Wait." Everyone turned their heads to Carson. "The Marked One. I've heard that before. That victrolic called me that the day I met you." Carson looked up at Evelyn. "And last night, I heard it again. What is that? What does it mean?" she asked.

"Car, listen. I didn't get to finish explaining everything—"

"Clearly," Carson interrupted. "Either you tell me what she is talking about, or she gets to finish. By the sounds of what's going through her head, I'm assuming you wouldn't want her to tell me the truth. You have thirty seconds to start talking, Evelyn."

Evelyn stared blankly for what seemed like a lifetime before finally forming words. "In 2017, you thought you talked a woman off the ledge on the top of Warden Hall, but she disappeared before you could see her face."

Confused, Carson shook her head. "I don't understand. What does that have to do with..." She met Evelyn's gaze again and stared in astonishment. "That was you?"

Evelyn nodded. "Yes."

"Why didn't you ever tell me? I thought the first day we met was with that victrolic."

"It was, formally, I guess. I was protecting you. He knew who you were."

"What do you mean he knew who I was?" Carson asked.

"You could say I was having a bad day. In all the years I've been alive, I've never come across someone who spoke to me the way you did. You made me feel...*human*. Normal, even," Evelyn explained. "After that day, I just wanted to know who you were, so I followed you."

"Pshh. Stalk much?" Rikki's sarcastic comment was blunt enough to make the twins giggle. They stopped immediately, though, once Rudy flashed them a warning just by the look on her face.

"Anyway, I thought I was protecting you. Taking care of a few dangerous strangers here and there and preventing a car accident," Evelyn said as she took a few steps backward. She began to circle the table slowly. "I was giving back to you what you'd given me. I didn't realize what I was doing, but it felt like I was drawn to you, and I couldn't help it. I know how selfish that sounds, but it was more than that. I didn't know that I had..."

"Marked me," Carson whispered softly, finishing Evelyn's sentence.

CHAPTER 18

Evelyn towered over the small city as she walked along the thin ledge of the rooftop of Warden Hall. She wished she could just fall—plunge thirty stories down and be consumed by death once she met the bottom like a normal person—but that was never going to be the case. There were *always* consequences with any decision she made when it came to dying. One of the elemental god's words rang through her head as if she'd just heard them yesterday: "*And if you ever try to end your life, Light One, you'll forever live on shamefully with the reminder of that very day.*" Hence the fact that she was now a walking lightning bolt.

Plus, there was the fact that every human down below would be traumatized by the fall, not to mention what would happen once they realized she wasn't dead. Maybe she'd surrender herself to become the perfect experiment for scientific studies? No, she couldn't do that. Humanity would someday wonder if there were more out there. They'd search for others like her, and she wasn't about to do that to Bhumika and the others.

Evelyn then wondered what type of fateful outcome this particular suicidal fall would entice. Perhaps her bones would pierce through her skin and she'd actually physically look like the monster she knew she was.

"Hey there," a soothing voice called out from behind Evelyn, dismissing her thoughts.

Evelyn left her hood up and kept her back turned, remaining in the shadows. She wasn't big on being noticed these days, but hadn't realized there was anyone else around.

"Are you okay?" the stranger asked.

Panicking, Evelyn spat out, "Um, I'm fine."

"You're a little close to the edge, you know. I'm afraid of heights and you're making me nervous just seeing you up there," the young woman said.

Evelyn rolled her eyes. Someone actually thought she was going to jump. *If only it was that easy.* She turned around to face the stranger, remaining secure in the shadows. "Look, I'm..." She stammered and searched for words as her eyes captured the beauty of the woman standing multiple feet away. "Er...I'm...I'm good, I—" Her words were cut short as her foot slipped, but just as quickly she caught onto the metal rods of the large sign beside her.

"Hey! Oh my God, hang on!" The woman began to race toward her until Evelyn stopped her dead in her tracks.

"Wait! Don't come any closer," she warned. "Listen, I need you to back up. I don't want to, um...have to let go." Evelyn watched as the young woman threw her hands up and took several giant steps backward, but kept her eyes glued upon her.

Evelyn finally swung her body like an acrobat and landed back on the ledge effortlessly. "Just stay there, okay?"

The woman nodded. "Um, how did you do that?" she asked.

Evelyn remained silent, then answered with a question of her own. "I should be asking *you* what *you're* doing up here. I didn't realize there was anyone else around." There was something about the young woman that triggered her curiosity. Maybe it was the innocence in her eyes or the friendly, soft voice? It was difficult to put her finger on.

"I'm at a meeting here for work. I came up here for the fresh air, and the view," the woman explained.

Evelyn turned around to face the view to which the woman was referring. "It looks the same as everything else to me," she muttered.

"Does that mean you do this often? Stand on the ledge of tall buildings?" the woman joked, obviously trying to suppress the tension.

Evelyn stood there, not sure what to say.

The woman persisted, "So do you have a name?"

I do, but not one that I can ever tell you. Evelyn turned her head briefly to face the stranger again, but kept her distance so she could not see her face. "Do you?"

"I'm Carson Miles," she said, then waited for Evelyn to reply with her own name. Again, Evelyn did not say a word. "Whatever's going through your head right now, whatever reason you have to do this...it's not worth it," Carson exclaimed.

Evelyn blinked. This woman, Carson, actually thought she was going to jump, which was probably a benefit for Evelyn. She figured in Carson's mind, Evelyn was just some depressed human ready to give up on life, which was basically true. Except for the human part.

"Death doesn't scare me. Living does," Evelyn finally replied. *Probably shouldn't have said that, because she's just going to keep asking questions.*

Carson looked puzzled at Evelyn's comment. "What part of living scares you? There are so many things to be thankful for: friends, family, love," she insisted. "Living is a blessing."

Evelyn shook her head. "Someday they'll all die, too, so how are any of those things worth it? Watching everyone around you die isn't a blessing." She noticed that the woman didn't say anything right away.

"You're right," Carson finally admitted. See, that was it! Evelyn knew she was right. There was no justification for that. "Everyone is going to die someday. You may not be around to see it, or you just might be. It hurts, you know, when we have to let someone go. But making every single day special and worth it for that particular person is worth living for."

Evelyn was stumped. She didn't expect an answer like that...one that she could honestly relate to. All the gratitude

Bhumika had shown Evelyn throughout the years for saving her life, the compassion Rudy had expressed for keeping them all safe. Those things had truly been worth living for. Carson was right.

"It was nice to meet you, Carson Miles," Evelyn whispered.

All of a sudden, the rusty door to the rooftop swung open, banging loudly on the wall behind it. Carson spun around to face the disruption.

"Hey, Carson! What are you doing up here? We're about to begin again!" a young man shouted.

Ignoring him, Carson turned back around, but to her surprise, found no one there. The mysterious woman had disappeared. She hurried over to the edge, but there was nothing on the ground below, and no sign of her. The woman was gone.

Chapter 19

"This is why those things are after me, isn't it, Evelyn?" Carson shouted angrily as she got up and headed for the door.

"Please, Carson, just let me explain the rest," Evelyn urged as she scurried to stop Carson from leaving. Grabbing her arm, she physically turned her to face her.

"Ev, no. Don't touch me. I don't trust you when you touch me. As a matter of fact, I don't trust you at all," Carson exclaimed, and rushed out the door. Before she could open the door to Rikki's car, Evelyn appeared in front of her, obviously using the advantage she had over speed.

Carson shook her head and glared. "Don't do that." She turned around to face the restaurant, where Rikki and the rest of the crew stood quietly. "Rik, let's go. It's gonna be late by the time we get home."

"Car, can I see you again?" Evelyn asked. "Please?"

Carson crossed her arms. "What I don't understand, amongst everything else I don't understand, is just exactly why me?"

"Because they're trying to get to me," Evelyn replied. She glanced down at the crystal around Carson's neck. "Please make sure you always have that on. I'm here, Car, if you want to see me again," she advised. She turned around and walked back to the restaurant.

As irate as Carson felt at that moment, it was like she couldn't look away. Her eyes just lingered on Evelyn until she disappeared into the restaurant and was no longer in view. Was it because she thought that could actually be the last time she saw her again? Was that the closure she needed?

Shortly after that, Rikki joined Carson in the car. They drove home in mostly silence until Rikki finally spoke.

"You know, it's obvious how in love with you she is."

"Do you really have to say that right now?" Carson snapped.

Rikki shrugged. "Just saying. Just affirming the obvious. Just stating a fact—"

"Rikki," Carson said firmly, "I get it. I'm confused beyond measure right now."

"And you think I'm not?" Rikki argued.

Carson sighed. "You're absolutely right. I can't imagine. I'm being selfish and I'm sorry." She shook her head in shame. "How are you feeling about everything?"

Rikki smiled. "Hey, look. We've both learned a lot about ourselves this weekend. I mean, maybe not completely by choice, but still." She giggled, which made Carson relax a little. "I'm not sure how I feel about it yet. I'll let you know before we go back next weekend."

Carson turned to face her friend, who was still facing the road as she drove. "Funny."

A few minutes passed before Rikki spoke up again. "Do you still love her—I mean, even after finding out *what* she is?"

Carson glanced back out the window and slipped her fingers around the crystal hanging loosely on her chest. "Of course. What kind of person would that make me if I didn't?"

Chapter 20

Carson groggily opened her eyes to some obnoxiously loud bangs on her apartment door. Dazed, she looked around to regain her focus; she'd fallen asleep on her couch. Rikki had dropped her off hours earlier, and the first thing she'd done once inside was lay down, not realizing how tired she really was.

"Car? Are you home?" Graham's firm voice called out on the other side of the door.

"Yeah, Graham, hang on." Carson pushed up off the couch with weary arms, reasserting herself. She unlocked the door and, as she turned the knob counterclockwise, Graham darted in.

"Where have you been?" He stood in front of her, an irate expression on his face. "I've come by a few times this weekend. I saw your car here, so I figured you were home." He crossed his arms and spoke as if he was disciplining a child. "I've texted you and you've ignored all my texts. What's going on?"

Carson began to panic inside. *Crap. I can't tell him that I went to see Evelyn. He would never forgive me.*

"Um, I spent the weekend over at Rikki's," she lied. "I'm sorry, Graham. I guess I didn't look at my phone much," she explained, and that was the truth. She really did forget to check her phone. She picked it up and swiped through her unread messages, discovering that most of them were from Graham. But there was another text from a number she didn't recognize.

I'm right here whenever you're ready to talk.

Carson knew who it was. She didn't have to guess. It had been sent at 9:40 p.m. She looked at the time now—12:15 a.m. She had been asleep for hours.

"Car?" Graham's displeased tone pulled her out of her temporary distraction.

"Um, yeah?" She continued to stare at the message on her screen as if afraid it would randomly delete itself.

"Are you even listening to me?"

Carson finally lifted her gaze to her brother. "I was going through your texts, Graham," she fibbed and looked back down at her phone. She immediately opened the few texts Graham had sent her while she was at "Rikki's." His texts, of course, weren't as intriguing.

I stopped by.

Saturday, 2:12 p.m.

Hey, where are you?

Saturday, 5:14 p.m.

As Carson was peering at his messages, she spotted one from the previous Saturday before her attack outside the hospital parking lot. She had forgotten to text him back, let alone bring it back to his attention.

Hey Car, I'm coming over. I wanted to ask you something.

"Um, Graham, a week ago, you texted me. With all the things that happened last weekend, I completely forgot to bring it up. What did you need to ask me?" Carson flipped her phone around, revealing the message to him.

Graham eyeballed the text. "Uh, it—um," he stumbled through his words, "it wasn't really important, so never mind." He shifted uncomfortably as if he was the one now being disciplined.

"Graham, you usually always talk to me about anything," Carson stressed. "What is it?"

He paused for a few seconds before he spoke. "I wanted to ask you about a door."

Carson was beyond confused. "A door?"

"Er, I mean not just a door. A painting of a door. A *water-color* painting of a door," Graham emphasized, moving his hands while he explained as though that would clarify his vagueness.

Carson shook her head. "I'm still not picking up what you're putting down."

Graham rolled his eyes. "The new project that Rikki is working on is a door," he blurted out.

"Ohh," Carson gathered. "So?"

"I was just curious if you saw it," he said. "Like what it looks like."

Carson shook her head again. "I haven't seen this one yet. As a matter of fact, she hasn't shown anyone." She shrugged her shoulders. "I think she said she wanted to wait until it was done."

Graham nodded as though that was all the explanation he needed.

"Care to elaborate on this?" she asked him.

"It's nothing, Car," he insisted. "I caught her before she left the picnic that day and we were just chatting. I was just curious about it. I've seen all her other ones, you know?"

Carson sighed, unsatisfied with his answer. "Sure, Graham."

"Anyway, I'll let you go back to sleep. I was just concerned because I didn't hear from you." He headed to the door and grabbed the knob, but instead of turning it, he glanced back to face her one more time. "It sort of scares me when you don't answer me like that. I mean, it reminds me of how you wouldn't answer us for days when Evelyn left," he explained. "We would have to physically come over and get you out of your apartment, so here I am."

Carson froze. *If only you knew where I really was this weekend.* She truly hoped he couldn't see right through her. She finally forced out, "You don't have to be afraid, Graham. I'm okay now."

He flashed her a smile. "See you later, Car."

"Good night, Graham." Once Graham made an escape, Carson plopped down on the couch and pulled her phone back out. After some deep thought, she brought Evelyn's message back up on her screen and replied:

I'll see you next weekend.

Chapter 21

"Arghhhhh!" Screams of fury echoed throughout the large cave as objects were thrown and glass was shattered on the cold walls. "I'm going to *kill* her!"

"Amadora," a man's unwavering voice called out, "You're wasting your energy." Raz, along with many other victrolics, emerged from the shadows to join her.

"He was my brother!" Amadora's eyes flashed an illuminating bloodred as she spoke in furor. "It was the Light One, Raz! Loki is dead! I just found him...lying here."

Raz stood silently for a few moments before speaking. "I know, my love. He went after the Light One himself."

Amadora tightened her fist as if preparing for a fight. "What did you just say?" She turned to confront him as dark, morbid veins underneath her eyes began to stiffen and crawl across her face, almost matching her long, soulless-black hair that dangled down over her shoulders. "You knew he was going to do this?"

"Yes."

"He didn't stand a chance one on one with her, but you let him go anyway?" She pointed to the still, lifeless body lying close by, her fingertips proceeding to turn black with the same protuberant features dispersing up her arms. "Just look where it's gotten us—where it's gotten him!" she shouted. "She's already taken so much from us!"

"I sent him," Raz stated coolly.

"You did what?" she hissed, more furious than ever.

"I'm not the one to blame, but you know who is." He pulled out a large, sheathed dagger. "We shall have our revenge," he said through a vicious grin.

As Amadora observed the weapon in Raz's hands, the treacherous storm inside her began to calm. The poison running through her veins, which was so visual just below the surface of her skin moments ago, slowly faded. "Is that…"

"The end of the so-called everlasting Light One?" He sneered wickedly. "Yes it is."

"How did you…"

"Why do you think we've made so many trips to Nepal, my love?"

"You never explained that, Raz." Amadora glared. "You left me in the dark."

"You know I needed you here," he stressed, "watching Carson closely, making sure she didn't figure out what she's capable of as the Marked One. It's enough of a problem already that she is in contact with the Light One."

"You sacrificed my brother," Amadora fumed, her eyes beginning to glow in a boiling craze once again. "You sent Loki after the Marked One. You knew Evelyn was too strong, and what the outcome would be."

"It was a grave mistake," Raz said as he inched nearer to her. "But it was the only way." He turned his back to her as he continued to explain, and shook his head in repentance. "Loki knew what he was getting into, as he strived to avenge us. He ultimately sacrificed himself. If we wouldn't have made some sort of distraction, Evelyn and her worthless elemental clan would have followed us, and discovered what we've—" he glided toward Amadora and handed her the dagger, "acquired. I didn't need any interruptions. You, my love, may have the honors when the right time comes."

"When is the right time?" she asked, clenching her jaw and squeezing her fingers around the sharp blade.

"Very soon. You know what you have to do."

After a long week of fundraising activities, managing donations as well as non-profitable budgets, and educating visitors and volunteers at several shelters, Friday had finally come. Carson had one thing on her mind all morning, and it had become obvious she was distracted when Rayna caught her zoning out while they were going over an upcoming charity event plan. Who could blame her, though?

Carson was to be meeting Rikki at her house by noon so they could get on the road and be there before dark. This time, Carson offered to drive. Once she pulled into Rikki's driveway, she beeped her horn seven times obnoxiously, watching and waiting for Rikki to poke her head out of one of the windows and flip her the bird like she normally did.

Thirty seconds later, her phone rang; it was Graham. She proceeded to answer by clicking the green button, and then held the phone up to her ear. "Hello?"

"Hey, Car. What are you up to? Want to have lunch with Amy and I? She has been persistent in getting us together," Graham emphasized, not letting Carson sneak a word in.

Carson paused for a moment, deciding on the best way to reject his invitation. The last thing she was concerned with was spending time with Amy, but she couldn't tell Graham that. *What am I supposed to say? I can't because I'm going to visit the one woman that broke my heart years ago and Rikki needs to learn how to control her supernatural abilities?*

"Um, I'm sorry, Graham. Rikki and I are actually about to head out of town. Rain check?"

His end of the line was silent for a few moments. "Where are you going?" he eventually asked.

Carson watched as Rikki finally exited her house, carrying a bag and, of course, her ever-so-casual smirk along with her. Rikki opened the car door and hopped in the passenger seat. Before Carson had a chance to tell her who was on the phone, words began ricocheting from Rikki's mouth. "Ohh, is that Evelyn? Hey, you 300 year old bi—"

Flustered beyond belief, Carson quickly cut Rikki off by replying to her brother on the phone, "Graham, hey, listen, I have to go. I'll call you when I get back. Right now Rikki needs my help with something." She hung up before she even heard a sound from him, and turned to face her best friend.

Rikki now offered the expression of a criminal who had just been caught in the act. "Insert foot in mouth here?" she asked as she pursed her lips.

"Let's hope he didn't hear that." Carson shook her head.

About a half hour away from the cabins, Rikki began complaining. "Car, I feel hot."

Carson, taking her eyes off the road for just a few seconds, cast a peek at her friend. "Well, I don't see any flames at the moment," she joked.

"Very funny." Rikki smiled faintly. "I'm serious, though. I feel like I'm burning up again."

"Are you sick? What is going on?" Carson asked. "Does it feel the same as the other times?"

"Yes, and it's getting worse," Rikki blurted. In a matter of seconds she was smothered in sweat. She placed both her hands on her head. "My head, Car. It's killing me."

"That's it, I'm turning around. You look awful! You need to go to the hospital."

"No, Car," Rikki snapped, "I can't go there. The best place for me right now is with the others. Just hurry, please. Something is wrong." She grimaced in pain.

"Okay, Rik. Try to do what Evelyn told you last week. Think of something that calms you. We'll be there soon," Carson stressed as she sped up the car. "She'll help you."

As Carson pulled in front of the three large, resplendent cabins, Rikki threw open her car door and collapsed to the ground. "I can't—I can't breathe," she gasped.

"Evelyn! Rudy!" Carson shouted at the top of her lungs as she rushed to her friend. "Somebody help!" She crouched down next to Rikki. "Just keep trying to breathe."

"I—I feel like I'm burning on the inside," Rikki groaned.

Within seconds, Evelyn appeared, standing in front of them. "How long has she been like this?" she asked Carson.

"Less than an hour. Why? What's wrong with her?" Carson panicked.

"She's being attacked by a victrolic," Evelyn stated, kneeling over Rikki. "Or provoked, I should say."

"What?" Carson's brow furrowed. "How? What do you mean provoked?"

The loud slam of a car door stole their attention. Carson looked back to find Graham trampling toward them, his black car parked behind hers.

"Oh no. Not right now," Carson whispered. She stood up and attempted to meet him halfway.

"Are you kidding me, Carson? Please tell me that's not who I think it is!" he exclaimed in utter anger.

"Graham, stop, please!" Carson held her hands up as if that would calm him down, and struggled to stall him. "You don't understand. You can't be—"

"You!" Graham stormed right past Carson's attempt at a forcefield, aiming directly for Evelyn. "I can't believe I am seeing *you* again! Haven't you put this family through enou—"

He stopped immediately once he saw Rikki lying helplessly on the ground. "Rikki?" He scrambled down beside her. "Car, what's wrong with her?" He peered up at Evelyn. "Did you do this?"

"You all need to go inside, now! Graham, pick Rikki up and take Carson inside, please!" Evelyn firmly instructed.

"Are you crazy? Rikki needs to go to a hospital!" Graham shouted at her.

Rikki softly touched Graham's arm. "Please, Graham. You can trust her," she urged. "Help me up."

Although Graham was obviously confused, he nodded courteously. He managed to pull Rikki upright, holding her there.

At that very second, the passenger door of Graham's car opened, and Carson witnessed a slim figure slip out and head in their direction.

"Um, Graham?" Carson murmured. "Did you bring somebody with you?"

Graham didn't answer. He didn't have to answer. Carson knew who it was before she even asked. They all watched as Amy joined them.

This time, though, Amy wasn't who she claimed she was. Dark, grisly veins slithered down her arms, meeting black fingertips that conformed with sharp, bloodred fingernails. She reached up and gently snatched the pair of sunglasses from their resting place on her nose, revealing hellish-red eyes accompanied by a diabolical expression. More grotesque veins crept across her face. She sneered as they all took in the image in front of them.

"Amy? What the..." Graham could barely speak. He was so overly astounded that he didn't move.

"Her name isn't Amy," Evelyn informed him. "It's Amadora."

Amadora smiled wickedly. "Graham, baby, could you do me a favor and hand over your sister's necklace?"

Evelyn took a step forward, her eyes flashing with electrical sparks. "You need to leave," she warned her.

"Where's the fun in that?" Amadora mocked. She directed her attention to Carson. "This would have been so much easier if you would have just met up with Graham and I today." She shook her head in disappointment. "So here's the plan. You're going to give me that necklace, or I'll kill Graham and Rikki in front of you, and I'll do it slowly." She flashed Carson another evil grin. "I've already done a number on your best friend, haven't I?"

"Don't listen to her, Carson. Keep it on." Evelyn spoke assertively.

Amadora glared at Evelyn and then back at Carson. "Do you really want to test me?" she asked daringly. "She's a new pyrobanant, right?" Amadora placed her pointer finger and thumb on her chin and cast her eyes upward and to the side as if in deep thought. "Hmm. Now, correct me if I'm wrong, Light One, but can't brand-new pyrobanants go off the deep end pretty easily?" She snickered. "I mean, just a little push from me, and I can cause her to explode."

"Ev, what's she talking about?" Carson turned to face Evelyn.

"Carson, Rikki is a strong pyrobanant. You know this and *she* knows this. She's trying to get to you."

Carson quickly looked over to find Rikki leaning on Graham, still pretty out of it, but her eyes were locked on Amadora as well. Graham, on the other hand, appeared as though he was going to faint from disbelief. He held Rikki closely, almost as if he was afraid she'd just slip out of his arms.

"Can't you make a stop at Kay Jewelers?" Rikki disrupted them. "I mean, all this for a necklace?" Of course Rikki needed to get her two cents in—she always did.

"Don't say I didn't warn you," Amadora scolded.

Rikki dropped to the ground, screaming in agonizing pain. Her skin began to transform into ashes and slowly flake off.

"Evelyn!" Carson shouted. "Please! Do something!"

Graham instantly reached out to grab Rikki's arm, but instead retrieved a handful of soot particles. "What is happening to her, Car?" he asked, clearly in distress.

"Rikki, fight this. You have it in you!" Evelyn yelled.

Rikki continued to cry out in anguish.

Carson realized she had two options: give Amadora the necklace that protected her from elemental harm or watch her best friend die at her feet.

"Okay, Amadora. Here!" Carson shrieked, and rapidly unclasped the necklace. She tossed it over to Amadora. "It's yours. Just stop hurting her, please!"

"Carson, no!" Evelyn yelled, panic evident on her face.

Amadora chuckled in bemusement. "You fool. You have no idea what you've just given up. And for what, a premature pyrobanant?"

Rikki moved slowly on the ground, attempting to regain her strength. "I'm—I'm going to..." She whimpered.

Amadora shook her head in vile laughter as she picked the necklace up and clasped it around her own neck. She appraised Evelyn. "I hear this necklace even protects against you," she sneered. "I'm looking forward to killing all of them, and there's nothing you can do about it."

Evelyn glared at her in obvious hatred, as if Amadora had just told the world one of her biggest secrets. Lustrous, raging bolts of lightning launched over Evelyn's entire body.

Carson watched as the one and only woman she'd ever loved transformed into something else; something with the strength of a *million storms*.

"I'll die myself before I ever let you touch any of them," Evelyn declared.

"Good, because that's what I'm counting on," Amadora spat back. Her body immediately blackened and her eyes boiled. Those same hideous veins crept across every inch of her skin, and the intoxicating smoke she caused in the air thickened around them. "I think I'll start with Grahamy-boy!"

All of a sudden, Rikki was no longer on the ground. And she was no longer—well, Rikki. Her skin smoldered with a burning ember-like appearance while hot, effulgent flames replaced her long, ginger curls. She stood beside Evelyn, indignation in her blazing eyes as she glowered at Amadora.

"Well, isn't that precious," Amadora said derisively. "The new pyrobanant has a thing for the Marked One's brother." She tilted her head back and sniggered loudly. "Oh, I'm going to have fun with this!"

Amadora didn't get very far, though; she immediately stopped dead in her tracks. Falling on her knees, she coughed and gasped for air. "What...is...happening..." She heaved between words as she yanked at the suffocating invisible grip around her throat.

The bolts around Evelyn's body waned. She stomped over to Amadora, who was hunkered on the ground struggling to breathe, and halted before her. "I never said the necklace protected elementals." She knelt in front of her, just inches away, and spoke solemnly as her ice-cold eyes met Amadora's. "The necklace was created for the Light One." Evelyn proceeded to remove it from Amadora's neck. "And the Marked One only. You put it on, you'll only receive a significant repercussion." She stepped back.

Once the necklace was off, Amadora regained her normalcy. She took in deep breaths and rubbed her neck as she stood up, planting both feet on the ground. The thick poison in the air dissipated. Amadora appeared defeated.

"I suggest you leave now. The others will be back soon and I can guarantee they won't be as lenient with you as I was today." She perked up like a dog realizing his owner just pulled into the driveway. "I can't always control the pyrobanant's behavior. You said it yourself; they *explode* easily."

Before Amadora had a chance to reply, as if on cue, the others arrived within a heartbeat. Abellona, Leo, Paxton, Chiraz, and Avani and her twin brothers circled Amadora; she was completely surrounded.

Amadora spun around steadily, eyeballing each elemental as they cornered her in the middle. "Oh, aren't we just one big happy family?" she scoffed.

"Are you deaf?" Rikki, nearly back to her normal self but with eyes that still blazed vigorously, spoke up. She marched a few steps toward Amadora. "Did you not just hear what Evelyn said? Get out of here."

Amadora ignored her and stared straight at Evelyn. "Quite the group of followers you now have, Light One."

Rikki clenched her fists with the determination to intervene again when Amadora lifted her hand, ceasing and precluding any next move.

"Relax, Ginger Snap, I'm leaving. I just have one more thing to say to your puppet master here." She turned her head to face Evelyn again. "We'll never stop coming after you. I'll never let you forget what you did to us. I will take from you—" Amadora nodded in Carson's direction, "like you took from me."

Within a millisecond, she was gone. The sweet scent of ether that lingered in the air was now all that remained of the ominous perpetrator.

"Car?"

Carson turned around to face her traumatized brother. She opened her mouth to speak, but no words formed.

Graham shook his head, then quickly marched off toward his car.

"Graham, wait! Please don't leave yet!" Carson begged as she began to move in his direction.

Evelyn gently grabbed her arm to stop her. "Carson, let him go. He's going to need a little time. I can promise you his safety."

Carson shook her head. "I can't let him leave like this."

"I'll talk to him, Car," Rikki offered, and then proceeded to chase after Graham. "Graham, hold on!" she pleaded desperately. "Please, wait a second! We can explain."

He spun around reluctantly, bitterness apparent on his face. "You both have been lying to me! About where you've been, about Evelyn, about everything!"

"Graham, how was I supposed to tell you something like this?" She gestured toward herself. "You wouldn't have understood."

"You never gave me the chance," Graham replied, pulling his car door open and slumping inside. "Who am I supposed to trust with my sister if I can't trust you, Rik?"

"You can trust me, Graham. How long have we known each other?"

He shook his head in disappointment. "I feel like I don't know you at all right now."

The offensive words from Graham's mouth left Rikki nearly speechless. Eventually, she shrugged and mouthed "*I'm sorry*" to him, but all she got in return was the same pained expression as before. Discomfited, Rikki backed off and let Graham leave.

After Graham's exit, Avani broke the group's ear-splitting silence. "This is exactly what I was talking about," she stressed, disrupting everyone's thoughts. "Of all victrolics, it's Amadora who has been here all along. We're all in danger now. Especially *her*." She pointed at Carson.

"Avani, please. We'll figure all this out," Paxton responded. "We're strong as a team. Let us not divert from that."

"I say we fight back," Leo blurted. "She says they'll never stop, so we must fight."

"I agree," Abellona said, joining the conversation. "What if they decide to attack when we're the most vulnerable—when Evelyn leaves again?"

At that moment, everybody chimed in, agreeing and disagreeing, debating without compromise.

"You're all right," Evelyn interrupted. "This is all my fault. I'm putting every one of you in danger."

"What if you trained us, Ev?" Rikki asked loudly, silencing the conversation. "You were all already planning on 'showing me the ropes,' remember?" She air-quoted with her fingers. "Why can't we make it a real lesson for everyone?"

"We don't need the training like you do, Ward," Leo retorted.

"I'd have to disagree with that," Evelyn countered. "You're all very young. You may have the basics down, but there's much more all of you still have to learn when it comes to being an elemental."

"Rubbish. Abe and I can handle ourselves," Leo argued. "As a matter of fact, I believe I could have easily taken care of Amadora myself."

Evelyn's eyebrows shot up. "Is that so?" she asked him.

Leo nodded in response.

Evelyn walked over and stood a few feet away from him. "Let's test that theory, shall we?"

Leo nodded and shrugged his shoulders. "Sure."

"Did I ever tell you how I met Amadora, Leo?"

He shook his head.

Evelyn crossed her arms and slowly paced in a circle around him as she spoke. "Some of you know the reason the victrolics despise me so much. Amadora, along with her family, believes I had something to do with the disappearance of their older sister, Eleanor." She continued to pace, stopping now and then to speak directly at Leo. "Years upon years ago, I could sense the torment that Amadora and Loki were causing a young pyrobanant to undergo because they knew I was in range; they could sense the necklace around my neck that night. They tortured him, pushing for him to break. This young pyrobanant had no idea he was an elemental, similar to Rikki's situation.

"Once I got there, the pyrobanant, whose name I later found out was Brandon, was lying on the ground face down—completely shot, completely powerless. He was groaning, hardly moving." Evelyn swallowed, attempting to remove the lump in her throat as the painful memory flooded her brain. "He looked up at me, and his eyes were like yours, Leo, although more out of control. Amadora and Loki stood there watching while they purposefully taunted me with Brandon. A pyrobanant's ability should never be forced to the surface when they aren't at the proper maturity in their life. Brandon was..." Evelyn shook her head and forced her eyes shut for a moment. "Far less advanced than most, which is probably why they chose to use him against me. I remember encouraging him to fight through it."

The group exchanged looks of confusion.

"Did he?" Abellona asked.

Evelyn stopped pacing and stood a few feet away from Leo once again. "He eventually got up, yes."

"What happened?" Leo asked her.

In a matter of seconds, Evelyn knocked the legs out from under Leo, and down on his back he went. He groaned and winced as if in pain, but it was evidently more from the stun itself.

"That was a cheap shot!" he coughed out. "I wasn't ready."

Evelyn stood over him. "Do you think Brandon was?"

Abellona leaned down and grabbed her boyfriend's hand to help him up.

Leo briskly dusted his pants off with his virile hands. "Okay, I get it. Your point is understood." He nodded.

"Brandon didn't make it, did he?" Carson interrupted.

Evelyn glanced at Carson. She frowned before replying, "He wasn't ready either."

CHAPTER 22

After the commotion subsided, Evelyn, Rikki, and Carson stood in front of the shop and conversed privately.

"This is the seventh time I've tried calling him," Carson said apprehensively, her shoulders drooping as she lowered her phone from her ear. "How is he ever going to understand any of this?" She crossed her arms and gazed out into the woods. "And how can I even expect him to?"

"He's your brother. He's confused, yes, but he will come around," Evelyn stressed. "He loves you very much." She cast her gaze over to Rikki. "Both of you."

Rikki cleared her throat loudly, intervening before Carson could reply. "What Evelyn means is we've all been close for years. He'll eventually calm down. He's just a little upset with us right now." She folded her arms as well, copying Carson's stance. "Besides, he will come looking for some answers sooner or later."

"You're probably right, but he may need someone to talk to. He just found out his girlfriend is—"

Evelyn cut her off. "An immortal being?"

Carson, now mute, only nodded.

"How did you take it when you found out about me, Car?" Evelyn questioned.

Carson smiled dolefully. "I'll give him some time."

"He knows he can call you, Car," Rikki confirmed. "He will when he's ready. He doesn't want to speak to me either at the moment."

"What about the victrolics, though? What if they go after him? Or my parents?" Carson exclaimed as she threw her hand up to her mouth and began to pace back and forth.

Evelyn drifted over and placed both of her hands on Carson's shoulders. "What Amadora did today was feed on your fears. The victrolics cannot harm innocent humans. They'd risk our existence and eventually have to answer to an elemental god." Evelyn backed away. "Besides, it's not Graham or your parents they want. It's me. And to get to me, they toy with you because you're the 'Marked One.' I promise I won't let anything happen to any of you, anyway."

Carson began to reply but was disrupted by the sudden barging of Avani through the front door of the shop. She stormed past all three of them, quickly making her way to the familiar path in the woods.

"Um, is she okay?" Rikki asked Evelyn.

"Avani is very angry with me. Especially for bringing you here," Evelyn answered.

"For someone who kept an eye on me, she doesn't seem like she's very fond of me at all," Carson commented.

"Actually, she watched over you the most," Evelyn clarified.

Carson peered back in the direction in which Avani sprinted off. "I'll be right back," she said, then rushed off to follow.

"Car, what are you doing?" Rikki hollered after her.

"I just want to talk to her," Carson yelled back without turning around.

"Okay, but don't come crying to me if she strangles you with leaves!" Rikki shouted.

Evelyn only shook her head.

Carson trotted through the woods, following the dirt path faithfully. The breeze blew gently against her skin and rustled the leaves throughout the forest around her.

Carson cut her hike short to peek around. There was no sign of Avani anywhere. Although she didn't see her, she spoke aloud anyway.

"If you were in my place, would you change anything? Would you have decided not to come here?" She squinted through the wooded greenery. Tree branches danced back and forth while leaves fluttered peacefully onto the ground. "Do you blame me?"

Still, no answer. Only relentless silence.

Carson stood firmly and spoke again. "I may not know everything about Evelyn or the others, and especially you, but I do know you all have given up a great deal to protect me. If that's the case, you must have realized the person I am. Your generosity will not go unappreciated." She turned back around, waiting for some sort of reply. She sighed. "I just wanted to say thank you, Avani."

After moments of quiet, Carson decided to give up and began back in the direction from which she came.

"I don't blame you," a familiar, strong voice echoed above Carson's head.

Carson turned around and looked up at the large tree in front of her. Avani sat contentedly on one of the branches, similar to how Carson had seen her twin brothers do the weekend before.

"But yes, you do not know everything. My mother has sacrificed much to keep this family safe—to even have this business where it's at right now, around the mortals."

"The last thing I wanted to do was cause any problems for any of you," Carson informed her.

"The problem I'm having right now is trying to protect my family."

Carson nodded silently.

"Carson, everything that is going on right now is out of your control," Avani elaborated. "In fact, it is out of everybody's control. I can complain all I choose, but who am I to impede the cycle of fate?"

Carson's brows furrowed. "Um, fate?"

Avani's once-stiffened expression transformed into a small grin. "Can you really stand there and tell me you don't love that woman as much as she loves you?"

Carson stood awkwardly for a minute and grabbed the back of her neck, fumbling for words. "I don't know what to say right now."

Avani giggled. "Yes, you do. You just don't want to admit the way you feel. You have more pride for your broken heart than security in yourself to let your guard down again right now, and that's okay."

That was the first time Carson heard any sort of positive response from Avani since they were introduced.

"But let me tell you this." Avani swooped down onto the ground and stood a foot away from Carson. "Everything that woman does is for you. She has put herself in more danger than anyone else I know, and that's to protect you. I may not always agree with her decisions, but I do know it's out of pure love."

Carson swallowed. "How do you know this?"

Avani sighed a long, expended sigh. "Because I was in love once, too. I see the way you look at each other, even after all this time," she explained. "It reminds me of the way he used to look at me."

Carson offered a warm smile, but said nothing. Although she had many questions, she didn't want to pry into Avani's personal business. She decided to change the subject. "So, um, why are you out here?"

"I'm waiting for someone," Avani replied, and perked her head up to look behind Carson's shoulder. "And it looks like they just got here."

Carson didn't have to turn around to know there was something massive behind her. She could see its shadow. Once she finally twisted her body to face the stranger, she felt her heart shift into fast gear.

A humongous brown bear stood before her, grunting and sniffling, staring her up and down.

As if sensing the tension immediately, Avani settled her hand on Carson's shoulder, which the bear seemed to take as permission to sit down comfortably. "He won't hurt you. He's just unsure of you; probably more afraid of you than you are of him."

Carson took a big breath in and let it out slowly, trying to steady her startled heartbeat. She'd never been this close to a wild bear before.

Avani glided over and placed her hand on the bear's head. She began caressing his face, which he thoroughly enjoyed. She rested her head against his as she introduced him to Carson. "This is Micah. He lives in these woods. I found him when he was a cub. He'd gotten hurt, and I revived him. He's been my best friend ever since."

Carson swallowed, still attempting to calm down. "He is beautiful."

Avani smiled. "Would you like to say hello?" she asked.

"Um, I'm okay. It doesn't seem like he's really all that comfortable with me here yet."

Avani's eyebrows spiked up at Carson's decline, as though she was surprised. She then looked back at Micah and quietly whispered something in his ear. Carson couldn't make out what it was.

Micah rose and slowly sauntered over to Carson.

"He knows you're nervous, but you don't have to be. He wants to welcome you," Avani explained.

On that note, Micah nudged Carson's hand, encouraging her to pet him. Carson gently stroked his fur, soaking in his approval. Micah continued to grunt and snort, but in a more placid manner.

"He likes you," Avani emphasized, smiling in clear gratification.

"What did you say to him?" Carson asked her.

"I just told him the importance you hold in our family," Avani replied. "But I didn't have to say too much. He can tell when someone has a good heart. All animals can."

After Carson headed back, Avani lingered behind a little longer, thinking back on the past few years, when she kept an eye on Carson as Evelyn slumbered. She reminisced particularly on one memory as if it had just happened yesterday:

Avani had stooped quietly behind some large bushes in the woods near Carson's parents' house. She knew Carson slept overnight there, and she knew she was safe, but she just wanted to make sure today was going to be an easier day for her.

She had watched as Carson finally slumped onto the back porch and sat down in one of the chairs. Tears rolled down Carson's face; it was obvious today was going to be no better than the rest. Avani couldn't blame her, though, because Evelyn had left just a few weeks ago. This heartache was fresh, and as excruciatingly raw as it could be. Carson had no idea why the departure had happened, but Avani did, and that was probably the most difficult part of watching this entire thing. Well, that and the fact that Avani too had to go through something similar. She had watched Lucas go through this for months after she'd demanded they go their separate ways. He never understood why she did what she did. Avani knew Lucas felt rejection but she felt it was in his best interest—for his own safety. At least that's what she'd had to tell herself every day to reduce the pain to the bare minimum. *We can't fall in love with humans. It only brings danger to them.*

"I just want this to stop. It hurts so bad," Carson had whimpered to herself, not knowing Avani could hear every word.

Avani had the urge to just barge out of the woods and tell Carson everything; why Evelyn left, and why it had to be this way.

"It will get easier," Avani had whispered.

Avani eventually realized how she could help Carson for the day. Carson was not wearing the crystal that morning, which meant Carson was susceptible to all of the elements. Avani was, of course, a terradescendant, and Carson just so happened to be sitting on the porch surrounded by her mother's splendiferous, unrestrained hanging baskets and potted plants. What better way to mend Carson's heart for the time being than to do it telepathically with nature's sweet help?

Avani's discerning thoughts and feelings crescendoed to the plants on Jan's porch. A vine cascaded out of one of the baskets and began to act. Ever so slightly, and without alarming Carson, the vine touched her shoulder. Nature spoke solemnly to her. Waves of assuasive relief swarmed Carson, alleviating her heartache for a short while.

"Let your mind and your heart find peace today, Carson," Avani had murmured.

CHAPTER 23

Once Avani and Carson arrived back at the cabins, Carson discovered the whole group had joined Rikki and Evelyn outside. They all appeared to be arguing again.

"I'm only looking out for the safety of you all," Evelyn was explaining.

"How's that?" Abellona accused. "If they can be as dangerous and vindictive as you say they are, then we're all screwed."

"Yeah, especially if there are more of them than there are us," Leo chimed in.

"We need to be prepared for the worst, Evelyn," Abellona remarked. "No offense to Carson, but you exposed us the minute you led her here."

"We aren't going to go looking for a fight. I won't allow it," Evelyn said, a hint of irritation in her voice. "I'm trying to protect you, so that means we need to leave. Get out of this area so none of you become targets," she continued.

"No," Avani cut in.

Everybody stared at her in silence, probably in shock.

"No more running. No more hiding," Avani said. "You're the Light One. We—" she gestured to the group, "aren't weak. We're strong as a group. I'm with them." She walked calmly while speaking until she stood directly in front of Evelyn. "You don't have to protect us. You can teach us how to protect ourselves and one another. This ongoing battle between the elementals needs to stop."

"Avani, where did this come from?" Abellona asked her.

Avani glanced over at Carson. "You can say I've had a change of heart."

"This isn't about fighting. This is about control," Evelyn emphasized to the crew. "Each and every one of you needs to be in control of your inner self." She cast her eyes upon Rikki, Abellona, and Leo. "Control the temptation to lash out every time you're angry. Reel yourself back in when you know that diminutive flame is about to convert into a tenacious wildfire. You are all capable."

"Haven't you ever heard the phrase 'If you can't take the heat, stay out of the kitchen'?" Rikki asked sarcastically.

"Take Rikki for example," Evelyn continued, disregarding Rikki's humor. "It's much easier to feed the anger than it is to block it out, am I right?"

"What do you mean?" Rikki asked.

"She means that it doesn't take much to get under your skin, Ward," Abellona suggested. "You know, the way I brought up your relationship with your mother."

Rikki rolled her eyes. "This again?"

"Hey, we're all thinking it. How was your visit back to see her last week? The same as always?" Abellona neared Rikki. "Let me guess. She was disappointed in you, correct?"

"Abellona, stop." Rikki's skin reddened. She clenched her jaw and tightened her fists.

"No, Rikki, you stop. This is what Evelyn is trying to explain." Abellona crossed her arms. "I'm not out to get you. But the victrolics will be. They'll push you to the breaking point, just like Amadora did to that young pyro."

Rikki loosened her fingers. She sighed. "I'm an easy target."

Evelyn placed her hand on Rikki's shoulder. "Control, Rikki. It's about control. You're only a target if you allow them to target you. You're the only one in control of yourself, remember that."

Rikki nodded. "I can do this." She turned her head in the

direction of Leo and Abellona. "I'll try harder with both of you."

"Ward, come with me. I want to talk to you," Abellona urged.

This time, Rikki wasn't reluctant. She followed Abellona willingly while Leo remained with the rest of the group, offering his girlfriend what seemed like a palliative expression just before the two girls disappeared into the woods.

"Why aren't you going with them?" Carson asked Leo.

"Because this is something Abellona needs to explain to Rikki by herself, and I respect that," he replied. He watched as Carson's face transitioned from concerned to apprehensive in a matter of seconds. "Carson, everything Abellona and I do is to teach Rikki to be a better pyro."

"What do you mean better?" Carson questioned.

Leo shook his head slightly. "We have both made some mistakes in the past. It was all before Evelyn found us. She has her story, and I surely have mine."

Rikki followed Abellona all the way down the dirt path to the bench. Abellona sat down and patted the open spot next to her, signaling for Rikki to sit next to her. As Rikki settled, Abellona began to speak.

"You don't really know me that well, so I want to explain who I am."

Rikki nodded, silently encouraging her to continue.

"You may not believe this about me, but I was very quiet and secluded years ago."

"I can see that," Rikki remarked sardonically.

Abellona nodded, offering a subtle smirk. "It's true. When I was in college, I was private and I focused on my academics. I did what I could to please the professors but didn't quite fit in with all the rest of the kids." She crossed her legs as she continued, "Many of the other students didn't really understand me. I was the teacher's pet."

She inhaled deeply and then let it out slowly. "There had been some rumors about my social sciences professor. He was well-liked and famous on campus. Then I had heard he'd done things to other students in the past. Other girls."

Rikki's brow furrowed prominently. "Things?"

Once again, Abellona nodded. "Bad things." She shifted uncomfortably. "I shouldn't have ignored the rumors; I should have said something sooner." She shook her head disappointedly. "And eventually, he cornered me too."

"What?" Rikki's eyes widened. "Did you report him then?"

"I did. His money got him out of most of it. His trial lasted months. During that time, I couldn't get what happened to me, and the other girls, out of my head. I built up an anger, a fury; more so than a normal person. It started with night sweats, dreams of fire."

Rikki's mouth dropped open. "You converted during all this?"

Abellona closed her eyes as if she was attempting to block out her memories. Once she opened them, two minuscule flames swirled vigorously where her irises once resided. "Yes. At the time, I thought he deserved more than just a few months behind bars. He deserved to pay. So after weeks of isolating myself in my dorm, I mastered my abilities. I decided to use them for another purpose...a *vengeful* purpose. I began setting fires on campus starting with his classroom, and then his office. Days after that, I covered his house in flames. Lucky for him, he wasn't there. He hadn't been home in weeks."

Engaged entirely, Rikki listened, waiting for more.

"I tracked him down. He was staying in a hotel north of the campus. One late night, he got into his car, not knowing I was in there. I tied him to his seat and told him he wasn't getting away with what he had done to all of us."

Abellona swallowed and paused for a few moments. She closed her eyes again and once she opened them, they were back to normal. "I stole his phone and recorded his screams as I sat in the car and watched him burn. I sent it to every one of those girls and titled it '*Enjoy the Show.*'"

Rikki sat quietly. It was the first time she didn't know what to say.

"He lived," Abellona stated. "Someone heard him screaming. They pulled him out of his car. He suffered severe third-degree burns that became so infected, doctors had to amputate his legs."

"Do you still think he got what he deserved? Think about how many girls he raped, Abellona."

Abellona shook her head contentiously. "He would have gotten what he deserved regardless if I didn't step in." She turned her head to face Rikki. "A lifetime in prison."

Rikki stared at her, confused.

"The night I did this, he had just finished up court that day. He finally pled guilty, and was sentenced to prison. His sentence started after he healed up and was released from the rehab facility. While there he was beaten to death by a boyfriend of one of his victims." Abellona stood up restlessly and crossed her arms. She trudged forward a few steps as she carried on. "I put him in the shape he was in and he couldn't defend himself or get help. Justice would have eventually taken its course, but I let my need for vengeance take over."

"You didn't know he was going to pris—"

Abellona immediately cut her off. "Rikki, no. Don't find excuses for me. I know he was a bad person. He was evil for doing those things to me and the other students, but what I did makes me no better." She sat back down. "You have a chance to become a great pyrobanant. Evelyn is right—control is the most important part of it. Don't make the same mistakes I did. Don't let your anger take over."

"Wait a sec," Rikki blurted out. "When did you start calling me Rikki?"

Abellona giggled and rolled her eyes. "Don't get used to it, Ward."

Rikki smiled. "So...what now?"

Abellona jerked her head in the direction of the cabins. "Now we go back, and we learn how to kick some victrolic ass."

"Wait, let me get this straight. You want *all* of us to attack you?" Leo asked, perplexed by Evelyn's request.

"Yes," she answered confidently, standing motionless in the center of the group.

"At the same time?" Chiraz questioned.

Evelyn nodded. "Precisely."

Leo scratched his head, and Paxton shook his. The twins, Chiraz, and Avani exchanged confounded expressions, wondering if they misunderstood Evelyn's instructions.

Carson, who sat on a large rock with Rikki several feet away from the group, watched as the team stared blankly at Evelyn.

"I don't think this is a good idea, Ms. Evelyn. What if we hurt you?" Paxton asked.

Evelyn offered a sly grin. "I wouldn't ask this of you if I couldn't handle myself, Paxton."

Leo and Abellona gazed at each other intently; a guileless yet cunning smile passed between the two of them.

"Hey, Ward, watch and learn," Leo exclaimed.

"You got seconds to impress me," Rikki retorted. "Getting bored here."

As if on cue, the entire bunch transformed from normal-looking young adults to bright, energized beings of perpetual power. Leo, his body ablaze with smoldering flames, commenced the attack and released a significantly expanded fireball, targeting Evelyn's back. Abellona unleashed sizzling streaks of fire out of her hands and toward Evelyn as well. Evelyn swung her body around and to the side, dodging Leo's attack, and then moved swiftly the other way as she backflipped and missed Abellona's.

"Any day now, guys," Evelyn said wryly. "I'm waiting."

The twins cackled at Leo and Abellona's failed efforts. The rest of the group didn't hesitate; they all took her sly comment as a challenge. Everyone launched their attacks on Evelyn.

From where Carson was sitting, it seemed just like a scenic display of fireworks. She watched as Evelyn jumped and flipped, moving with the speed of light away from every blast. Nobody was able to hit her, let alone keep up with her.

"This is amazing, isn't it, Rik?" Carson commented, mesmerized. She turned her head to find Rikki had left her side. "Rikki? Where did you go?" Carson locked her eyes back on the group, finding Rikki nearing Evelyn on her opposite side. "What the—" Her eyes widened in panic.

"Ev!" Rikki yelled, waving her arms as she attempted to get Evelyn's attention. "Hey, Ev! It's Carson! Something is wrong!" Rikki shrieked.

Everybody halted immediately. Evelyn froze, all of her focus on Rikki.

"It's Carson, please, she needs your help," Rikki exclaimed.

Evelyn quickly turned around, eyes locked on Carson. "Car, what's wrong? Are you—"

Rikki, transformed into her fierce, fiery side, dove to the ground rapidly. As if sliding to home base, she took Evelyn's legs out from underneath her. *SWISH! CRACK!*

Just like that, Evelyn fell flat onto her back.

Rikki stood above her. "It's all about control, Evelyn, right?" She grabbed Evelyn's hand, helping her up. "How are you supposed to control yourself when it comes to Carson?"

The team hooted and hollered, cheering Rikki on.

"Nice, Ward! I underestimated you!" Leo choked out through giggles.

"I have to give it to her, Ev. She used your weakness against you. That was spot on," Abellona quipped.

Carson, out of breath from scrambling over to join them, could barely form words. "What in the world was that?"

"I just got my ass handed to me by a newbie." Evelyn smiled.

CHAPTER 24

Later that evening, after what seemed like endless rounds of training, everybody joined Pakruti and Bhumika in the restaurant for dinner.

"Thank you for this, Rudy," Carson said. "You make it feel like home here."

Rudy smiled appreciatively. "You're very welcome, my dear." She patted Carson gently on the back. "That was my goal."

As the conversation progressed during dinner, Rikki snuck a peek at her phone. She hadn't mentioned to Carson that she had a text typed out to Graham, but had anxiously refrained from hitting the "send" button. She watched as the cursor blinked and blinked, as if it was egging her on, expecting her to finally work up the guts to tell Graham how she was feeling. She read her words over and over.

Everything Amy said about my feelings is true.

As Rikki burned an invisible hole into her screen, a text message popped up from her mother. *Great,* she thought. She would get back to staring at her ridiculously thought-out message later. She clicked on her mother's message.

I expect to see you at the Ridgeburg Charity Fundraiser tomorrow.

"Shit," Rikki blurted. "I forgot." She quickly wound herself back into reality, looking up to find all eyes on her.

"What's wrong, Rik?" Carson asked.

"I forgot about my mom's speech tomorrow. The one in Ridgeburg."

"That's tomorrow?" Carson's eyes widened with panic. "Oh no. The one we also invited Graham to? I can't believe I forgot about that." She shook her head anxiously.

"You both have had a long few weeks," Evelyn said sympathetically. "It's easy to forget things when you're distracted."

Rikki stood and crossed her arms. "I agree, but I can't get out of this. I have some legal documents for the event. Accountant stuff." She looked over at Carson. "How's it going to look if I don't show up?"

Evelyn tilted her head. "If the victrolics know you're going, it could be unsafe," she said.

"Do you think they'd do that in front of a bunch of humans?" Carson questioned.

Evelyn shook her head. "They'd find a way to get you alone."

"Wait, light bulb!" Rikki cried as if she had just figured out the last clue to a profound mystery. "I got it!" She looked over to Evelyn. "Come with us. You can keep an eye on things. It's a public event."

Evelyn glanced at Carson, watching her reaction to the suggestion. "Um, I could do that," she replied, "as long as Carson approves."

Carson put her hands up, stalling. "Hang on a second, Rik. What about Graham? And your mother knows Evelyn. How do I explain to her where she's been the past two years?"

"It's none of my mother's business," Rikki replied. "As for Graham, if he shows up, Evelyn will protect him. As a matter of fact, Evelyn can protect everyone there."

Carson hesitated a minute before finally agreeing. "Okay. For everyone's safety."

"Great!" Rikki clapped in approval. "It's settled. I'll take care of my business with my mother, and Evelyn will keep Carson company." She smiled with satisfaction. "Everyone stays safe."

That night, Carson lay restlessly in bed while Rikki snored peacefully beside her. Sleep had been forcefully postponed by heavy thoughts flooding her brain. She knew she'd be bombarded with questions by at least Rikki's mother—if not anyone else—at the event tomorrow. Questions about Evelyn and about their current relationship. She could hear them now:

Did you really forgive her after what she did to you? Was there somebody else? Are you two now back together? What does the future hold for the both of you?

Carson sat up in bed while the reality of the last question hit her hard. *What DOES the future hold for the both of us? Evelyn supposedly dies every two years. This is going to happen again, isn't it?* She pondered for a bit before making a final decision. She was going to get that answer right now.

Carson hurried out of bed, determined for the truth, whether it could hurt her or not. She impatiently but quietly slipped her sandals and a jacket on and snuck out the front door of the small cabin.

The moon gleamed fiercely overhead, making it possible to see feet in front of her. She flew down the steps and into the open, where the moon shined brightest. After everything that had happened so far, she knew for certain Evelyn was watching her at that moment.

"Ev, I need to ask you something," she said with confidence.

Not even thirty seconds passed, and she felt a presence behind her, but wasn't startled. She knew it was Evelyn.

"Can't sleep?" Evelyn's voice was soothing and calm.

Carson turned around, face to face with her. "I need to know something. Please answer me truthfully."

Evelyn nodded.

"The same thing that happened to you two years ago—it's going to happen again, isn't it?" Carson interrogated. "Two years from now?"

Evelyn lowered her gaze to the ground, obviously refraining from answering.

Carson slowly inched closer to her, stopping just short of their bodies touching. She had significantly drained herself of all energy to keep some distance between herself and Evelyn these past few weeks. It was starting to get difficult, and it was much harder when there was no one around to distract them.

She gently placed her hands in Evelyn's. "Ev? Can you look at me, please?" She then softly lifted Evelyn's chin with her hand, forcing Evelyn's eyes to lock with her own.

"There's nothing I can do to change it," Evelyn eventually replied. "It's been happening for so very long."

Carson swallowed back the fear and fought off the dread Evelyn's response was bound to cause. She nodded in silent submission, accepting the fact that her strength was going to fail her. Evelyn was going to disappear again in two years, and Carson would have to recover all over again and repeat the cycle. The truth was that she knew this was going to be the answer, but it was something she had been trying to avoid talking about until now.

Carson stared into Evelyn's ice-blue eyes, losing herself piece by piece. Before she knew it, the moment was taking advantage of them in their vulnerable states.

Carson felt the heat radiating from Evelyn's body. She watched as Evelyn's eyes delicately wandered down to her lips. Carson noticed the refulgent glow emanating from those eyes. The light...she couldn't describe it. It drew her in, and it was mesmerizing.

Evelyn must have realized what was happening, because she flinched and jammed her eyes shut, pulling precipitously away from Carson. "I'm sorry," she said frantically, "I didn't mean to get carried awa—"

"Evelyn, look at me," Carson whispered. "Open your eyes." She reached out and pulled her in again, but waited for Evelyn to look back at her before she ultimately said what she'd been thinking for days. "I think I always knew."

"Knew what?" Evelyn asked.

"That someone as rare as you couldn't only be human." Carson brushed her fingers lightly against Evelyn's sides, and didn't stop until she found the bottom of her shirt. Her heart, she was sure, was going to beat out of her chest with every tender touch. She gradually allowed her daring hands to guide themselves under the piece of fabric and onto warm, familiar skin.

Looking into Evelyn's eyes, Carson thought she had never witnessed anything more exquisite. It was as though with each subtle move she made, the light in Evelyn's eyes evolved, became brighter, more powerful. They were radiant with angelic blue hues, and piercing with an intensity so strong that Carson couldn't look away.

Carson felt Evelyn move in closer; so close that she felt her breath on her lips. The combination of Evelyn's natural scent, the feel of her skin on her fingertips, and Evelyn's lips barely touching her own caused her to feel lightheaded.

That's when Carson gave in. She pushed herself completely into Evelyn, closing all distance and finally pressing her lips into hers as if a magnetic force took hold. Evelyn's arms wrapped around Carson, holding her tightly as she kissed her. She snaked her hands underneath Carson's shirt and onto the small of her back.

Old feelings rushed back to Carson, unrelenting and profoundly overwhelming. It felt as though Carson had found home again after being homesick for far too long. The last two years began to dissipate in her mind, as if they never happened.

The moment availed itself as Carson dug her nails into Evelyn's skin after feeling Evelyn's tongue slip inside her mouth.

"Well, that didn't take long!" Rikki's voice could have been heard miles away.

Carson withdrew from Evelyn's lips just as the slightest chuckle left them. "Been there long?" she asked Rikki.

"Long enough," Evelyn answered.

Rikki strolled over with a giant smirk on her face as she eyeballed Carson wiping her lips. "I mean, I totally get it now," she remarked.

Carson shook her head and smiled. She knew more was coming from her quick-witted friend.

"Why you used to say she's a good kisser." Rikki pointed at Evelyn. "I mean, she *is* ancient. Therefore, lots of time to practice."

Carson grabbed Rikki by the arm, ripping her away from the dreadful conversation at hand. "All right, well, I'm tired and I think it's time to go to bed now," she exclaimed.

"Oh, I bet you *are* tired! Woo! I'm tired after watching the two of you. I mean, I could honestly feel the heat from where I was standi—"

"Good night, Evelyn, see you in the morning!" Carson yelled as she pushed Rikki back into their cabin.

"Hey, you can go to bed now but you're so gonna spill it as soon as you wake up in the morning," Rikki snarked.

Carson jumped in bed. "I can't hear you, I'm sleeping." She fake-yawned.

After about fifteen more minutes of bantering and obnoxious smooching noises, Rikki finally fell back asleep. Carson, however, couldn't focus on sleep. She still felt Evelyn's lips on hers and the tingle in her body was not letting up, not even the slightest bit. She could still feel that elegant but vehement grip on the bare skin of her back.

It was going to be a long night.

"Wakey, wakey," Rikki shouted in Carson's ear.

Carson's eyes fluttered open, taking in the rays of sunlight in their room. She began to stretch. "What time is it?" she asked her best friend.

"Time for you to spill the beans," Rikki replied, handing Carson a cup of coffee. "And I'm dying to know," she added while taking a seat beside Carson on the bed, "did you get zapped?"

Carson sighed and rolled her eyes. "I'm scared, Rik."

"About what?" Rikki asked. "Did it hurt that bad? Maybe you need to put a shock collar on her so she can see how it feels!"

"What?" Carson shook her head. "No, she doesn't scare me like that. She scares me because she could disappear again in two years. I can't go through that again."

"Hm," Rikki murmured. "Then why don't we figure out how to keep her here?"

Carson shrugged. "But is it even possible? All I know is it wouldn't be simple. I know she hasn't told me everything yet, and I have so much to learn about her."

"Car, you know much more than you did two years ago. That's a start."

Carson nodded in agreement but didn't say anything else. She decided to get up and get ready. They had another long day ahead of them.

Once in the car, Carson did her best to relax as she sat beside Evelyn in the back seat. Abellona had offered to go as well, so she accompanied Rikki in the front of the car while she drove. It had only been about twenty minutes and they had already covered just about every topic; boys, college, work, etc. They laughed and shrieked. They gasped and shouted. It seemed as if they had actually become friends.

Carson watched as the trees zoomed by the window. She thought about the chaos of the last few weeks and how things from here on out would probably always be this way. That's when she realized she needed to text Graham. She pulled her phone out and typed a few words.

I don't expect you to meet us at the fundraiser. I know you're upset. I just wish you'd at least let me know everything is okay. I want to know you're safe. Can we please talk when I get home?

"Is everything all right?" Evelyn asked.

Carson smiled and nodded. "Just texting Graham. I just want to make sure he's okay. I doubt he'll come today after what happened yesterday."

"I checked on him late last night," Evelyn informed her. "He's safe."

Carson couldn't hold back the tears that began swelling behind her eyes, much less the relief she felt knowing her brother was okay. "Thank you," she told Evelyn. How much more did Evelyn take care of when they were together?

Carson carefully slid her hand up against Evelyn's so as to not draw attention from the front row of the car. She caressed the side of it with her pinky and noted the small, amused grin on Evelyn's face.

"You guys alive back there?" Rikki asked.

"For hundreds of years," Evelyn confirmed.

"True. You got me there," Rikki replied. "We'll be there in a few minutes."

Once parked, Carson stumbled out of the car and began to stretch. The warm sun beat down on them as they traveled to the pavilion set up nearby.

Sandra Ward hustled over to the four of them. "There you are."

"Hello, Mother." Rikki's greeting was rather dry.

A wave of astonishment cast itself over Sandra as she grasped the fact that it was Evelyn who stood before her. "Oh, wow. Hello, Evelyn. It's been...years." She couldn't have spoken in a less displeased tone.

"Mrs. Ward," Evelyn greeted her. "It's lovely to see you again."

"Alrighty then. We are gonna go this way." Rikki pointed in the direction of their destination, walking past her mother, who quickly caught up to her after saying hello to Carson and introducing herself to Abellona.

Carson overheard Sandra whispering to Rikki as they walked several feet in front of them. "Why didn't you tell me they were back together?"

Rikki must have said something to her mother that Carson speculated had much to do with minding her own business because Sandra stopped peeking over her shoulder at them as they walked.

Once everyone was inside and accounted for, Rikki and Sandra disappeared into the back, probably so Rikki could take care of her paperwork for the event.

Carson recognized a few people from fundraisers and charities over the years. She engaged in some conversations, but kept talking to a minimum as best she could. Evelyn and Abellona spoke to some groups as well, attempting to blend in. Everybody at the event seemed to be having a pleasant time.

Rikki reappeared after about an hour, rushing to Carson's side. "Car, something is wrong. I feel weird again." She pressed her hand over her abdomen as though in pain.

Carson realized this could only mean one thing, and that was when they saw her.

Amadora emerged through the entrance, wearing snug black pants and a sheer red tank top. Dark sunglasses hid her eyes from view. She halted once she discovered Carson and displayed a sly, evil grin.

Carson quickly looked around for Evelyn and Abellona and found them standing close behind her and Rikki already.

"Rikki, she's doing this on purpose because you're in front of people. She's going to try to break you," Evelyn whispered to her. "Ignore her."

"I'm...trying..." Rikki groaned through gritted teeth.

"Ward, you're strong—you can get through this," Abellona assured her.

Amadora sauntered over to the four of them. "What a surprise, seeing you all here. I would have never expected it. I feel as though I just saw you yesterday," she said smugly as she used one hand to slide her sunglasses slightly down to take a peek at Rikki. "Oh, dear. What's wrong with her? Is it contagious?" she snickered.

"You're...gonna be...sorry..." Rikki hissed between breaths.

"I highly doubt that." Amadora crossed her arms. "Anyways, I came to speak to the beloved 'Marked One.'"

"Um, yeah, that's not gonna happen," Abellona barked at her. "What you're gonna do is turn around and leave, before I *make* you leave."

"Hm, where's the fun in that?" Amadora countered. "Oh, look," she said, examining the table at the back of the pavilion. "O'derbs. Well, I'll be in the back helping myself when you decide to come to your senses—you know. For your friend." She winked at Carson as she brushed by them and started for the trays of appetizers in the back.

"Ugh, I can't...let my mom...see me like this," Rikki moaned. She sunk down into a chair, rocking back and forth.

"Maybe I should just go talk to her," Carson considered aloud.

"Carson, no. She's dangerous," Evelyn said.

"You said it yourself; Amadora isn't going to do anything here. Not in front of all these people."

Evelyn shook her head in disapproval.

"Rikki?" Graham's concerned voice interrupted them. Everybody turned to see him standing there, eyes glued on Rikki. He sat down beside her.

"Hey, I didn't think you...were coming..."

"I wasn't going to, but here I am." He smiled for a moment, then looked at Carson. "She's doing this, isn't she?" He nodded his head in Amadora's direction.

They all turned around to look at her. She waved malevolently and pointed to her imaginary wristwatch to let them know time was of the essence.

Carson nodded. "Yes, she is. But I'm gonna fix it." She

turned to face Evelyn. "Listen, I'll be okay. I won't be that far away from you."

The apprehension on Evelyn's face was evident, but she nodded anyway. "Don't take this off, please." She pointed to the necklace around Carson's neck.

"I won't." Carson squeezed Evelyn's hand before she walked away, approaching Amadora.

"Ah, you came." Amadora smirked, then pulled off her sunglasses, revealing her near-red irises. "You aren't such a dumb girl after all."

"Whatever you're doing to Rikki, please stop," Carson demanded.

"Relax. The ex-boy toy over there is taking the edge off. If you didn't already know, he keeps her mind occupied." She slid the sunglasses back on.

"I'm not sure what that is supposed to mean," Carson said as she cast a look over at Rikki and Graham. She watched as Graham kneeled in front of Rikki, obviously worried. Whatever Graham had been saying to her was working, because Rikki appeared to be better, much to Carson's surprise.

"Oh, you'll figure it out. Like I said, you aren't a dumb girl. It doesn't take a genius to figure that one out," she scoffed.

"What do you want?" Carson glared at her. "I'm not sure why you're harassing Rikki."

"Oh, it doesn't have anything to do with the pyro," Amadora drawled. "Tormenting her is just for amusement." She shrugged her shoulders innocently.

"And why Graham?" Carson asked.

"Don't take this the wrong way, but maybe you *are* stupid." Carson's glower persisted.

"I mean, come on. I was only trying to get to you." She nodded her head in Evelyn's direction. "And of course by getting to you, I can get to the Light One."

Carson eyed Evelyn, who was offering Amadora a signified death glare.

"Here's what I want." Amadora swiveled her body so that she was facing Carson and ripped her sunglasses back off. "Talk your girlfriend into surrendering herself to us, and I'll let you all live."

Amadora's crazed expression began to intimidate Carson a bit. "I don't understand why you are doing this." Carson shook her head. "Why are you so angry with her?"

A few blackened, prominent veins appeared just below Amadroa's smoldering crimson eyes. "Why don't you ask her?" Once again she slipped the sunglasses back on, hiding the transformation on her face. "You think I'm bad? Ask her about what she's done."

Before Carson could respond, Evelyn appeared beside her. "That's enough, Amadora."

Carson noted the blatant eye-roll Amadora offered Evelyn.

"I suppose I've overstayed my welcome." Amadora leaned a little closer to Carson. "Hey, if you ever get sick of this one, give me a call. The old ones tend to get stuck in their ways. I could show you some *real* fun." She winked at Carson once more, then moseyed back the way she had entered.

"What did she mean?" Carson's attention shifted to Evelyn."I know you listened to every word of our conversation. What's she talking about? What have you done?"

"Can we talk about it all in private?" Evelyn asked, looking unsettled, and gently took Carson by the hand so she could lead her back to the others.

"That depends." Carson pulled away. "Are you gonna tell me or avoid this conversation?"

After a few moments of silence, Evelyn nodded. "I promise I'll explain everything, but it's going to take some time. You probably need to get back home soon. Maybe next weekend?"

Evelyn was right. Carson and Rikki both needed to head back to Tree Heights. They had work in the morning. "Yes, next weekend."

They returned to Rikki, Graham, and Abellona.

"Hey, Car." Rikki smiled faintly. "You missed all the fun."

"Trust me; I was dealing with my *own*. Are you okay?"

Rikki nodded. "I'm good." She nudged Graham playfully with her shoulder. "I think Graham has some superpowers we didn't know about."

Carson centered her eyes on her brother. "Graham? Can we talk?"

Graham stood up. "Sure, but I think we need to get Rikki out of here before her mom sees her. Or, worse, Amy—er, whatever her name is—comes back."

"He's right. People have been staring. We need to go," Abellona added.

Everybody, including Graham, walked outside, back in the direction of the parking lot.

"I'll be a few minutes. I want to talk to my brother before we go," Carson told Evelyn. She took Graham aside. "Graham, I know how confusing this must be for you. It isn't easy to explain. I don't even understand it myself."

"I'm extremely confused; you're right," he agreed, a look of bewilderment on his face. "But what I'm most upset about is the fact that you didn't tell me what was going on." He nodded his head in the direction of the others.

"Graham, how do I even begin to explain something like this? I just learned about this entirely new existence last week," she clarified.

"As truly fascinating and unbelievable as that is, I'm actually talking about her." He pointed at Evelyn.

Carson looked at Evelyn, who looked back at her, but the eye contact only lingered for a second before she turned back to Graham. "Oh. Um, that's also pretty complicated to explain."

Graham crossed his arms. "Human or not, she still hurt you, and I'm still your brother."

"Believe me when I say there's a perfect explanation for that."

Graham's brow furrowed. "Uh-huh. So what is it?"

"Graham, that's not something I can actually get into right now. I'll be home in a few hours if you want to come over. We can sit down, and Rikki and I will tell you everything we know so far."

Carson watched as her brother glanced over at Rikki, contemplating. He rubbed the back of his neck as if releasing tension. "Actually, can it just be the two of us? And maybe sometime this week. I have a lot going on at work tomorrow." He appeared uneasy and restrained. "But I do need to tell you something."

"Um, yeah. Is everything okay?" Carson asked, a bit more unsettled.

He grinned. "Besides the fact that I just found out there are superhumans in this world?" He giggled lightheartedly. "Yes, besides that, everything is okay."

Carson hugged her brother before seeing him off. She watched as he waved awkwardly at Rikki before getting into his car. Rikki returned the gesture with a light smile on her face. Then it finally clicked.

Ah, I get it now. What Amadora was trying to tell me.

After Graham pulled out, Carson walked back over to their car impatiently, something new on her mind. "Do you like my brother?" she asked, focused on Rikki.

Rikki, taken aback by the question, stumbled over her words until she found the right ones to spit out. "What—er, why would you think that? I mean, it's Graham. It's your *brother.*"

"Graham isn't the least bit broken over finding out his ex-girlfriend is a monster." Carson crossed her arms. "He was never really invested in their relationship, or any others for that matter. I now understand why. He's always had feelings for someone else, and I'm shocked I never figured it out."

"Car, this is ridiculous. Come on, think about what you're saying. It's Graham."

"Yes, Rikki. It is. I suppose it has always been for you. Have you even admitted it to yourself yet?"

"I don't know what you're talking about, Carson. Graham and I are just friends. He's a *good* friend," Rikki elaborated.

"Ward, I don't think there is any way out of this one," Abellona chimed in.

"This is ridiculous. Can we go now?" Rikki turned around, desperately reaching for the car door. She awkwardly fumbled with the handle before eventually getting inside.

Carson smirked, silently giggling in her head and maybe feeling a little proud of figuring it out before Rikki or Graham had admitted it. She walked over to Evelyn and Abellona.

"Well, I'm really hoping she doesn't blow the car up on the way home," Abellona joked.

The driver's side window glided down and Rikki popped her head out. "Real funny. Hey, I got an idea that will fix all of this. Why don't you all walk home?" She slid the window back up, obviously unwilling to wait for anyone else's wry remark.

Carson, Evelyn, and Abellona laughed in unison.

"She does have a point," Evelyn noted. "Abellona and I can get back just fine. Why don't you spend some private time with Rikki on the drive home? You both have quite a lot to talk about."

Carson nodded in agreement, but it was then her turn to become awkward. "Um, so next weekend?" She crossed her arms, looking down at the ground. "I mean, Rikki does need to come back to train with you guys." She began to fidget with a rock near her shoe.

"I'm already counting the days," Evelyn assured her and offered her ever-so-compelling smile that made Carson long to kiss those full, sensual lips.

Before Carson had a chance to say anything else, Abellona interposed. "See you later, Carson. Tell Ward the real work starts next weekend." She turned to Evelyn. "Come on, Ev. I'll race you back."

"I'll give you a head start," Evelyn challenged.

Abellona smirked, then off she went, leaving what looked like dying embers in her wake.

"That's going to be quite the head start," Carson said, amused by their interaction.

"I like to let her think she can win," Evelyn snickered. "I want you to know if you need me between now and next wee—"

"I think I've finally figured that one out," Carson intervened.

Evelyn smiled. "See you very soon, Carson."

Carson nodded and smiled back. And then, in a blink of an eye, Evelyn was also gone.

Carson heard the car window slide down. She looked over at Rikki, who had an utterly befuddled expression on her face.

"Should I tell them I was only kidding about making them walk home?"

CHAPTER 25

The drive home was quiet for the most part. The prolonged silence began to eat at Carson while she sat in the passenger seat, feeling slightly restless. She ultimately decided to speak up, but kept her gaze focused out the passenger window.

"I want you to know it doesn't bother me," Carson stated and patiently waited for Rikki to say something back, anticipating a caustic reply. Minutes went by with no response, and Carson realized it was probably the first time Rikki Ward was speechless. "And I approve, Rik." Still nothing, so Carson pushed a little more. "I know this might be weird for you to talk about, but—"

"It *is* weird, Car," Rikki informed her best friend, interrupting her mid-sentence. "This is your brother, and I didn't expect something like this to happen." She paused before eventually sighing. "For me to feel this way, it's...different." She shook her head, obviously in disbelief. "Can you do something for me, Car?"

"Of course, Rik."

"Can you promise to keep this between us? I'm not ready to talk about this with him yet," Rikki explained. "I need some time to think."

Carson smiled, determined to lessen Rikki's tension. "Your secret is safe with me, but I have one important question."

"What's that?" Rikki asked, curiosity evident in her voice. She looked back and forth between the road and Carson, expectant.

"Should I wait to get Graham a fire blanket for his birthday?" Carson giggled hysterically.

Rikki pursed her lips. "Yep, should've made you walk home."

That night, while Rikki lay awake in bed, she replayed bits and pieces of the conversation between herself and Graham in her head. She closed her eyes and thought back to something Graham had said as he knelt in front of her, attempting to comfort her from the severe pain Amadora had been causing. She reminisced as if the last several hours of the day had rewound itself.

"Rikki, you are a fighter. Don't let her win. She doesn't get to steal your strength, or your power, or let alone anything from you. She can't have what's yours. You are Rikki Ward, and no one can steal anything from you."

Rikki recalled her feelings at that exact moment, while one distinct thought crept in surreptitiously after he had spoken those placatory words to her.

Except you, Graham. You've completely stolen my heart.

It most definitely wasn't something Rikki had the guts to say aloud. She'd never been the type to find love, want love, be in love...until recently. Was it true that her heart was indeed allowing in much more than just some unfathomable empty void that her mother had caused her to feel most days?

CHAPTER 26

Tears streamed down Evelyn's face as she read Gregory's last letter yet again. Gregory Walsh, her distant nephew, had been executed by means of an electric chair for conviction of murder one week ago; a murder of which Evelyn found out Gregory had been wrongfully accused.

Years after the remainder of Evelyn's immediate family died off, Evelyn didn't think she could handle losing another family member. She distanced herself from them for years—until she met Gregory and bonded closely with him. She ultimately decided to stick around to protect him throughout his life. He reminded her of her father, of his humble nature and accustomed magnanimity.

One day, after getting into a heated argument with the mature, fifty-five-year-old Gregory, she fled. A few years passed, but she refused to reply to his letters or visit.

Evelyn thought back on the argument they'd had that fateful evening before she'd rushed out the door. She didn't turn back once as he called her name, begging for her to stop.

She now sat there in Gregory's abandoned home, reading the last letter he sent to her, one she'd read a little too late.

My Dearest Evelyn,

The day you left, I never got to tell you how proud I have been to know you. You were my protector, and for that, I am grateful.

I will be leaving this place soon, and all I ask of you is that you please help others in need. You have so much Light in your eyes; I believe you can diffuse it wisely.

With endless love,

Gregory

Evelyn repeated the words out loud. "'Light in your eyes... diffuse it wisely...'" Evelyn knew what Gregory meant. For many years, she refused to devote herself to being the Light One. Gregory was requesting she fulfill her moral duties and be the great elemental guardian he thought she was.

As for the unjust accusation, it didn't take long for Evelyn to discover that Gregory had been at the wrong place at the wrong time. He had come across a woman purposely left for dead in the dark streets of downtown Tree Heights, but before help had gotten there, she passed. He was sentenced to death by the electric chair without a fair trial per none other than the new, deceptively ignorant mayor who now possessed control over Tree Heights—Clarence Howard.

Evelyn glared at the mayor's face printed onto the newspaper in front of her. Indignant rage dispersed itself through Evelyn's now-ice-cold soul. The mayor was going to pay.

That night, Evelyn followed Mayor Howard and his goons to the town's new Business Hall, where she zeroed in on their conversation. Loud and obnoxious laughter arose from the group. They were obviously inebriated.

Evelyn had been listening to their disgusting conversation for hours as they discussed the affairs they were having, the money they laundered, and so forth. Finally, one of the men changed the subject.

"How about the poor bastard that took the fall for us last week? What was his name again?"

Smack! Another man slammed his hand down on the table

in excitement. "Ah, yes! Walsh, wasn't it?"

"Poor bastard, you say? Ha! Ralph, he was a nobody!" This particular man took a long gulp of his drink before continuing. "That was spot-on timing, though, wasn't it? Walsh made it easy for us to get away with it. He walked right into that one. It was too easy to pin it on him."

Evelyn began to shake in anger, clenching her fists. She realized the distinct, evil voice speaking was Mayor Howard himself. She proceeded to listen to their conversation.

"Anyway, he didn't hang on for long. Clarence only got to pull the lever once. Walsh was killed instantly," Ralph explained.

"Unfortunately, that's true. I was hoping I'd get to pull it a second time, you know. Really have some fun," he snickered. "The guards told me it releases 2,000 volts of electricity to your body. I suppose we could call that electric shock therapy, eh?" Clarence bellowed in amusement.

Evelyn gripped the crinkled letter that her beloved nephew had written her. She opened it slowly, letting tears splash down onto the thin material, watching as the ink smeared. She listened to the group of men in the background as they cackled and exchanged a few more stories before finally agreeing to depart for the night.

Evelyn observed the languid flickering of a distant streetlight, and instantly decided upon a plan. Her life as the Light One was no longer worth it, and she would forcefully withdraw herself from the title. She spoke aloud. "I'm sorry, Gregory. I cannot be the person you think I am, but your death will not go unpunished to those who harmed you."

Evelyn watched the mayor and several other politicians stumble one by one out of the building. She stopped them on the sidewalk, primed for the encounter.

"Good evening, Mayor," she greeted, her arms crossed. "May I have a word?"

He smiled. "You can have whatever you want, sweets, for the right price."

"How about justice?" she asked.

Clarence, utterly taken aback, replied, "Excuse me?"

"The man whose life you unrighteously stole one week ago, Gregory Walsh, was a close relative of mine. And for the woman you murdered in cold blood in this very spot on the street three weeks ago. Did you already forget her name?"

Mayor Howard turned to look at Ralph, an angry expression on his face. "I thought you said Walsh had no family, Johns? I really don't have the time for this."

"He doesn't. I don't know who this young hussy thinks she is," Ralph spat, eyeballing Evelyn intently.

"Let me show you," Evelyn scolded, a crazed expression on her face. In moments, she had snatched the mayor from where he'd been standing alongside the others. She hardened her grip around the mayor's throat, squeezing vehemently.

"Any of you soulless morons move, and I'll kill him now," she warned.

The group of men said nothing between each frantic breath they took, startled by Evelyn's erratic, insane behavior.

Evelyn pushed the mayor down by her pointer finger. "Onto your knees, Mayor. Let's show your gang how tough you really are." She clasped her hands behind her back and paced a few steps, contemplation on her face. "Let's play a game. You enjoy games, right, Mayor? Oh, and answer honestly. You don't want to see what happens if you don't."

Clarence didn't speak. The only reaction Evelyn received from him was a trembling head nod.

"Wonderful. I'm going to ask you three questions. If you get them all right, I'll let you live. Deal?" Evelyn stood in front of Clarence, waiting for his reply.

"Please, miss, I'll give you anything you want," Clarence stuttered, fear loud in his voice. "Ju-just st-stop this. Please!" Sweat trickled down the side of his head.

Evelyn shook her head in disapproval. "Now, now, now," she tutted as she sauntered around him. "I haven't even asked you anything. You can't give up just yet. First question." She halted behind him. "How many people have you sentenced to death by the electric chair?"

"Pl-please. I—I don't know. Please stop," he begged her.

"Answer me, Mayor. Don't test my patience."

"Ma-maybe 100?" he choked out.

"Okay, then. Question number two. How many of them were innocent?" Evelyn asked. Once again, she strolled around him as he kneeled, shivering in terror. "Maybe you'd like to ask a friend?"

She turned around to find the others standing there in apparent trepidation. They were as quiet as mice. Some were even shaking their heads in refusal.

"Sorry, Mayor. Looks like you get to answer this one on your own. Now answer!" She forcefully pushed him over onto the ground.

"I-I-I d-don't know," he stammered. "Maybe a few?"

Evelyn bent over to whisper in his ear. "Mayor, remember what I said about honesty?"

"Ye-yes. Um, I-I think maybe forty? Ple-please forgive me. I am sorry," Clarence pleaded.

"Last question." Evelyn faced him again. "Do you know what it feels like to have 2,000 volts of electric current running through your body like Gregory did?"

Clarence slowly raised his head to look Evelyn in the eyes. "N-no."

"Let's find out," Evelyn snarled, and then suddenly grabbed him again. In seconds she was stationed at the top of the street lamp, one arm wrapped around the large pole while the other held Clarence, dangling him in the air. She tightened her grip around his neck as he coughed out pieces of words.

"Ple—give...me 'nother chance..." he gasped.

Thunder boomed in the distance. Shortly thereafter, raindrops began to crash down around them, soaking them entirely. Evelyn could hear the others screaming in the background.

She knew they were still watching; she could sense their fear.

"Here's the thing, Mayor. Those innocent people never got another chance. My *nephew* never got another chance." She pulled him in toward her, so close that their noses almost touched. "So neither do you!" she hissed.

Evelyn then violently slammed Clarence into the lamp, shattering the glass globe where he ultimately met his fate. It didn't take long before she felt his heart stop beating from the intense electric arc that proceeded to rush through his now-limp body.

All of a sudden, a humongous, jagged streak of lightning plunged down from the dark clouds straight through Evelyn's body.

A series of excruciating jolts of pain seized Evelyn, but the hunger for death allowed her to push through, determined to finish the job. She held out, feeling the electricity racing through her entire body, lingering in her veins as charged particles rushed through her blood until she was near the point of depletion.

Before she blacked out, she heard powerful, disembodied voices echoing around her.

"Light One, you will be cursed for eternity for this."

"Every two years you shall receive this very death."

"Punished forevermore in your own mental dreamscape."

As Evelyn's weary eyes fluttered open to the minuscule raindrops tapping the skin on her face, she grimaced in agony. Sharp, consecutive twinges of pain incessantly ran through her chest, but seemed to diminish gradually once they reached her extremities. Her body felt as though it was vibrating, as unusual as that was. She blinked her eyes forcefully a few times, attempting to take in her surroundings. Her eyesight was blurry. She sluggishly turned her head, discovering a bright light near her, but couldn't make out what it was exactly.

She was uncomfortably soaked from the rain. Evelyn began to push herself up off the ground, onto her knees. In a muddled state of mind, she carefully held her hands out in front of her, realizing the brilliance was, in fact, coming from them. Once more she blinked, noticing her eyesight had cleared.

That's when Evelyn saw it. She gasped. The light emitting from her hands was in actuality electricity; the piercingly intense, concentrated sparks raced statically around her hands and up her arms.

Evelyn stood up in panic, rushing to the first puddle she found.

Staring back up at her through the murky, dappled reflection was a monster; an anomalous freak of nature. She watched as bolts of electricity rushed around her, originating from her very core.

"What did you do to me?!" she yelled, searching for some sort of response from the elemental gods, but nothing ever came.

Fury reigned in Evelyn's mind, causing the electricity clinging to her body to grow more rapid and mighty. She trembled in outrage.

BANG! CRACK! BANG!

Small, igneous pebbles of some sort pelted her in the back. She turned around to find the other men who'd been with Clarence Howard aiming their guns directly at her. She flicked her eyes over to Clarence Howard's lifeless body.

"You filthy witch!" one of the men screamed.

"Monster!" another spat out.

Evelyn's eyes narrowed on the men, glaring in hatred. "I'll show you monster," she whispered.

Blood-curdling screams echoed through the dark streets of downtown Tree Heights that night, just as they had three weeks earlier.

CHAPTER 27

Carson lay down, ready for another exhausting evening to end. It had been five long days since Carson had brushed her lips against Evelyn's the previous weekend. She thought back on that night when she let herself go, giving into her never-ending feelings for this woman; the feelings she'd attempted to relinquish over the last few years. Tonight, the hungry anticipation to see Evelyn again was tormenting her and occupying all her thoughts. Carson wanted her.

Carson opened her eyes, realizing she wasn't in her bed anymore. Somehow, she'd been transported outside to a strange place she didn't recognize.

She scouted the area, finally grasping that she was sitting on the side of a cliff, her feet dangling over the edge, thousands of feet above the water. She found the cliff oddly similar to where Evelyn had rescued her from the victrolics' attack. How had she gotten there?

Panicking, she tried to scoot back, but it was as if her arms and legs weren't registering what her mind was telling them to do.

"I thought you got past this," a woman's pleasant voice commented beside her.

Carson turned to face a woman sitting next to her.

"I mean, come on. This is just a dream, and you've already done this before. It can't be *that scary* anymore," the mysterious stranger added, her scarlet eyes fixated on Carson. She rocked an obsidian-colored, edgy but tousled pixie haircut, and she possessed fine yet sharp facial features.

"This is a dream?" Carson asked, fidgeting her arms anxiously as if the attempt at finding a more relaxed position would calm her nerves.

"Someone once told me the key thing to remember about heights," the woman continued, ignoring Carson's question, "is that there is always somewhere higher."

Carson, leaning away from the edge, decided to sit upright. This wasn't the first time she'd heard those words. Carson bent a little more at the waist and planted her hands beside her. *It's just a dream. It's just a dream.* She repeated the words in her head. "Somebody I know told me the same thing."

The woman studied Carson intently before sighing. "I used to wonder who she would choose," she chuckled as she rolled her eyes lightheartedly. "Thought it would never happen. She used to be so miserable—that is, until she found you."

"Who are you?" Carson asked the stranger.

"Just an old friend."

Carson woke up suddenly as if she'd been deliberately pushed into reality. She felt as though she'd been awake for hours and was significantly energized. She cast her eyes over to her clock, which read 4:38 a.m.

Friday was about to begin, and she was eager to get her half-day at work over with and eventually get on the road to see Evelyn.

Carson planned on mentioning this peculiar dream to Evelyn. *What did it mean? Was it only a random dream that coincidentally served no purpose at all?*

She remembered something Evelyn had told her a few weekends ago. Victrolics had the ability to interfere with dreams. This stranger did have similar eyes; piercing, bloodred eyes.

Surprisingly enough, Carson did not feel threatened. It was as though she knew this woman.

Rikki listened to her mother's insulting rant as they sat outside on her back patio, discussing her odd recent behavior.

"You've been just disappearing lately, which is absolutely uncalled for. You are supposed to be a responsible adult, Rikki. It would help if you started acting like one."

Rikki glared at her mother's reproach but gave her her full attention, quietly taking in every word.

"One minute, you're at the event, and the next, you are nowhere to be found." Sandra shook her head and stood up, placing her hands on her hips. "There were some potential clients at the event who were asking questions about your work. Imagine my surprise when I went to introduce you and they told me they saw you leave," she barked.

Rikki took a deep breath in as she tried to calm her temper, and it indeed required much effort.

"As if that's not bad enough. You actually brought Evelyn to the event?" Sandra took a step toward Rikki, pointing her finger at her. "What is wrong with you? And, for that matter, what is wrong with Carson?"

Rikki could feel the heat rising inside drastically with every disparaging verbal missile Sandra launched at her.

"Are you even listening to a word I am saying?"

Finally, Rikki could not control what surfaced.

"Stop it! Stop it! Stop it!" she screamed at Sandra.

Suddenly, Rikki exploded into a fierce, fiery being, standing there on her back patio.

Sandra backed away quickly, unable to believe what she was seeing. Her mouth was open, but she couldn't speak.

Rikki, immediately realizing what she had done, simmered down and back to her normal, human appearance. She lurched toward her mother. "Mother, I—"

"I don't believe it..." Sandra leaned forward, staring at Rikki as if she was discovering her child for the first time. "You're a pyrobanant."

"I can expl—wait, what?" Rikki blurted. "How do you know what a pyrobanant is?"

"I know a pyrobanant when I see one," Sandra clarified.

Rikki's brow furrowed. "What? How?"

Sandra sighed, a spent expression on her face. "I didn't think I would ever have to have this conversation with you, Rikki. Frankly, I never thought this would happen."

"I'm still not following," Rikki said, baffled.

"Darling, come here." Sandra held out her hand, silently reassuring her daughter to take it.

Rikki sat down in the chair beside her. She hesitated a moment before eventually placing her hand in her mother's.

"Rikki, I think it's time I tell you who your father is."

"What do you mean *is*? I thought you said he died when I was just a baby."

Sandra shook her head in shame. "I, like most mothers, was trying to protect you from a life I didn't quite under-stand." She sat back as if attempting to get more comfortable. "Out of curiosity, have you ever wondered why I don't talk about my childhood?"

"Actually, yes," Rikki answered.

Sandra drew in a deep breath and let it out slowly, prepar-ing herself. "Growing up, we didn't have much. My mother could hardly keep a job due to her drug addiction, and my father only came around when he needed money for his next drinking endeavor." She shook her head in shame. "You can imagine what my childhood was like dealing with both of them and their lowlife friends. When I turned sixteen, I got a job to help pay the bills. If my parents got wind I brought any money home, they'd steal every last cent. I didn't have a choice; I had to give it to them since I wasn't eighteen. But upon turning eighteen, I finally moved out and began making a new life for myself."

Rikki listened to her mother's story intently. Anytime she mentioned her grandparents, her mother would pretend like she didn't hear her questions. After so many attempts, she had given up. She didn't know much about any of her mother's family, for that matter.

"I hadn't spoken to them for three years. By that time, I had made a nice name for myself. One day, shortly after turning twenty-three, my mother called and told me that my father was ill and was on hospice there at home. She said he wanted to see me again before he passed away. Guilt ate at me, and I couldn't live peacefully without doing the right thing. So I went to visit." Sandra locked her hands together and intertwined her fingers. She looked downward as she continued her story. "When I got there, my father was fine. And it wasn't only the two of them there waiting for me. Five of their disgusting friends were there too. It was a trick so they could rob me."

Sandra looked back up at Rikki as she spoke. "I was surrounded and couldn't even make a run for it. One of the men pushed me to the ground, screaming at me for my purse. When I told them I left it at home, well, it was as if my life flashed before my eyes—the anger in all of them. I've never seen rage like that...until your father showed up."

Rikki's eyes widened. "He saved you?"

Sandra nodded. "Your father kicked in the door. He'd been walking nearby and heard the whole thing. He told them he would allow them their lives if they let me go, but you can't negotiate with the addicted."

"So they didn't let you go?" Rikki asked.

Sandra shook her head. "Big mistake on their part. That's when I watched your father turn into this powerful, fearsome, fiery *thing*..." Sandra repositioned herself on the patio chair. "He took them all on without even a scratch. The house was on fire, and by that time, I was beginning to pass out from smoke inhalation. The last thing I remember is your dad picking me up and walking me out of the house. I heard fire whistles as I watched the house I'd grown up in burn down."

"Your parents?"

Sandra shook her head slowly. "The police report stated it was a drug deal gone wrong, with homicide and arson involved. How could anybody prove otherwise? The town knew who my parents were."

"I'm sorry, Mom," Rikki whispered.

Sandra shrugged her shoulders. "Don't be. He gave them a chance. If he hadn't stepped in, they would have killed me. I realized they'd never been a family. Only strangers who lived with me my entire life."

Rikki nodded in understanding. "So, um. What happened with Dad?"

"He stayed with me the night this happened after dropping me back off at my apartment. Gosh, the excitement he made me feel. We were together for a few years. He lit something in me I can't explain. But after I heard about the fires that destroyed our local banks and other businesses, I began to question him. He would get angry, so that only proved he was involved. He began to remind me of my family, and I didn't want those memories back, so I left. I drove so far that I knew he wouldn't find me. Then I found out I was pregnant with you."

"Really? So, um, he has no idea that I'm even alive?"

Sandra shook her head. "Rikki, he was dangerous. He killed people. I didn't want that life, so I moved away, and I started my own life with you. I promised to keep you from harm, and I've done that."

Rikki didn't say a word.

"Darling, please say something."

"This is a lot to take in."

Sandra nodded slightly. "Rikki, I know I have been hard

on you. I'm so sorry. It's just that I never wanted you to have the life I lived growing up. I wanted you to go far and much farther than me, for that matter. As you can imagine, I didn't have nearly any sort of upbringing, so I wanted yours to be perfect."

"Mother, you could have been a little less strict and a bit more understanding," Rikki blurted. "I needed a mother. Not a drill sergeant."

Tears swelled behind Sandra's eyes as she nodded in response.

"With that being said, you are not those people. You are not Dad. You are not your mother or father. You are Sandra Ward; Tree Heights' *outstanding* mayor."

Sandra giggled through sniffles. "Don't forget the proud mother of one amazing young woman."

Rikki hugged her mother for the first time in a long time. It felt natural; like this was a new start.

"Um, Rikki?" Sandra backed away momentarily.

"Yes, Mom?"

"Do me a favor, please? Promise me you'll never go searching for your father." Sandra appeared desperate.

"I promise, Mother. All I need is right here."

Sandra pulled her back in for a hug. "Darling, I love you. I only want the very best. Forgive me for everything I've done in the past. I promise you I'll be better."

Now it was Rikki's turn to cry. Tears gushed out. She couldn't stop them if she tried. She realized she'd been waiting for this moment her whole life.

CHAPTER 28

Carson tossed her bag in the car, finally finished with her day. She'd now rush over to Rikki's to pick her up and race to those extraordinary cabins so she could engulf herself in this new part of her life; the part where majestic, near-invincible people occupied her time. Feelings of excitement fluttered through her. In a few hours, she would get to see Evelyn again.

When her phone rang, Carson peered down at the caller. *Mom.* She answered immediately.

"Hey, Mum. I'm just about to head out the door. Can I call you when I'm on the roa—"

"Dream Queen. Glad I caught you." The female voice on the other line sniggered.

"Who is this?" Carson asked, befuddled.

The voice laughed again. "Come on now. Can you really forget a pretty voice like mine?"

It suddenly hit Carson. "*Amadora?* How did you get my mom's phone? Where are my parents—"

"Relax, they're fine. I'm outside their house watching them right now. Your mom is watering her plants and your dad is watching the news. They're quite boring, actually. I snuck right past them. They have no idea they're about to get a surprise visit from *moi.*"

Carson shuddered, struck with panic. "Amadora, please. Don't hurt them! What do you want?"

Another mocking scoff sounded at the other end of the line. "You know, Car, I told you what I wanted. Ha, I was even semi-nice about it."

Carson swallowed the lump in her throat, making her best

attempt at staying calm. "Amadora, please don't do this."

"However, I'm willing to make a deal. Actually a *trade*."

Carson inhaled deeply. "What is it?"

"You. We want *you* in place of your precious, soul-sucking *Light One*. Come to me or your parents die, and I won't stop there. I'll move on to Graham, and then Rikki. Oh, and lose the necklace. I'll know if you have it on. Don't test me, either. You have twenty minutes. Need I say more?"

Tears swelled in Carson's eyes as she listened to Amadora's sinful words. Following her command, she unclipped the necklace with dread and chucked it on the ground in front of her. "I'll be there in ten."

Carson slowly pulled into her parents' driveway to see that all the lights were off in the house. She apprehensively stepped out of the car and quietly shut the door. Carson crossed her arms as if she felt cold and took a few steps toward the house she'd grown up in.

"You are fast, you know, for a human," Amadora's voice said behind her.

Carson turned around to face the victrolic that had been making her life miserable for the last few weeks. "I'm here—now where are my parents? Why does it look like there is no one home?"

A sly grin spread across Amadora's face. "You've been so caught up in Evelyn that you completely forgot your parents were going on vacation."

Carson's brow furrowed. "Wait..."

Amadora giggled. "Even I remembered they were going to the Bahamas this week. They told you and Graham weeks ago."

Carson shook her head. "Then how did you get my mother's phone?"

"Really, Car?" Amadora placed her hands on her hips. "All that time I spent with your brother. What makes you think I didn't sync her phone to mine? I'm kind of an evil genius, remember?"

"I'm not going anywhere unless I know my parents are okay." Carson glared at Amadora.

A gaudy cackle escaped Amadora's bloodred lips. "As if you have a choice." She threw her hands up in mock defense. "But I will submit to your amusing little threat. Call them, go ahead."

Carson watched Amadora intently, silently questioning whether this was another one of her tricks.

"Oh, for God's sake!" Amadora pulled out her own phone and prodded a few buttons before holding it in front of her mouth.

Carson heard it ring a few times on speakerphone before somebody picked up.

"Hello? This is Jan."

"Janet! Hello!" Amadora's voice changed from wicked to surprisingly genuine in seconds. "I'm so sorry to bother you while you're away, but I just wanted to tell you myself that Graham and I are back together. He was so excited that he asked me to call you."

"Awww. That is great, honey! It's no bother at all. I am glad he found such a nice girl. I was hoping things would work themselves out. He doesn't tell me much."

Carson listened as her mother opened up to this nefarious traitor with absolutely no idea what she had planned. She wanted to yell something—anything—but held back for her mother's safety. She didn't want to pull her parents in this any deeper.

"Thank you, Jan. I hope you are having a splendid time. Maybe we can all get together when you get back. Oh, I hear Carson is just *dying* to get together with me." Amadora's eyes flickered devilishly up at Carson as she spoke the last sentence.

Amadora no doubt loved the drama, because she blew Carson a kiss before she finally got off the phone. "See? I told you they were fine. I was at least honest about that," she joked. "But anyway, we shall be on our way."

Amadora hustled over beside Carson, intertwining their arms as if they were best friends, and softly pulled her in the direction of Amadora's car, which Carson realized had been out of view when she pulled in.

A chill ran down Carson's spine as she felt the skin of Amadora's arm against hers. Although she feared her, the feel of her skin wasn't what she expected. She pictured coarse, brittle skin. The kind that obviously matched her heart. Much to her surprise, it was soft, warm, and satiny. And below the sweet odor of ether, she could smell a hint of Earl Grey and oranges.

Carson realized Amadora was guiding her a little too gently, as if she was afraid Carson was fragile. Instead of making eye contact with Amadora, especially while she was this dangerously close to her, Carson focused on the path straight ahead. The smell of ether grew, burning her nostrils. It was beginning to make her woozy.

At the vehicle, Amadora opened the door. "Inside," she demanded. She slammed the door shut once Carson got in and strolled around to the other side, slipping into the driver's seat.

Carson surveyed the inside of Amadora's car. It was dark and gloomy, which was no shock to Carson. It matched Amadora's demeanor so well.

What really caught Carson's eye was a photo on Amadora's dashboard behind the steering wheel. Amadora and another woman sat together on a bench, submerged in the sunlight. The expression on Amadora's face in the photo couldn't have been mistaken. There was a brightness in her eyes that was real, sincere. She seemed...*happy.* Carson inspected the photo as closely as she could without being too obvious. She examined the other person in the photo. The dark, pixie haircut and those pointy facial features. She was oddly familiar.

"I lost her six years ago," Amadora said, interrupting Carson's thoughts.

Carson turned her head to face Amadora, who was motionlessly gazing at the picture on her dash. "Who?"

"My sister, Eleanor. I'll never see her again because Evelyn took her from me. I'm going to make her pay," Amadora declared.

Finally, it struck Carson. It was the same woman from her dream that morning. It all clicked. The woman in the photo was Eleanor, the victrolic whose disappearance Evelyn "supposedly" had something to do with. Carson remembered Evelyn mentioning it. But why did she have a dream about her? Was she really even dead?

"Amadora, I've seen he—"

"Ah, just in time," Amadora stated, cutting her off.

Carson watched as Rikki appeared in front of the car, engulfed in rapid, deadly flames. She was exquisite, but the expression on her face was anything but delightful.

One by one, the others encircled the car as their ultimate elemental sides overtook. Carson spotted Abellona and Leo, who inched nearer to Rikki, eventually standing beside her as they glared at Amadora. They appeared as ferocious as Rikki did, with smoldering amber-colored flames surrounding them. Chiraz and Paxton glided to the passenger side of the car, hovering closely as if assuring Carson's safety. The tempestuous, crystal-blue water pervaded their serene bodies as looks of disgust flooded their faces. On the driver's side, three sparkling, verdant female beings levitated as snake-like branches slithered unobtrusively across their bodies. Their prominently pointed ears complemented their dazzling green eyes. It was none other than Bhumika, Pakruti, and Avani, who floated calmly, repulsion planted on their faces.

Carson cast her gaze into the rearview mirror as two more

beings drifted behind the car, much in the same majestic state of being, only male—the twins.

The only person Carson couldn't find was Evelyn.

"Amadora, let her out of the car now!" Rikki screamed.

Amadora laughed, almost lightheartedly. She glanced over at Carson. "They're adorable, really, Car. Your own set of Christmas bulbs."

"Now!" Rikki yelled.

Before anything could happen, Amadora's phone rang. "Ah, just a sec." She answered and hit the speakerphone button. "Okay, go ahead."

"Carson, it's a pleasure to finally meet you. You are famous around here," a stranger said over the phone.

"Who is this?" Carson asked.

"None other than Raz himself."

Carson felt a hard drop in the pit of her stomach, as though she was going to be nauseous. She was speaking to the leader of the victrolics. Whatever Amadora was doing, it was because Raz instructed her to do so. "What do you want with me?" Carson murmured.

"Ah, well, now that you ask, nothing. We got what we wanted. This all worked out so perfectly thanks to you," he said, ostentatiously jaunty.

"What worked out?"

"It only took a few pushes by Amadora for Evelyn to finally give in and surrender herself to us. She cares so much about your pathetic human life, it's despicable."

Carson felt as though she was going to pass out. "You... have Evelyn?"

"Oh yes. She was quite willing to give herself over when she found out Amadora had you."

"I don't believe you. If you have her, I want to speak to her," Carson blurted.

"Certainly."

A few moments went by. Carson heard fumbling on the

other end of the line before Evelyn's voice sounded on speakerphone. "Car?"

"Evelyn? What is going on?"

"Carson, I'm sorry for everything. I put you in danger so many times. I've put the others in danger. This is the only way I can keep you all safe. If they have me, they'll leave you all alone." Evelyn spoke woefully until the tone of her voice changed as she uttered her next few words, assertive and unambiguous. "I want you all to let Amadora go, and don't come looking for me. When you get out of the car, make it clear to the others this is my wish. Forgiveness, Car. Remember forgiveness."

Carson, completely taken aback, could hardly get her thoughts in order, let alone speak them. She finally let one overpowering thought escape her quivering lips. "But Ev, I love you."

The silence was deafening, but Carson knew Evelyn felt it, because she was feeling it too.

"I love you too, Carson. Live your best life. You deserve everything."

CLICK.

"Between us, we were never going to harm you. *I* was never going to harm you. Know that I am no more a monster than Evelyn is for what she's done," Amadora clarified. "Now pull yourself together and get out of the car. You have some instructions to give your squad."

Tears rolled down Carson's face as she turned away from Amadora without a word and slowly opened the door. She put her hands up, motioning for Rikki to stop. "I spoke to Evelyn."

"What? How?" Rikki asked.

"On the phone. Please," she stammered through small sobs. "I'm going to tell her to go. I need you all to let her go, too. Evelyn's request." Carson watched as they all exchanged perplexed looks. "Please," she cried.

The flames surrounding Rikki gradually dimmed, then dissipated fully, but the others did not let up.

"You heard the girl. Evelyn's request. Carson would not lie about this. Now everyone back up," Bhumika commanded, briskly transforming back into her human appearance. Seconds later, the others followed.

Amadora rolled her window down.

"You can leave safely," Carson said. "But *you* can leave knowing that the difference between you and Evelyn is this: she's already forgiven you."

<h1 style="text-align:center">CHAPTER 29</h1>

Carson sat sluggishly on her mother's back deck while Pakruti handed her a hot cup of tea. The others joined them. Everybody was quiet.

Carson finally shrugged in disbelief and looked over at Rikki. "How did you know where I was?"

"Evelyn called me. She felt you take the necklace off, but before that she sensed fear. She told me the others were already on their way and that she would be also." Rikki blinked as if in shock. "I expected to see her when I got here. All of us did."

"We all rushed here. Evelyn knew what she was doing. She knew our loyalty would get the better of us. It was a distraction. None of us caught it in time," Abellona added.

Rikki scooched closer to Carson. "Did Amadora hurt you?" she asked.

Carson shook her head. "Believe it or not, I don't think that was her intention. I was just used as leverage."

"I wish I knew exactly why Amadora hated Evelyn so much," Rikki expressed.

Rikki's words immediately launched Carson into fast gear, assisting her in recollecting the image she'd witnessed while in Amadora's car. The disbelief that Evelyn had willingly surrendered had been the only thing on her mind before that; she was unable to rationalize that she would never see her again.

"Rikki, you just reminded me of what I saw in Amadora's car. It was a picture of Eleanor. I didn't get a chance to tell you, but I had a dream about her this morning. It can't be a coincidence." She turned to face Bhumika. "Bhumika, what really happened with Eleanor? I need to know the truth. I think Eleanor is the person who can stop all of this. I just need to figure out how to find her."

"Maybe it'll come to you in a dream, my child," Bhumika said softly.

Before Carson could answer, she noticed she was beginning to feel exceptionally tired. Her eyelids were so very heavy, so she blinked forcefully a few times, attempting to stay awake. "Wha-what was in that tea?" she muttered, her speech slurred, just before giving in to sleep.

When Carson awoke, she was back at the edge of the cliff she'd been sitting on in the dream earlier that morning. She stood up, clear-headed and knowing exactly what had happened.

"Thank you, Bhumika." She looked up at the sky and whispered as though Bhumika could hear her, then swiveled around. "Eleanor, I need to talk to you. Please! Evelyn is in danger."

"She's always getting herself into something."

Carson whirled around to find Eleanor standing near the edge.

"Although this time it's my fault," Eleanor explained.

"What is?" Carson questioned.

Eleanor paused before replying, "Evelyn has known me for a long time. She's seen me at my worst. We met each other here on this cliff one day. I was sitting here thinking about how awful things were getting with the victrolics and the other elementals. I couldn't believe it had actually come to that." Eleanor walked over to stand in front of Carson and spoke gravely. "It was never like this. Years ago, we all got along. Now there's always a fight."

"What could have caused such a war?" asked Carson.

"I believe Raz ruined the relationship we had with the pyrobanants, the hydrogracers, and the terradescendants. Raz wanted full control and power as a leader, and what better way to get that than gain loyal followers? They always say there's strength in numbers, right? He even tried to tell us we were better than the others. He beat it into our heads. He really got to Amadora and especially Loki."

"What about you?"

"I would listen when he spoke, but I never committed to it. I just didn't think we were all that different. We weren't more special than them, and they aren't more special than us. We are all the same. We should have been helping each other," Eleanor stressed, and then she sighed. "I tried to talk to Amadora. She wouldn't budge. She thought Raz had all the answers. And Loki, well, he was so far gone too. They would have done anything for Raz."

"I don't understand how it involves Evelyn; why Raz has so much hatred for her."

"For so very long, years to be exact, the Light One was nowhere to be found. Raz knew he could get away with anything. One day, she began to protect and guard the elementals and that set him off. He couldn't stand the thought of someone being stronger. He wants to dominate the elementals completely, and the only way to do that is to have the power of the Light One."

Carson gasped. "He's gonna steal her power?"

Eleanor's gaze dropped to the ground. "I believe he's found the Dharo Dagger—the dagger that is rumored to destroy the Light One while also absorbing the power itself. That's how Evelyn's immortality was created. She was stabbed by an elemental god, but she agreed to fulfill her destiny as the Light One. That's the thing; Raz can absorb Evelyn's power through the dagger, but he has to be created by an elemental god to ensure he receives the powers. My speculation is that Raz is working with a corrupt elemental god, and I don't think this god wants a 'Light One,' per se, anymore. I think they want something dark, evil."

Carson's mind, running through more questions, decided on the most important one as fear crept in. She was afraid to learn the answer, but knew she needed to ask anyway. "What's going to happen to Evelyn when Raz does this?"

Eleanor shook her head, confirming Carson's main concern. "It's going to change her back into a human, but it will kill her. Her age will catch up. She's 300 years old."

A pool of tears surged behind Carson's eyes and swarmed down her flushed cheeks. "No," she croaked, "I can't let this happen. I can't lose her for good."

"There's something else you should know," Eleanor voiced, and swallowed before proceeding. She crossed her arms and cast her eyes away from Carson's as if embarrassed to make eye contact. "I fell in love with another elemental, a terradescendant. Raz found out, but before he could punish me, I fled to Evelyn. She reassured me of my safety but I didn't want to live apart from Tellus. Evelyn understood. She encouraged me to go and live a long, happy life with him. She said she'd take care of the problem here."

Carson's jaw dropped. "Evelyn took the blame for your disappearance, didn't she?"

Eleanor nodded in utter disgrace.

"Amadora doesn't know about this, does she?"

Eleanor shook her head. "My relationship with Amadora became a little rocky because of her strong admiration for Raz and my aversion to him. Raz didn't mention Tellus and I to anyone. Why would he expose the truth when he had Evelyn right where he wanted her? Amadora, Loki, and the rest of the victrolics despised her for my disappearance. Raz was blissfully fueled."

This was it. Carson realized what had to happen.

"Eleanor, you need to come with me. You can sense Amadora, so you can find where they're keeping Evelyn. If we show your sister you're still alive, and you tell her the truth, we can save Evelyn. Please help me. I love this woman," Carson begged.

Eleanor took a long breath in and upon exhale, her pumiceous eyes grew a chromatically darker hue before transforming altogether into hardened, crimson-red stones. "Then it's time for you to *wake up.*"

Carson's eyes jolted open, finding Rikki and the others hovering over her. She bent at the waist, sitting up slightly. "We need to go. We need to save Evelyn," she gasped.

Rikki's brow furrowed. "What? How? We don't even know where she is."

"I do." None other than Eleanor herself spoke from behind them all.

"A victrolic!" Abellona growled.

Without hesitation, Carson jumped up in front of Eleanor. "Stop this!" She thrust her hands up toward Abellona. "You're so quick to fight! What about what Evelyn has taught you? You defend, but you don't dishonor!" she yelled. "This is Eleanor, Amadora's sister. She's on our side. We'll explain everything on our way there. You can trust her. I do, and so does Evelyn."

"How did she find us?" Rikki questioned, shock evident on her face.

Carson turned her gaze on Bhumika, who was sitting next to Pakruti. "A little help from a new friend," she answered.

Bhumika smiled dashingly.

"I have a plan. You aren't going to like it, but, well, it's a plan," Eleanor informed them.

"Then we best be going, my children. We don't want to be late," Bhumika emphasized.

Chapter 30

SMACK! Amadora viciously slapped the forcibly restrained Evelyn across the face. Evelyn was bound by an indestructible confinement device formed out of leather and enchanted to keep the Light One secured.

"Tell me, Light One, does it hurt?" Amadora slunk around Evelyn, speaking mockingly. "Knowing that you'll never see your precious Marked One again?"

Evelyn, whose face was barely bruised thanks to her extraordinary ability to heal, had been beaten by Amadora for the past twenty minutes. She hesitated between breaths. "She's better off without me," she muttered.

Amadora's feverish eyes lit up. "Hm." She placed her pointer finger on her chin as if in thought. "First smart thing I've actually ever heard you say." She then swiftly smacked Evelyn across the other side of her face.

"Amadora," Raz shouted across the rocky field of Dark Valley, "that's enough. Let our pest relax for the last several minutes of her life."

Amadora snickered. "Sure thing." She derisively patted Evelyn on the cheek before hurling around, giving Raz her undivided attention.

"Besides," Raz continued, "I want to see her tremble when I tell her that her marvelous Marked One will be next."

Amadora frowned. "What? I thought you said she was safe—"

"I know exactly what I said, and I don't need you to reiterate a thing. Do not dare undermine me!" Raz exclaimed before stomping off.

"Please, Amadora," Evelyn implored, "don't hurt Carson. You have me, isn't that enough?"

Amadora shook her head, disconcerted. "Shut your mouth, Walsh," she snapped. "I have it under control."

"Eleanor wouldn't want this for you," Evelyn yammered.

Amadora halted in her tracks. Within seconds, she had a vigorous grip around Evelyn's throat, choking her. "Do not even say her name," she growled through gritted teeth as obtrusive, inky veins slithered out from her eyes and oozed down her cheeks under the fluxed surface of her skin. "Say another word and I'll take care of Carson myself."

"No you won't."

Amadora twisted around to find Carson standing there.

"Carson, what are you doing here? This is dangerous," Evelyn implored. "You need to leave!"

Amadora put her hand up toward Evelyn, warning her to back off. She looked back at Carson. "I hate to admit it, but she's right. This isn't the place you need to be, especially right now. I'm finding it very hard to believe that you came alone. How did you even find us?"

"With my help," Eleanor said, coming into view and standing beside Evelyn.

Evelyn peeked over at Eleanor. "It's good to see you again," she said with warmth in her voice.

"Likewise." Eleanor winked at her.

Amadora froze as she stared at her sister. "El?" She rushed over, throwing her arms around her in desperation. "I thought you were dead," she exclaimed.

"I'm so sorry. I left when you needed me the most. I'm here now," Eleanor cried as she embraced her sister. "Listen," she said as she pulled back to look into Amadora's eyes. "There's a lot I need to tell you, but first, Raz is lying to you. He's planning on not only killing Evelyn and taking her power, but he's planning on taking over. He will kill all of us to get what he wants," she explained.

"Ah, Amadora. You did not inform me we had guests," Raz drawled as he and several other victrolics surrounded them. "And you!" He glared incessantly into Eleanor's eyes as he spoke, indignantly waving the Dharo Dagger at her. "What makes you think you are welcome here after your volitional abandonment? You are a disappointment to victrolics everywhere!"

"As far as I'm concerned, it's not a crime to fall in love with another elemental," Eleanor replied.

Amadora's jaw dropped. "What?" she questioned.

"Oh yes, Amadora, my dear. Your sister left us to run off with a filthy terradescendant!"

"No, Raz. I ran because you were planning on punishing me for not following along with your plan to divide and conquer."

"Raz, you knew she was alive, and you didn't tell me?" Amadora shouted, turning to look at her sister. "And you...left me willingly?"

Eleanor shook her head. "Amadora, I am so sorry, I should've warned you—"

"I wouldn't have even cared about the terradescendant. You left me here thinking you were dead this whole time. I took care of Loki by myself and he's dead now, Eleanor!"

"What?" Eleanor gasped, bringing her hand up to her mouth. "How?"

"Her!" Amadora pointed ferociously at Evelyn.

"No," Evelyn countered. "I didn't kill him. The night he attacked Carson, I knocked him out and dropped him back off with the victrolics."

"Liar!" Amadora cried out.

"She's not lying, Amadora," Raz interjected. "I killed Loki."

A gasp escaped Amadora and Eleanor both.

"Yes—when he awoke, he told me everything. I had asked him to attack Carson, of course. You knew that part, Amadora. But what neither of you realized is that you were both pawns."

Raz continued to explain as he sauntered around the group. "The only use Loki had was to aid in reassuring me the Light One was back, so by attacking Carson, it was confirmed. Loki, though, of course didn't know she had returned yet. I had only asked him to bring me Carson. He didn't question me or talk back. He was too foolish and stupid, your brother."

"You lied about *everything*!" Amadora spat. "You son of a—" Before she could even take a step in his direction, the other victrolics wrapped their strong, virulent hands around her and Eleanor both.

"And, well—you, my dear, were just as easy to distract. With Eleanor gone and unable to fill your head with silly ideas, this was so easy." Raz walked in a full circle until stopping in front of the victrolic sisters.

"What Eleanor is saying is completely true, isn't it? You are trying to take control of all of the elementals," Amadora breathed.

"You'll never get away with it. The Light One will live on forever," Eleanor insisted. She turned her head, making eye contact with Evelyn and winking at her again.

"Huh." Raz drew his mouth into a thin line as if thinking momentarily. "Is that so?"

Evelyn shook her head in disapproval, mouthing *"Stop, El. No, please"* to Eleanor. She knew she was instigating Raz, and Evelyn knew this wasn't going to turn out good.

All of a sudden, Raz stabbed Eleanor with the Dharo Dagger, spearing it through her abdomen.

"NO!" Amadora screamed as she watched Eleanor drop to her knees. Smoke dispersed from Eleanor's body as she barely held herself up.

Raz placed his finger under Eleanor's chin, lifting it gently. "What was that, you dumb human?"

Eleanor only giggled in a mocking manner. "You are the dumb one, Raz."

Carson, who had been attempting to remove Evelyn's chains, yelled, "Now!"

Almost instantaneously, Rikki, Abellona, and Leo emerged from the darkness, forming a boundary circle of ferocious flames, pushing all the other victrolics out. The victrolics who had been retaining Amadora and Eleanor let them go, now fixated on the attack.

Chiraz and Paxton appeared, unloading gallons upon gallons of water on the victrolics who were asinine enough to attempt to pass through the fire.

The wind, mighty and brisk, blew so powerfully that it toppled Raz over. Struggling up onto his knees, he jerked his eyes up to find five terradescendants surrounding him. Bhumika, Pakruti, Avani, Mayo, and Rush trapped him in a whirlwind of rageful gusts.

Amadora hunkered over her now-human sister, Eleanor. "El? Are you okay?" she asked loudly over the mayhem.

Eleanor pushed herself up and onto her knees. She pointed over to Carson, who still couldn't manage to free Evelyn from the confinement device. "Free Evelyn. We need her help to fight him. You know this."

"I'm not leaving you like this. Do you know how dangerous this is for you now?" Amadora argued.

"I'm fine. Please, Am. I'll be over in a sec."

Amadora nodded and rushed over to Evelyn and Carson in the blink of an eye.

Raz, who had been taken off guard, had dropped the dagger in the midst of all the chaos. He glared at each of the terrasdescendants above him. The Dharo Dagger wasn't far from his reach. He had an idea.

Carson fought with the straps wrapped firmly around Evelyn's wrists. As much as she tried to pull them loose, they wouldn't budge. "I don't understand this. There are buttons around these straps. I can't figure out how they come off."

"Let me help you with those," Amadora interposed, placing her hands on the cuffs that were holding Evelyn hostage. "It's a numerical code. Raz and I are the only ones who know it. I'll get them off of you."

Carson watched as Amadora slipped the cuffs off, finally freeing Evelyn.

Suddenly, without warning, Raz unleashed an explosion of ether, knocking the terradescendants backward. He grabbed the Dharo Dagger and shot up onto his feet in rage, fully transformed into something grotesque. His eyes burned with bloody fury. Incongruous, grisly veins bulged under his skin, covering his body. Casting all of his evil energy into one solid strike, he launched the Dharo Dagger straight toward Evelyn.

Carson watched the next several seconds play out as if in slow motion; that scoffing smile on Raz's malevolent face as he released the Dharo Dagger that would soon destroy the love of her life. The profoundly hopeless despair in everybody's eyes merged with the gut-wrenching fear in the pit of her stomach, and there was nothing she could do to stop what was coming. She jammed her eyes shut, giving in to the darkness. She waited for the screams of panic that would soon occur and confirm her worst nightmare; Evelyn's death.

There were gasps. Carson opened her eyes apprehensively. Much to her surprise, the Dharo Dagger never reached Evelyn at all. Instead, Eleanor stood in front of Evelyn, shielding her from the attack. Eleanor dropped to her knees with her hands wrapped around the dagger that impaled her chest. Just as quickly as Eleanor dropped to her knees, Evelyn zapped Raz, knocking him out.

"No! No! No! No!" Amadora screamed as she frantically scurried over to Eleanor's side, placing her arms around her.

Evelyn knelt beside the both of them as Eleanor lay there limp, her blouse saturated in her new human blood.

Black tears poured down Amadora's face as she held her dying sister in her arms. "El, please. I just got you back. You can't d—"

"Hey...you. Don't...cry," Eleanor whispered breathily. She reached up to hush her sister, gently resting her hand on her cheek. "I love you. Now it's my turn to take care of Loki."

Amadora softly settled her hand over Eleanor's, attempting to comfort her. She looked up at Evelyn. "Ev, please, can you help her? Please," she cried.

"You know I can't heal a prior elemental. But I can make sure she goes peacefully without pain," Evelyn informed her.

Amadora nodded tearfully. "Please."

Evelyn rested her hands over Eleanor, the feel of warm blood on her fingertips. "Rest easy, old friend. Your death was not in vain." The bright light emitting from Evelyn's hands appeared to transmit to Eleanor's body.

"Long live our everlasting Light One," Eleanor whispered. Her eyes closed slowly, and she lay there lifeless as Amadora sobbed above her.

Amadora carefully lowered Eleanor's hand down beside her exanimate body.

The chaos around them subsided, and everybody was quiet as if paying their respects to Eleanor for sacrificing herself for Evelyn's safety.

Carson inched nearer to Evelyn, tears in her eyes. She thought back to when Eleanor said that she wasn't going to like what she had planned. Eleanor was right, and she knew all along what she was plotting.

Fully engrossed with indignant anger, Amadora yanked the dagger from her deceased sister's chest and sprang to her feet. She glared in hatred at Raz, who had finally gotten onto his knees. "You did this," she snarled. Her veins swelled with liquid ether, seemingly near bursting.

Raz only snickered as he watched the other victrolics join him. One even helped him up.

Evelyn rose to her feet as well. "You will be taken to where the elemental gods can judge you themselves. I wouldn't take that lightly," she declared.

"Is that right?" Raz laughed sinisterly. "Do you really think after all of this that I am afraid of them?" He shook his head and snickered wickedly once more. "After all, I was promised a place among them once I take you out."

Evelyn glared. "That won't be happening. I won't be leaving any time soon. As for the rest of you," her eyes flickered to each victrolic as she continued, "if you leave here now, you're free. I will act as though Raz's foolish yet baneful influence never clouded your moral judgment, which each and every one of you is capable of. We are better together, remember that. Here's your fresh start."

On that note, the victrolics on either side of Raz appeared to corroborate just by exchanging looks, and were gone. Raz glowered at Evelyn.

Carson watched Amadora closely while Evelyn convicted Raz. Amadora shook in fury, and Carson knew she was about to lose control. Carson took a few steps over, ultimately standing beside Amadora, and slipped her hand into hers.

Amadora jolted, surprised by the brave yet sudden touch.

"I know it hurts and this is hard; you're craving revenge. But believe me, you don't want to do this. You don't want to be like him," Carson said to her.

"You don't know what I want," Amadora spat out, but she did not pull away.

"I know as much as you think you despise humans, you were willing to protect your human sister with your life," Carson replied.

Another tear rolled down Amadora's face as she lowered her head. "I was so distracted by Raz, I didn't see what he'd been planning this whole time. I was fighting against my sister, not fighting beside her like I should have been."

"And if you kill him, are you really following her wishes?" Carson asked.

Amadora forced her eyes shut. She let go of Carson's hand. "No. But who said I was going to kill him?" she whispered.

"Evelyn, darling. Do you really believe this ends here? You are defying a future elemental god," Raz hissed.

"You're no god. And you're no longer an elemental," Evelyn said solemnly, closing her eyes and lowering her head as if deliberately ignoring what happened next.

In seconds, Amadora appeared behind Raz. "Enjoy your new life as a human." She stabbed him with the Dharo Dagger.

Raz screamed. Smoke dispersed from his body, much like it had done with Eleanor, and he fell to the ground, choking and gasping for breath. "What...have...you...done?"

"Does it sting?" Amadora towered over him, her eyes a bloodred hue. "I imagine it burns quite profusely." She smiled in heinous satisfaction before looking up to discover Evelyn standing in front of her. The grim, dark veins that were once spread across her face diminished, leaving her vulnerable, mascara-smeared face to be witnessed by all.

Carson studied Amadora's expression. She watched her intently, curious what was going through her mind at that exact moment, knowing Amadora was fully capable of the unpredictable.

Amadora willingly handed the dagger to Evelyn and offered her a slight nod as if thanking her before reaching down to pick up her sister and leave. Before she departed, though, she gazed for a few moments in Carson's direction. There was no mistaking the misunderstood, empty eyes Amadora cast upon Carson, and Carson could feel the sadness burn right through her.

Evelyn gently reached down to bring Raz, who was now groaning in deep humiliation, to his knees. She stooped down in front of him, speaking to him at eye level. "What you're feeling right now—well, it's called emotion. You'll be getting used to it, living as a human. There is a lesson to learn in every decision we make, elemental or not, Raz."

Raz began to cry in shame.

Evelyn paused momentarily while she looked over at Carson, pondering. Carson sensed the strong, embracing connection as their eyes made contact. Although it was brief, the overwhelming feelings were perpetual.

Evelyn turned to face Raz again. "Raz, you're free. I want you to take this as an opportunity to start over," she urged. "Don't make the same mistake again. Too much power will eat you alive, even as a human."

Raz's eyes widened in utter surprise. "Y-you mean you're letting me go?" he questioned.

Evelyn nodded. "I'm letting you go."

"Why?" he asked.

"Because a smart, amazing person once told me even the most evil of people can be forgiven; they're just misguided, misunderstood." Evelyn cast her gaze over her shoulder at Carson again as she elaborated.

Carson felt her smile grow.

"There's something I need to tell you, Evelyn," Raz informed her. "It's important, but it's as though my memories are fading."

Carson took a few steps closer so she could hear what Raz had to say. "What's wrong with him, Ev?"

"There's a downfall to becoming human. You begin to lose your elemental memory. I've seen it happen in the past. Most emotions flood your thoughts right away. He's experiencing a lot right now." Evelyn turned to face him again. "What is it, Raz?" she asked.

"The god I was working with—forgive me, I cannot remember his name. He holds the power to send you back into your dreamscape early."

Carson's heart sank. "He can do what? Please, Raz, tell us who he is."

Raz grabbed and rubbed his head as though he was in pain. "I—er, it hurts to think. I can't remember."

Evelyn placed her hand on his shoulder. "It's okay, Raz."

Raz shook his head in fear. "It's not. Danger is coming."

CHAPTER 31

Rikki slipped her spare key to Carson's apartment inside the keyhole and shoved the door open. She'd texted Carson to let her know she'd be stopping by just to grab a few things she'd left there. Carson was at work—however, the apartment wasn't empty. Rikki caught movement on Carson's couch in the corner of her eye. She looked up to find Graham there, sitting quietly, fidgeting on his phone.

"Hey, Rik," Graham greeted her.

"Hey, um, do you do this often?"

"Do what?" Graham asked, puzzled.

"Hang out in other people's empty apartments?" Rikki joked.

Graham offered her a friendly smile, but she could tell something was on his mind.

"Are you all right, Graham?"

Graham continued to stare down at his phone. "I, uh, knew you were coming over here. I was having lunch with Carson when you texted her."

Rikki, incredibly confused, crossed her arms. "You're scaring me a little now. Did someone die?" she joked again. "Is this an intervention?"

Graham finally looked up at Rikki, who he thought at that moment looked more beautiful than ever with her red locks cascading around her face. "I came over here because I need to ask you something, Rikki. If I don't do it now, I don't know if I ever will."

Rikki watched him eagerly as she bit her lip, the anticipation killing her. She knew what was coming. Her heart was practically beating out of her chest from excitement.

He stood up and walked over in her direction until he stood face to face with her. "Uh, well, here it goes. I want to know if what Amy—er, Amadora I guess now—said was true. Um, about your feelings for...me."

Rikki could hardly hold her composure. Before she answered, she noticed the thick bandage wrapped around Graham's left forearm. "What is that from?"

"Oh, uh, that's from the stove this morning. I burnt myself. I wasn't being very careful," he explained.

Rikki was sure her heart had crumbled into tiny little pieces when she realized just what she needed to do. She was never going to introduce Graham into this sort of erratically dangerous life. Not after seeing what she saw a few weeks ago during the battle involving all of the elementals. It was never going to be safe for him. Having Carson around it was enough.

"Um, Rik?" Graham pressed. "Is it true?"

It was now or never. Rikki needed to do what was right, surely in Graham's best interest, whether it meant breaking his heart or not. Being with him, putting him in harm's way, would be selfish.

She finally shook her head. "No, Graham, I'm sorry. I don't feel that way about you." Rikki hurried to the door and made a run for it. She couldn't bear to look at his face after that. Tears streamed down her face as she got into her car and drove home.

The next few weeks were a blur for Carson as she attempted to get back to normal life. Raz's words echoed in her mind most of the time. *Danger is coming.* It was 7 p.m. on a Tuesday and raindrops trickled and tapped the glass of her apartment window as she lay in bed after a bad dream. Distracting herself by gazing up at the ceiling fan, she watched as the dark, wooden blades spun round and round. She wished, even for a few minutes, they'd hypnotize her out of the distress she'd been feeling. Could she actually lose Evelyn at any moment?

"Hey." Evelyn interrupted her momentary intrusive thought, bringing her back to reality.

Carson quickly shifted to face Evelyn, who'd fallen asleep in her bed that evening. "Hey, you." She placed her hand on Evelyn's cheek, caressing it softly. "Sorry, did I wake you?"

Evelyn smiled. "Your dreams did." She moved closer to Carson, wrapping her arms around her waist, and pulled her into her. "Please don't worry about this. You shouldn't have to feel like you need to save me," she whispered.

Carson gazed into her eyes solemnly before replying, "I can't imagine my life without you in it."

"So be with me here in this moment, right now, in the present. Don't worry about the future. I want to love you and I want you to love me," Evelyn confessed.

Although Carson was screaming on the inside, she would do anything for Evelyn. If Evelyn wanted to ignore their problems for that night, well, she could handle that. She pulled Evelyn on top of her, and they entangled themselves in her smooth, velvety sheets for several sweet, intimate hours that night.

Neither Carson nor Evelyn once noticed the smudged handprint from a stranger on the window. It faded before they'd even opened their eyes in the morning.

Acknowledgments

God – Without your guidance, I wouldn't get through the many struggles of life. Thank you for your unconditional love. I am truly blessed for this opportunity and everything you've given me. I love you.

Mom & Korr – Thank you for being my favorite lifelong fans. You inspire me to be a better person every day and have always been my motivation. I love you both so much.

Heather – Thank you for being a big supporter throughout the long process of writing this book. You have my sincere gratitude, and will always hold a special place in my heart.

Tony – You have been my most loyal and supportive friend since the day I met you. Thank you for your creative ideas and encouragement.

Kurt – Thank you for your suggestions, input and support with my writing throughout our friendship.

Atmosphere Press – You are a wonderful group of people who made this process easy for me. I am truly thankful that I had the honor to work with you.

ABOUT ATMOSPHERE PRESS

Founded in 2015, Atmosphere Press was built on the principles of Honesty, Transparency, Professionalism, Kindness, and Making Your Book Awesome. As an ethical and author-friendly hybrid press, we stay true to that founding mission today.

If you're a reader, enter our giveaway for a free book here:

SCAN TO ENTER
BOOK GIVEAWAY

If you're a writer, submit your manuscript for consideration here:

SCAN TO SUBMIT
MANUSCRIPT

And always feel free to visit Atmosphere Press and our authors online at atmospherepress.com. See you there soon!

About the Author

Kasie Shobert is a huge animal rights activist and is very involved in her local town's cat organization. She has two dogs and eight cats, and fosters cats for the organization. She knows she couldn't get through life without the love and support of her mother and identical twin sister. She believes moral integrity is her best quality.